scrAtch

scrAtch

RHONDA HELMS

KENSINGTON BOOKS
www.kensingtonbooks.com

KENSINGTON BOOKS are published by

Kensington Publishing Corp.
119 West 40th Street
New York, NY 10018

All Kensington titles, imprints, and distributed lines are available at special quantity discounts for bulk purchases for sales promotion, premiums, fund-raising, educational, or institutional use.

Special book excerpts or customized printings can also be created to fit specific needs. For details, write or phone the office of the Kensington Special Sales Manager: Attn. Special Sales Department. Kensington Publishing Corp., 119 West 40th Street, New York, NY 10018. Phone: 1-800-221-2647.

eISBN-13: 978-1-61773-121-1
eISBN-10: 1-61773-121-8
First Kensington Electronic Edition: October 2014

ISBN-13: 978-1-61773-120-4
ISBN-10: 1-61773-120-X
First Kensington Trade Paperback Printing: October 2014

10 9 8 7 6 5 4 3 2 1

Printed in the United States of America

This is dedicated to my husband and kids,
the best support system a girl could ever hope for.
You guys make my world so much brighter.

Chapter 1

"Do you have that one new song by Dogface Thirty?" The girl tilted her overly tanned face and gave me a patronizing smile as she hollered up at me, one high-heeled toe tapping on the steps leading up to my booth. "I'm sure you've heard it. You know, where he says in the chorus, 'I wanna bounce your big—' "

"Yeah, I got it," I interrupted with a polite smile in return. I hated that song and its misogynistic, stupid lyrics, but that didn't matter. "I'll cue it up to play as soon as I can fit it in."

"You really should. People want to hear that one, and sooner rather than later. Oh, and here." She dug into her purse, flipped through a massive wad of cash, peeled off and tossed a single dollar bill on the corner of my equipment. Then she waggled her fingers and walked away, swaying hips encased in the tightest, shortest skirt I'd seen so far tonight.

"Thanks so much," I said to her retreating figure, fighting the urge to roll my eyes about her cheap tip. Oh, well—she didn't have to give me anything at all, so I guess it was better than nothing.

She either didn't hear me or didn't care about the edge of sarcasm in my tone, having disappeared back into the sweaty, raving crowd, which was currently tangled and dancing en masse to the deep, thrumming bass blasting out of my speakers.

I popped my headphones back on and transitioned to the next song, a dub-step that recently came out and was hitting the indie charts big-time. While a few of the club's patrons were full of themselves, like the lovely Oompa-Loompa chick, most of them were awesome and enjoyed my varied music mix. They would shimmy up to my table, drinks in hand and smiles on their faces, and toss me a ten just for playing a song they love. Being here made my weekend nights fly by.

And I had to admit, there was something hypnotic and empowering about being the person to bring dancers to a fevered pitch. Whenever I deejayed here and fed the crowd's craving for good music, we connected in a way. Something I didn't allow myself on campus or anywhere else. Up here I could watch them without actually being a part of their chaos.

I took a swig of the dregs of my lemon water, fanning my plain blue tank top to cool the streams of sweat slipping down my torso. Gently, so my shirt wouldn't pull out of my waistband and show my stomach scars. The Mask, one of the Cleveland area's most popular dance clubs, typically heated up fast due to being packed, but tonight it was warmer than normal. Only an hour into my gig and I was already dying in these clothes. Perhaps if my outfit were smaller and sheerer, like the other girls', I wouldn't be sweating like this. No way in hell was that gonna happen, though.

Justin, one of the bartenders, strolled over to me bearing a fresh glass of lemon water. "Here ya go, Casey," he said with a friendly smile. His red-tipped hair was styled to perfection, and he wore a slim-fitted black tee and skinny jeans. Smart guy, playing up his trim body—women came on to him all the time.

He was gay, but had no problem flirting with anyone to get a bigger tip.

"Oh, you're psychic," I replied, tugging out an ice cube and rubbing it across the back of my neck. My hair was pulled up, but the thick tips of my ponytail clung to my wet skin. "It's extra hot in here tonight."

"Sal said the air conditioner is on the fritz." He snorted. "Let's see how long it takes him to get it fixed."

"Probably never." I chuckled. "He'll make more money off these people by keeping them sweaty and thirsty. Clever man."

When I'd answered the ad in the paper three months ago looking for a part-time DJ in an up-and-coming dance club close to my campus, Sal had instantly struck me as a savvy businessman. Short, squat and completely unapologetic for his brashness, Sal had taken one look at me, rubbed a thick hand over his bald head and said, "*You're* a DJ? Ain't you a bit young, sweetheart?"

Yeah, I looked younger than a freshly minted twenty-one-year-old, which made it hard for people to take me seriously. But when I'd assisted my older cousin John two years ago as he deejayed a distant relative's wedding, I was instantly hooked. I saved up my spare money for several months to buy my own refurbed equipment and music and started working with him regularly, doing parties and other gigs.

William had seen Sal's ad and encouraged me to give it a shot, though with the way Sal's eyebrow had crooked at me, I knew he was skeptical. So I'd looked Sal straight in the eyes and said, "I have an amazing music collection and I own my own equipment. I'm reliable, hardworking and I know music. If you want this club to be a success, fast, I can help you."

I had no idea where that had come from. Desperation? False bravado? I didn't know, but I wanted this job for some reason. Needed it. Enough to blow smoke up his ass and make myself sound amazing.

Sal had stared at me for a long moment, then laughed, clapping me on the back. "You ain't too bad, kid. We'll give it a trial run, see how it goes."

Three months later, I was still here.

A group of young women, wearing nothing more than tiny, stretchy dresses and wide smiles, stumbled into the club, arms thrust in the air and whooping loudly. They looked trashed already, and it was barely eleven. I hoped they wouldn't cause any drama. One girl had on a tiara and a sash—either she was getting married soon or it was her birthday. Odds were, one of her friends would come over and insist I *had* to put on an overplayed booty-grinding song just for her. Since they typically tipped the best, I accommodated their wishes as quickly as I could.

Justin came back over, a mysterious grin on his face and a light beer in his hand. He put the beer on my side table. "This is for you."

I squinted at him. "Uh, thanks, but you know I don't drink." Never while I was working and rarely any other time, even my nights off when I was at home. Drunk people lost control, said and did things they regretted.

"It's not from me." He nodded his head toward the bar. "One of the guys there bought it for you."

Someone had bought me a drink? I scanned the bar, looking over the crowd. So many people packed in there that I couldn't tell who it could be.

"Well, it was nice of you to deliver it personally," I said, giving him a wry smile.

He grinned back, winking boldly. "I wanted to see your reaction."

I knew why. No one ever bought me drinks. I didn't dress sexily, didn't flaunt my stuff or make myself front and center at the club. The music spoke for me, and I was happy that way.

But someone had noticed me anyway.

"He's *really* cute, too, by the way. If you don't want him, I do." Justin sauntered back toward the bar, waggling his fingers over his shoulder.

My heart thudded. I was flattered and uncomfortable at the same time. Who was my mysterious benefactor? Should I acknowledge it? Would it be rude to not do so?

My hand shook just a bit as I lifted the beer and nodded my head toward the bar. I couldn't see the guy, but I figured he could see me and my thanks. Then I took a tiny drink to be polite and put it back down on the table.

The next couple of hours flew by. Despite the growing heat, the club was packed and extra feisty tonight. A couple of girls in my business finance class had taken a break from the dance floor and came up to me to say hi, beer bottles in hand. I'd given them a polite smile in return and told them to let me know if there was anything they wanted to hear.

Break time. I needed a stretch and some fresh air, stat. I set up the mix CD to play through, gave a wave to Justin to let him know I was taking my break and slipped out the back door near my DJ booth. The air outside wasn't that much cooler than in The Mask, but a refreshing breeze slipped down the alley. I leaned against the warm brick, lemon water in hand, and sighed happily, taking a sip of my drink.

Normally the alley had a few smokers milling around and a couple of drunk people making out hot and heavy—not bothering to hide the sounds of their horniness—but no one was here right now, which gave me a moment of much-needed quiet. I took a deep breath and rolled my stiff neck.

Then a deep voice from about twenty feet away in a pitch-black part of the alley broke the silence. "Uh, is this spot taken?"

At the guy's voice, I nearly jumped out of my skin, sloshing my water all over my arm. I slipped my free hand to my back pocket and patted my pocketknife to make sure it was still there. I'd never had to use it, of course, but better safe than sorry—especially since no one else was around. "Who's there?" I was proud of the way my voice sounded smooth and confident, despite the tremor in my hands.

A tall, black-haired guy in faded jeans and a white T-shirt came out from the darkness, holding his hands up in front of him as a universal sign of nonaggression. I recognized him—he was in my philosophy class. Couldn't remember his name, but his green eyes struck me just as hard now as the day I'd first seen him in class two weeks ago. He'd cracked a couple of philosophical jokes with our professor that went over everyone else's heads, and they'd laughed for almost a minute, to the point of her practically wiping away an amused tear.

His odd sense of humor hadn't put off any girls, though—he'd already attracted two in our class who sat on either side and flirted nonstop. I sat right behind him, and despite my best efforts had noticed how broad his shoulders were, how nicely a T-shirt hugged his lean torso. I'd also noticed how piercing a girl's giggle could really get when she was in serious man-hunting mode.

The guy had a wry grin on his face as he stepped closer, stopping about ten feet from me. He ran a hand over his mess of black hair, and I could see the muscles in his arms flexing. "Sorry, didn't mean to scare you. It's hot as hell in there, and I ducked back here to cool off."

"Hot as hell out here too," I said cautiously, eyeing him. My upper lip beaded with moisture. I forced my shoulders to relax. He wasn't acting odd or anything, but I'd keep a close eye on him anyway.

He glanced at my water glass, the spilled liquid drying rapidly on my skin. "Sorry, I'd have sent something else to you if I'd known you weren't a beer fan."

My heart thudded in surprise. *He'd* sent me the drink? "Uh, thanks. But why buy me something at all?" I blurted out. God, I sounded so awkward. And unappreciative. I didn't want to give him the wrong idea about me, but I didn't need to be rude either. Grandma would have given me the evil eye for being so ungracious.

He crooked his head and a slow smile spread across his face. "Why not?"

I raised one eyebrow at him and pursed my lips, not really sure how to reply. Master flirter, I was not.

"You're Casey, right? We're in philosophy together," he said, tucking his hands into his back pockets and rocking back and forth on his feet. "I sit right in front of you, as a matter of fact."

I nodded, trying to ignore the way my heart rate kicked up a notch. So he'd noticed me too. For some reason, that realization made small tingles cascade across my flushed, damp skin.

"I've never met a DJ before. How do you pick what music to play?" he asked suddenly, sliding over to lean on the brick wall, facing me but not moving any closer. He crossed his arms in front of his chest as he studied me.

"Um, I . . . do a mix of stuff I dig and stuff the crowd wants to hear. Mostly top-played songs that everyone knows, but also some B-sides and indie hits," I replied, feeling a bit too off-kilter to sound intelligent. The way he was staring at me openly, yet giving me patient space, threw me off.

Sure, I'd been hit on before—pretty much any woman with working female parts would get picked up in a bar by some guy at some point—but after a couple of minutes of clumsy conversation, the guys backed off, realizing I wasn't going to be an easy lay. This guy was different, though. He ignored my awkwardness, keeping his mood casual, nonthreatening.

My body relaxed a touch more.

"I liked that one song where the bass line was echoed by the keyboard, back and forth like a duel," he said. "Haven't heard it on the radio before."

My throat tightened for a second and my cheeks burned hot

in a strange flush of pleasure. I knew exactly which one he was talking about.

It was my song.

This week I'd done something I hadn't dared try before. I slipped in one of my own compositions, a piece I'd worked on for weeks in my spare time. I'd loaded up another dance song just in case I needed to change it out due to poor crowd reception. But no one had seemed put off—they'd simply shifted their dance around the tempo and continued the musical foreplay on the floor.

The guy shoved off the wall and gave me a friendly nod. I noticed the well-worn Converse on his feet, and for some reason that made me smile. I had a pair of Chucks, too, stashed in my closet, in a neat row beside my other shoes. "I'd better head back in before my friends think I got my ass kicked in the alley or something," he said with a laugh.

I licked my lips. Sweat dribbled down my back, tickling my skin. "Uh, I have to also. Thanks again for the beer," I added.

He gave me that slow, wide grin again that flashed his bright teeth. Something about that smile made my breath hitch in my throat. Justin was right—this guy was *really* hot. Hot and unnerving. I didn't know what to make of him at all.

He turned around to leave.

"What's your name again?" I said to his back, embarrassed I had to ask but needing to know.

He paused his step and looked over his shoulder. "It's Daniel. See you in class on Monday, Casey." He stepped back into the dark, swallowed whole in the pitch-black early September night.

I took my half-empty glass and made my way back to my DJ booth. For the rest of the night, it took all my willpower to not look over at him with his group of friends by the bar.

In spite of my better judgment, I couldn't get him out of my mind.

Chapter 2

Mondays sucked.

I rubbed my forehead and smothered a groan as I stared at our class reading, unable to follow what the hell the text meant. Professor Wilkins had told us to quietly read the extended passage in our textbook on Nietzsche's concept of the *Ubermensch* and write a response on if that idea was relevant or irrelevant in today's culture.

Far too much thinking for a nine a.m. class. I made a mental note to start drinking a shot or twelve of espresso in the morning. Even if I didn't understand our class discussions, I'd at least be awake.

In front of me, Daniel hunched over his desk, wearing a dark green shirt, his back muscles flexing. I could hear his pen scratching away as he flew in his writing. Obviously *he* understood what our professor wanted. Even the two girls who sat on both sides of him were writing, though I had serious doubts it was about the class work.

I took a deep breath and exhaled slowly, rereading the passage, one sentence at a time. The class was just fifty minutes long, and there were only a few minutes left. My heart started to pick up a stuttering beat as negative thoughts crammed in my mind. If the material was this hard to understand just a couple of weeks in, how would it be in two months, when we were neck-deep in philosophical concepts and theories? Could I keep up? Yeah, I could drop it and take another elective next semester, but it would throw me off my master schedule. I was determined to stick it out.

"Please finish up your journal entry, and make sure to type it at home and bring it with you Wednesday," Professor Wilkins said from behind her desk, pointedly ignoring the low groan that came from a few rows behind me. She closed her notebook and started putting away her massive stacks of paper into a large woven bag. The fabric matched the pattern of her patchwork black and red skirt. As usual, she kept her wiry hair long and thickly braided down her back. I'd bet she had more hand-dyed peasant shirts in her closet than a Renaissance festival.

Professor Wilkins was an older woman who adamantly refused to accept most modern conveniences like cell phones or computers, claiming they were dumbing down the population and creating global addiction and self-centeredness. I'd heard from another student that she actually had an ancient typewriter in her office, having protested for a full year against being forced to use the school's computer system. But she was tenured, so the school had caved.

"There will be a quiz next class period, so study hard." She raised one gray eyebrow at the class, her thin lips pressed together as she studied us. "You're dismissed."

I was both relieved and dismayed to pack up my things and slide out of my desk. Looked like my philosophy textbook was going to be my best friend until the end of the semester. I scrolled through my phone to an upbeat playlist, dug out my earbuds and popped one in my ear.

"That was grueling," Daniel said with a grin as he rotated my way, flexing his neck. The corded muscles stretched from the movement, and I tore my gaze away to avoid staring, cheeks blazing.

I turned the music volume down a touch on my phone. "Yeah, I don't know how I'm going to get any of this," I admitted.

He picked up his book and crammed it in his bag, slinging it over his shoulder. Then he made his way down the aisle and out the room into the hall. I put in the other earbud and stayed a step behind, not wanting to look like I was following him, but it seemed he was heading in the same direction as me.

Then he slowed down to match his stride to mine. I pulled out one earbud and let it drape over my shoulder.

"So what do *you* think?" he asked me.

"About?"

"The *Ubermensch,*" he said, his face serious. "Our journal question."

"You tell me first," I shot back. I'd bet a hundred dollars he had a good answer. And if he shared it with me, maybe I could use it for my paper.

He barked out a laugh. "I like you," he said with a crooked grin.

I blinked. I'd never had a guy tell me that before—so easily, so smoothly. Like he was telling me he liked strawberry ice cream or kung-fu flicks.

I like you.

I found myself flushing again. "You don't hold anything back, do you," I said as he pushed the building door open and waved me through. Gentlemanly too. A surprise a minute, he was. I turned my music off and stuck my phone in my pocket, then my earbuds in my bag.

"Why should I hold back?" he replied. "Life's too short to not be upfront."

We walked in a strange, companionable silence down the sidewalk, a couple of cars slipping by. Birds chirped happily from their nests in thick, green trees lining the roads, but I was so distracted by his electric presence beside me that I didn't care. Plus I was in desperate need of coffee but didn't want to go back to my apartment, since my English class was at noon, so I'd decided to go to Coffee Baby, the best coffee shop in Berea. Not only did they give you large mugs of coffee, they also had *huge* pastries for supercheap. It was a studious college student's wet dream.

"Where are you going?" I finally asked him. Shouldn't he be heading away toward a class already?

He shrugged. "I don't have another class until early afternoon, so I'm just wandering around, killing time."

I stopped in my tracks. Hot sunshine poured over me, despite the midmorning hour. It was gonna be another scorcher today. "Um, so why are you here with *me?*" The attention made me itchy underneath my skin. I suddenly didn't want this guy to walk beside me, to nudge me gently into opening up in that manner of his.

My life was my own, private, and it was better that way.

He peered down at me. The dappled sunshine spilled through a nearby tree and cast gentle shadows and highlights on his face. His eyes glowed a strange shade of green. "Am I getting on your nerves, Casey?"

"No," I was grudgingly forced to admit, a bit embarrassed at my rudeness. I hadn't intended to come across that hostile. Yeah, I would meet his bluntness word for word, but for some reason I couldn't make myself lie.

Okay, he made me uncomfortable. But he also had this compelling air around him that made me want to listen to him, to have him turn those bright eyes on me. I'd felt it on Saturday night, when he was talking to me a little bit about deejaying. I felt it nearly every class period when he answered the professor's questions. And now that attention *was* focused on me.

And for the life of me, I couldn't figure out why.

Daniel shifted his bag strap to his other shoulder. I noticed a smattering of freckles across his forearms, the bridge of his nose. He had this oddly boyish charm about him, but his body was all man.

"Are you busy right now? Can I buy you a Coke or coffee?" he asked quietly.

I should pass on the offer, should keep our interactions the way they'd been so far—interesting but not invasive. Not personal. Yet I found myself saying, "No, but I'll buy you one if you help me with this philosophy assignment."

Where the hell had that come from? Probably the same place that had boldly asserted to Sal that I was his DJ. Some deep-down, balls-out part of me that would not be suppressed, despite my best efforts to stay on the straight and narrow track.

There was no harm in my sitting with a fellow student, I justified to myself. And if I could get a handle on philosophy, I could ease some of my stress. Nothing more, nothing less.

A slow smile spread across his face, and he gave me a nod.

We made our way to Coffee Baby, and he opened the door for me to step in. The air inside was tinged with the aroma of coffee and was blissfully cool, instantly chilling the thin layer of sweat on my skin. I sighed in contentment and followed Daniel over to a back table, where we dumped our bags on the floor and slipped into the rickety wooden seats.

Daniel leaned back in his chair, draping his forearms on the table as he eyed me with one brow raised.

I swallowed and glanced away for a moment. His scrutiny was so penetrating. How did he go through life with that level of intensity? Didn't he find it exhausting? "So, what kind of coffee do you want?" I asked.

His fingers stroked the swirls and dips of wood on the table, and I found myself unable to look away. He had artist's fingers, lean and long, and his left hand had pencil marks on the side.

"You're a leftie," I said.

He gave a low chuckle, and I glanced up at him. "Dun-dun-dunnnn! The sinister hand."

My brow furrowed. "What?"

"In the olden days, being left-handed was considered bad, even evil. Kids were beaten into using their right hands."

"That's jacked up," I said, blinking.

"The world is a cruel place," he simply said. "People are awful for no good reason sometimes."

Like he needed to tell me that. My mood soured instantly. I shouldn't be here. I would buy him a coffee and leave, and then I could go back to normal. I could—

"Where are you right now?" he asked, ducking his head down to meet my gaze. His eyes were fixed on mine.

I stood, cramming my right hand into my pocket. Goose bumps broke out across my exposed flesh. *It's just from the cold,* I told myself, my lungs tightening with each breath. *It's chilly in here. You're fine.* "What would you like?" *Get the coffee, get the hell out of here.*

Out of habit, I brushed my hand across the left side of my stomach, my fingers running over the familiar deep dimple that puckered a section of skin beneath my loose T-shirt.

His eyes darted to my hand, and I stilled. "Just black is fine, thanks," he said slowly.

I gave him a stiff nod and got in line. God, he was going to think I was a total freak, unable to keep a handle on my emotions. I needed to get myself back in control, now.

The barista, a supertall blond guy I'd never seen here before, gave me a polite smile, and I asked him for two black coffees. While he made them, I drew in slow, long breaths—in through my nose, out through my mouth. The way Grandma had taught me.

It worked. It always worked. I could hear her soothing voice in my ear, and the tension in my back faded just a hair. My arm and leg muscles uncramped one by one. Grandma had told me there'd be strange panic or stress triggers, probably would be my whole life. And the best thing I could do was be aware of it and not let it wig me out more.

Easier said than done. Then again, it was her son who'd done this to me, so no doubt her unique mental anguish was nearly as strong as mine.

My phone vibrated from my pocket. I dug it out and smiled as I saw I'd gotten a text from her. Sometimes I would've sworn she was psychic. Then again, Grandma did love sending texts now that she knew how to work her phone. She was surprisingly technologically savvy. Granddad, on the other hand, refused to even touch a cell phone.

I clicked on the message.

It's going to be warm out today, so don't forget to wear sunscreen. Can't burn that fair skin! Love, Grandma

A low laugh burst out of me. Never ceased to amuse me that she signed every one of her texts. Like I couldn't tell it was her. The rest of my tension melted away as I replied that I would.

The two coffee cups slid across the counter. I gave the guy a few bucks and told him to keep the change. His distant demeanor faded a bit as his smile grew genuine in thanks. If there was anything I understood, it was the pains of being in customer service.

My hands were smooth and steady when I brought the cups back to the table. I was proud of myself—I'd shaken off the beginnings of the panic attack. History told me the next time probably wouldn't be so easy, but I was going to revel in today's success.

One day. One hour. That was all I had to do—focus on the now.

Daniel took the cup and sipped, giving a smile. "This is great stuff," he said, looking surprise.

Had he never been here before? I nodded, taking my own drink. Strong with caffeine. The way I liked it. "I've spent many hours here over the last three years," I said. "If you come here around one, when everyone has food coma, the lines are almost out the door."

Since my panic attack had faded, maybe I could go ahead and talk to him about our philosophy class. Needed to get that done with anyway at some point. I put my cup down and pulled out my book and notebook. While I was grateful Daniel hadn't commented on my weirdness, I also didn't want to open the door to the conversation coming back to it. "Can I ask you some questions about the *Ubermensch* and take notes as we talk? You seem to have a better handle on this stuff than I do."

"By all means."

I cleared my throat and hovered my pen above the paper. "Okay. First, what the hell is an *Ubermensch*?"

He barked out a laugh and put his cup down. "I suppose that's as good a place to start as any."

For the next ten minutes, Daniel patiently explained the origins of the concept of *Ubermensch*. It took me a while to grasp the nuances of what he meant. Partly because the theory itself was rather difficult, but also partly because as he leaned over the textbook and pointed to various sentences, I could smell the ocean-fresh scent of his cologne wafting off of him. Having him this close made my stomach flutter uncontrollably.

I couldn't take my attention off his fingers. Or the way he shifted slightly in his chair, the gentle huffs of breath that came from his slightly parted lips. It was uncomfortable how aware of him every pore of my skin was.

I'd never been this hypersensitive about another human being in my life. Disconcerting, to say the least. And strangely magnetic.

"So basically," he summed up, "the *Ubermensch* is Nietzsche's ideal man. One who doesn't simply go with the crowd. He's not a follower, nor is he a leader. He has his own ideas and beliefs, but he doesn't force them on others. See, for Nietzsche, God didn't exist. So man has to create his own unique set of morals, standards." Daniel turned to look at me with a toothy grin, his green eyes glowing with enthusiasm for the topic. "Make sense?"

I gave a silent nod. The concept was coming together for me now, but I needed to get out of there before I did or said something embarrassing. Like how good he smelled or how awkward he made me feel.

"Uh, okay. I think I get it. But I need to head out now," I said to him, ducking my head to avoid his stare. I stuck my book and notebook in my bag. "Thanks for all the help. It might have taken me hours to get this far."

"No problem." Daniel leaned back and took a sip of his coffee, probably now cold. He'd ignored it the whole time he'd been talking. "I hope we'll hang out again soon," he added.

I cleared my throat. Did I want to? Surprisingly, I did. But I wasn't ready to admit that to him. Giving a noncommittal shrug and saying thanks again, I dumped my half-filled cup in the garbage on my way out. Then I turned to glance over my shoulder as I walked through the door.

Daniel was still looking at me, an unreadable emotion in his eyes.

Chapter 3

The song was *almost* there.

Squinting my dry, fatigued eyes, I scrolled through available tracks on my laptop, clicking and listening to different samples I'd created or bought over the last couple of years. Digital music composition was just as exacting and precise as any other type of composition, and I would sometimes spend hours hunting for the perfect sample. If I couldn't find it, I'd make it myself.

The piece I was currently finishing up was a little more melancholy than I normally did. My typical songs were heavy on bass and an echoing melody, meant for airplay in a dance club. But for some reason I'd been inspired to try something new. To be a bit more resonant.

I'd woken up just over two hours ago, shaking from a vivid nightmare. This one was even more brutal than usual. The room in my dream was dark, pale blue light casting a deadly pallor across the narrow twin beds, dressers and walls. My younger sister Lila's pale face, spattered with scarlet blood specks, had turned to look at me. We were both stretched out on our bedroom floor between our beds, limbs awkwardly positioned like dropped marionette puppets.

Lila parted her lips, but blood dribbled out the corner of her mouth and I couldn't understand what she was saying. I tried crawling to her, but the stabbing pain in my stomach was so severe, I couldn't do anything but lie there and press my hand over the spurting wound. She moved her lips silently and then her eyes went still as she exhaled her last stuttered breath.

Then I'd woken up. Covered in a clammy layer of sweat, cream-colored sheets and blankets kicked onto the floor, fists clenching my pillow. Tears streaking down my cheeks and throat aching from biting back my screams.

After almost eight years, one would think I'd be used to these torturous dreams by now. Could even grow to anticipate them and not be so freaked out. But they surprised and horrified me every single damn time.

I shoved the dream back into the far recesses of my brain and focused on the task at hand, taking a sip of water. I'd found that if I worked on music until I was so tired I collapsed, I could usually go back to sleep for another few hours. Enough to keep me running. That, plus a morning coffee, would let me have enough energy to make it through the day. And given that I had to go to work in eighteen hours, I needed all the sleep I could manage.

Adjusting my headphones, I cued up a sample I'd made of a woman singing. Her voice was light and airy, her soft French words a verbal caress. When I'd first heard her voice, it had given me goose bumps. Could be a nice complement to the strings track. I added her to my composition, which I'd tentatively titled "I'm Haunted."

A hand clasped my shoulder, and I jumped out of the computer chair, wheezing in fear, lungs the size of grapes. I ripped the headphones off and whirled around to see my attacker.

Megan, my roommate, stared at me in shock, her sleep-mussed, curly black hair sticking out in all directions. My bedroom door was open, a black, yawning stretch of hallway behind her. Since my slim, solid-wood desk was underneath my window, my back had been facing the door. I hadn't heard her at all.

"You okay?" she asked, dropping her extended arm to her side. She had a pillow crease along her smooth, dark cheek. "I heard some loud music coming from here and it woke me up. I tried knocking on your door, but . . ." She gave a meaningful look at my headphones.

My heart rate finally began slowing down. I pressed a shaking hand to my chest, letting out a surprised laugh. "Oh, you scared the shit out of me, Megan. I'm sorry. I was . . ." I glanced back at my computer, at the opened composition behind me.

Her perfectly arched brows knitted as she peered over my shoulder. "What is that? Are you doing homework or something? It's after one in the morning."

"Um, it's nothing important. Just playing around. Sorry to wake you up."

I'd never told Megan about the music I composed. Megan had stuffed animals on her bed and her walls were covered in pictures of her and her friends, where I barely had any decorations on my plain white walls or desk, except a couple of pictures of my grandparents. Needless to say, we were completely different.

She and I had started rooming together a few months ago when I'd answered an ad she'd placed in the school paper looking for someone to split an apartment off-campus. Though Megan liked to party at least two to three nights a week and was far more social than I'd ever be, she usually left me alone and didn't bug the hell out of me. I appreciated that.

But it also meant we knew very little about each other. We ran in different circles, since I preferred staying home most evenings and holing up in my room. Something I thought wasn't too bad . . . until now. Because according to the look on her face, I'd offended her.

Megan tilted her head to the side. "That looks like music. I was in band in middle school—played clarinet. Are you writing something? I didn't know you were into making your own songs." There was a strange thread in her voice, a note of wistfulness mingled with hurt.

My cheeks burned with embarrassment and guilt. "It's nothing, really. Just something stupid I do when . . ." I sucked in a shaky breath. I'd been about to spill the beans on my nightmares. God, what was *with* me lately? "Uh, when I can't sleep. I do a little bit of music to kill time." I picked up my headphones and fiddled with the cord. "There must be something wrong with these—I'm sorry I woke you up."

"Oh." She crossed her arms over her chest, her face falling. "Yanno, you usually just stay in your room whenever you're home, so I never know what you're up to. It's like you don't want to be around anyone—even me. And we've been roomies for months now."

Guilt hit me harder, whirling in my stomach. She was right. Whenever Megan's friends came over, I locked myself in my room and put on my headphones, listening to music as I stared up at my stain-splotched ceiling.

I swallowed and pressed my backside against my desk. "I wasn't . . . I didn't mean to . . ." Shit, I wasn't any good at this. Here I'd thought we had an understanding.

And Megan thought I was shutting her out. For good reason, I supposed.

"Um, I'm sorry," I finally said.

She gave me a curt nod. I could tell my apology hadn't done much to appease her bruised feelings.

"Maybe we can hang out?" I blurted out, wanting to make her feel a little better. "You know, sometime. Soon, I mean."

Megan came to the club where I deejayed a couple of times, but that wasn't us hanging out together.

She gave me a tentative smile. "Really?"

The tightness in my chest eased up a bit. I nodded. Hell, at this point I'd have climbed Mt. Fuji with her if she wanted. Seeing the disappointment in her eyes and knowing I'd caused it had made me feel awful.

She fluffed her curls and her grin spread. "I have the *perfect* idea. There's a party on Thursday . . ."

I groaned; I couldn't help it. This wasn't the first time Megan had asked me to go to a campus party with her. "Well, I thought we could rent a chick flick and overdose on ice cream or something." One-on-one at home, where I could avoid being reminded of how socially awkward I was. Or worse, possibly have one of my stupid panic attacks.

"But the guys there will be *so hot,*" she crooned, stepping closer. Her rich brown eyes sparkled from the light of my laptop monitor, which also glinted off her natural, unprocessed hair. "You have to come. Have to. I'll do your makeup and dig some clothes out of my closet for you to wear, and we'll turn you into a total tiger. Just one time, that's all I ask."

Ugh. If I turned her down, I would be the biggest asshole ever. I'd woken her up tonight, had shut her out for months, and then I would look like I was too good to even hang out with her in public. Maybe going to this party would get her to ease up a bit on me. She'd feel like I was letting her in, and I could keep my big secrets to myself.

"Okay, I'll do it," I said, making a mental note to update my planner for Thursday. I could get my studying done before the party. And if the gods were on my side, I'd only have to stay a couple of hours.

She squealed. "Yay! Okay, I need to go back to bed. I have a commutative algebra quiz in the morning. Not that I won't ace it or anything, but I can't go in there looking like shit."

I snorted. As if Megan could look anything less than beautiful. She was tall and statuesque, her skin unblemished. She could work a crowd like no one's business. And she was majoring in math. The girl had brains and legs for miles.

"You won't regret this," she added, apparently seeing the uneasiness in my eyes. "I'll be there the whole time. It'll be fun—you'll see."

Despite my discomfort, I gave her a quick hug and she closed my door behind her. I dropped back into my computer chair and whirled around, shutting everything down. The mood to compose had left me completely. In its place was a sense of disorientation.

To keep my hands and mind busy, I sorted the errant papers on my desk into their folders. The desk was old, but it was Granddad's, so I took care to keep it tidy and in good shape. Then I slipped back into bed, staring at the shadows on the ceiling until my eyes grew too heavy to stay open.

My life was supposed to be steady, comforting. Predictable. But it felt like this was going to shake things up a bit, and I wasn't sure whether I was ready for that or not.

"I wish you'd let me put you in a skirt," Megan mumbled as she eyed me over. We stood on the sidewalk of a frat house right on the fringes of Smythe-Davis's campus. Students flowed in and out of the doors, laughing. The strong pulse of a bass took over the air, slipped beneath my skin.

"Hey, I compromised," I protested. The skirt she'd wanted me to wear looked like a leather belt, and she'd suggested I pair it with a tiny thong. No way in hell was I going to show my vagina to the world. So I was in my requisite faded jeans, but I'd caved and worn a tight white T-shirt of hers with the words *I <3 Bacon* written in pink glitter letters across the chest.

Megan had done my makeup and hair—and happily, I didn't look like Hooker Barbie. My eyes were slightly smoky but not obnoxiously so. She'd pulled my hair into a messy bun and curled the loose ends, the 'do effortlessly chic. I'd have to have her make me over more often.

"Well, at least the rest of you is hot," she said with a smirk, then looped her arm through mine. We started walking toward the house, weaving between students. "Okay, let's go get you drunk."

"Whoa," I said, digging in my heels. "I'm not a big partier, okay?"

She eyed my set jaw and backed off. "Okay, okay. But just one beer to help loosen you up. One or two, that's it. All they'll have is that light shit in the keg anyway—college guys are cheap as hell, in case you hadn't noticed yet. Oh, my God, Bobby is sooo hot," she whispered under her breath as she eyed a super-tanned football guy wearing a big smile and his jersey. He stood with a group of football players on the front lawn, all of them raising their beers in the air to do a loud toast, complete with some kind of a football chant. Then the testosterone-laden cluster moved inside.

She and I headed in as well and stood beside a large crowd of girls talking and drinking. The music changed to a popular song, and Megan started dancing in place. Her gaze kept drifting over to check out Bobby.

After a few minutes of watching her watch him, I sighed and waved her off. "Go. Talk to him."

"But I don't wanna ditch you."

"I'll be fine."

She raised an eyebrow and gave me a knowing look. "The moment I leave your side, you'll bail on the party."

A flush swept over my cheeks. She totally called it. "Fine. I'll stay. For a little bit, anyway."

"Promise?"

I nodded.

Her face lit up, and she squeezed my hands. "Thank you. I

owe you. Now go get a beer—it'll help you relax." She sauntered over to Bobby, and I saw them start to talk.

The music was thick and potent, throbbing just under my skin. A little loud and off-balance, and the DJ could use better speakers, but I wasn't here to work. I was going to attempt to enjoy myself.

One beer. I could sip on it for a while and then duck out of here. Hell, it might help me relax a bit. Because right now, my stomach was twisted into knots and my hands were shaking like crazy. I took deep breaths as I scanned the packed room. I recognized a couple of guys from previous classes; they were hitting on a group of girls. Despite knowing ahead of time that the place was going to be full, I hadn't fully prepared myself for it.

As I looked around, I realized I was woefully underdressed. Nearly every female was dressed like Megan—tiny neon dresses or skirts, tube tops, halters, breasts practically spilling out.

"Hey, want a beer?" some guy said from behind me.

I spun around, and his eyes raked over my body, a grin widening on his face. He wasn't bad-looking, with spiky blond hair and blue eyes, but he was one of those guys who knew he was fairly attractive and used his charms to work his way into women's panties.

Or so I was assuming. Maybe I was being unfair.

"Um, I'm gonna go grab one," I told him with what I hoped looked like a regretful smile, "but thanks." A smart girl never took a drink from a stranger, no matter how nice he might appear.

"There's a wet T-shirt contest in the backyard in a little bit," he said, his attention zeroing in on my small breasts. "I think you should give it a chance. We're offering a hundred dollars to the winner." His grin widened, and I could practically see his molars sparkling in the overhead light.

Okay, so I wasn't wrong about him. He was a total creep.

"Thanks, but I'll earn my way through college the sanitary way." Before he could say anything else, I spun on my heel and headed to the backyard, where I figured the keg would be tapped.

I would have one beer. If I hung out for an hour or so, Megan couldn't complain about my effort. Then I could go home, curl up with a book and relax. Win-win.

On the outdoor patio, a short brunette's wedge heel tilted, and she twisted and fell into my side, some of her beer splashing on my hair. "So sorry!" she said with a high-pitched giggle as I caught her and helped her right herself. "Oh, heyyy, I know you!" She squinted her eyes at me.

Yeah, I knew her too. One of the chicks who routinely tried to get Daniel to copulate with her through the power of her seductive eye-batting. "We're in philosophy together," I filled in. A few drops of beer dripped down my cheeks; I swiped it away. All of Megan's hard work, ruined and now reeking of hops.

"Oh, that's right!" She smoothed a hand across her tiny tank top, her boobs ballooning over. "Are you gonna be in the wet T-shirt contest? It sounds like so much fun! I'm Amanda, by the way."

"Casey," I answered politely, edging along the side of the house.

Amanda stayed on my heel as I walked toward the keg and filled a cup. She stuck hers under the spout, so I filled hers too. Not that she needed it. Then again, I was currently sticky from the remains of her last beer.

"Ugh, that class is so boring!" she said, pouting her hot pink lips. "I don't understand anything our prof's talking about. I might drop."

The evening sun began to set, and as it dipped below the horizon, the edge of heat that had pervaded all day eased up just a touch. A gentle breeze slipped across my face, and I sighed in pleasure.

"So, what other classes are you taking? What year are you?" Amanda took several gulps of her beer.

I took a big drink, too, as I wove my way to the back of the yard, away from the thick crowd dancing and chatting in the middle. Maybe if I focused on drinking this beer, I wouldn't have to talk to her so much. Instantly I felt bad at the thought. It was obvious she was trying to be friendly, but she and I had even less than zero in common.

"I'm a senior business major, so it's pretty much all business classes now except for a couple of electives," I told her, gaze scanning the people milling around in the yard. Laughter was everywhere, people kissing and smiling as they talked. For some stupid reason, my heart squeezed a bit. Maybe because I wished I could shed my own personal darkness and be more like them.

"I'm a junior," Amanda replied as she eyed a tall African American guy walking by. "Holy hell, he's ripped. Check out those muscles." Then her attention turned to the door, and she sucked in a breath. "Omigod, look who's here. That sexy guy Daniel from our class."

My heart slammed in my chest, and I took another big gulp of beer to help ease my sudden nervousness. A liquid languor settled in my limbs. I looked down into my cup—nearly gone. In my distracted apprehension, I'd practically chugged the whole thing in minutes.

Shit.

Daniel, hovering just outside the back door, looked strong and tall and more compelling than usual tonight. His black hair was slightly mussed, and he had on jeans and a black T-shirt bearing the logo of a 90s grunge band.

"I'm going to go talk to him," Amanda said, oblivious to my sudden buzz. She fluffed her boobs and said, "Do I look okay?"

"You look like you're about to devour someone," I replied drolly.

She giggled. "Oh yes! I totally am. Ta-ta for now!" With that, Amanda strolled across the grass, stumbling a couple of times as her wedges caught divots in the ground and threw her off-balance.

I couldn't help but chuckle. Well, until she made her way to Daniel and slipped one hand up his chest. He gave her a warm smile in return and they started talking. Then my laughter died, and a sourness settled in my chest. I didn't want to see her flirting with him. Or vice versa.

I walked resolutely over to the keg and grabbed another beer. My senses felt a bit softer, yet more alert in a weird way as I sipped, determined to not chug this cupful. I could almost hear the pulse in my veins, skipping along in an offbeat melody.

And not just because of the alcohol. Because of him.

Had I known he was coming, I would have stayed home. Then I laughed at myself, sliding along the edge of the fence and trying so hard to not look at him. Yeah, right, like I could fight it right now. I'd been drawn to him from the start.

Daniel's focus left Amanda's face. He flitted from person to person, his eyes finally locking on mine. My throat squeezed for a moment and tingles spread across my skin as panic managed to resurface for a tiny second.

God, why was I doing this? Drinking, letting myself be drawn to him. . . . This was stupid. I had to fight these emotions and not let them take me over.

Daniel turned his attention back to Amanda, said something briefly, then headed toward me, slipping his way through the crowd. I couldn't tear my eyes away as I watched his progress. The alcohol buzz settled in stronger, my body now feeling light and airy. My limbs seemed stretched longer than usual. I felt strange, sultry, aware of everything around me. Contrary to how I thought it would be, the sensation was surprisingly pleasant.

As I waited for him, fingers of one hand digging into the wooden fence, the other clenching the red cup, I lost the urge to run away to safety. My stress dissolved into small pieces, then faded back into the depths of my mind.

In its place was a throbbing awareness that wanted him to come closer.

Chapter 4

Daniel's grin grew wider as he stopped just a couple of feet from me, peering down at my face. "What's a girl like you doing at a college party like this?" he asked in a light voice.

"Has that line ever worked on anyone?" I asked, tilting my head.

"Not even once," he admitted without any hint of shame. He walked over and grabbed a red cup, filling a beer for himself, then came back to my side. "So, seriously, I've been to a few of these and have never seen you."

I gave a casual shrug, fighting the swell of butterflies in my stomach. *He's just a guy,* I told myself. *Don't be so nervous.* "Just haven't made it to any, that's all." Understatement of the century. I sipped my beer. "Shouldn't you be home, coming up with some new theory of philosophy?"

"*Bibo ergo sum,*" he declared.

I raised an eyebrow. "Latin, huh? What does that mean?"

" 'I drink, therefore I am,' " he said in a teasing lilt, tapping the edge of his cup against mine. "Cheers."

I watched his Adam's apple bob as he drank, then tore my gaze away, focusing on his shoes. Those Chucks again. They were well worn, comfortable. The sign of someone who enjoyed being outside doing things.

"Did you get dragged here?" he asked.

I darted my gaze back at his wry grin. "Roommate," I admitted, a light flush crawling up my cheeks. My beer was warming me from the inside out, and I felt like I was glowing. "She's around here somewhere, being social and fun."

Squeals came from the back of the yard. Daniel and I turned our gazes to look at the chaos. Guys with buckets were dousing a row of girls in water, revealing outlines of breasts clinging to damp shirts. I saw Megan standing beside that football guy on the edge of the crowd, clinging to his shirt and pressing her full lips to his. He wrapped his arms around her and tugged her into his embrace.

The heat in my cheeks blossomed, and I turned back to look at Daniel's profile, his cheekbones highlighted in the warm glow of the early evening sun. He shook his head and gave a throaty chuckle about the wet T-shirt contest, and shivers of delight danced across my skin from the sound.

He took a swig of beer and sighed, turning those brilliant green eyes to me. "These parties always dissolve into some form of debauchery."

I gave a heavy sigh. "Wow. Now I *really* regret missing them all these years."

"Hey, was that a joke?" he asked, eyes wide, pressing his free hand to his chest. "Dare I think you might be warming up to me?"

I rolled my eyes and held up a hand. "Let's not get ahead of ourselves. You haven't said nearly enough Latin to warm me up yet."

Whoa. Who was I, this girl who was openly flirting with a

guy? So unlike me. But something about him made me want to meet his wit with my own. And the beer probably helped that too. Talk about a social lubricant.

"Casey," a shocked voice said from beside me. Megan stood beside the football guy, staring in open interest at me and Daniel. She gave me what she probably thought was a sly wink but was so obvious I cringed. "What's going on?"

"Talking," I mumbled, clearing my throat. "Um, this is Daniel Griffin. He's in philosophy with me. Daniel, this is my roommate, Megan Porter. And—" Crud, I'd already forgotten the other guy's name.

"Bobby Ellison," Megan filled in, her grin so wide that all of her teeth sparkled. "He's on the football team."

I fought the urge to roll my eyes. Like we couldn't tell by the jersey. But Megan was obviously infatuated with the guy and his rippling muscles, so who was I to judge? "Nice to meet you," I said.

Bobby gave me a curt nod, turning his attention back to Megan. He slid a hand along her side, tugging her closer to his hip.

"So, what are you guys talking about?" Megan asked, letting out a giggle when Bobby started nuzzling her neck. She swatted his chest. "Ooh, that feels good. But I'm trying to talk here!"

Oh God, this was awkward. I shot Daniel a glance.

"We were talking about Latin," he replied evenly. "And a little philosophy. We're studying Nietzsche in our philosophy class, and he has some fascinating theories on God and morality. Have you read any of his arguments? I'd love to hear your opinion on the subject."

"Huh," Megan said. I could almost see the exact moment her eyes started to glaze over. "Yeah, not really. I'm a math major, so I stick to numbers. Well, we're going to refill our cups and then mingle around a bit. Enjoy your conversation."

Bobby detached from Megan's neck long enough for them to scoot their way back into the crowd.

I couldn't stop the laugh that burst from me. "Wow," I said. "That was surprisingly effective. She ran right off."

Daniel shrugged. "She just doesn't have our refined tastes, is all. So," he continued, leaning his arm against the wood post, trapping me between his firm body and the fence, "are you enjoying the party?"

I rubbed my hand across the front of my upper chest. "Not really," I confessed. Not my scene. It was noisy here, and I kept getting bumped into. Even the beer glow wasn't helping me relax much.

"I have an idea," Daniel said. "Wanna get out of here?"

My heart stopped for a second, then restarted. I peered up into his eyes and saw no malice there. Could I trust him, though? It wasn't safe to leave a party to go out somewhere with a guy. Especially one I didn't know that well.

He stepped back just a bit, and I sucked in a small lungful of air. "I know somewhere we can hang out and talk," he continued. "And you can text Megan to let her know where we are."

Obviously I hadn't hidden my concerns very well. But he was thoughtful enough to help me feel comfortable. I drank the last of my beer and tossed the cup in a nearby garbage can. Should I go? Should I stay?

"Or you could just stay," he said. "I think I see another round of the wet T-shirt contest starting."

Ugh, he was right. That cinched it for me. I whipped out my cell and texted Megan that I was taking off and I'd check in an hour from now. Then I nodded and, pushing my suddenly shaking hands into my jeans pockets, I said, "Lead the way."

"A drive-in movie?" I asked in disbelief as Daniel's rust bucket of a car pulled into the lot forty-five minutes later. They still had those around? I thought they went out in the fifties or something.

He chuckled. "What, you don't like movies?"

Well, at least he'd been honest with me back at the party. It certainly was a public place, with a few cars scattered throughout the lot in front of the massive white screen. The gentle night breeze flowed in through my open window, caressing my hair and sending flutters of locks around my face.

"Of course I like movies," I stated primly, resting my hands in my lap.

Sure, I looked calm on the outside, but on the inside my stomach was a riot. And my heart hadn't stopped beating madly in my chest, despite Daniel being a perfect gentleman the whole ride here. He'd let music play softly in the background to fill the vast pockets of my awkward silence and kept his limbs on his side of the car.

"So, what's playing on the big screen?" I asked.

"I have no idea," he said, and I laughed, the band around my chest loosening a smidge. "They play movies around this time almost every night until the weather gets cooler, so I figured we'd take a chance and see what's on tonight." He paid our way in and found a spot in the middle of the lot. No cars immediately around us, but close enough that I wouldn't feel alone.

The tension in my shoulders unknotted bit by bit. He still kept to his side of the car, not trying to make any moves on me. His whole body was relaxed in the driver's seat as he shut the car off and tucked the speaker onto the door. His long legs stretched out, and he had an arm dangling over the side of the window, just in front of the speaker box.

Digging into the console between us, Daniel procured a massive bag of M&M's. "Hungry?"

"You keep chocolate in your car?"

"You don't?" he countered.

I gave the bag a skeptical look. "Doesn't it melt?" It had

been another scorcher today; surely that bag was nothing more than chocolately goo by now, despite the slight temperature drop over the last hour.

"Probably a little, but it's still good." He reached back into his console and grabbed two plastic sporks, still in the wrappers. "Here. This might help."

I stared at him.

"You haven't lived until you've eaten melted chocolate from a bag with a spork." His face was completely serious. "It's pretty much the best thing ever."

Well, I did love chocolate. With a small shrug, I took the spork and unwrapped it, tucking the wrapper in a pocket on the door. He opened the bag and scooped out a spoonful of chocolate mess. I pinched my lips and kept my still-clean utensil in my hand.

Daniel swiped his tongue out to lick the tip of the spork, his eyes locked on me; I swallowed, my body suddenly tense again, but this time with a heightened awareness of him. There was something sexy about the way he slowly licked the chocolate. With purpose.

With total pleasure.

A light shiver skidded across my flesh, and I dug my spork into the bag, desperate for something else to focus on. "Wow, this is pretty good," I conceded around a mouthful of chocolate. Still super messy, as I'd suspected it would be, but at least he wasn't wasting good food.

The movie screen flickered to life, and after a couple of commercials about concession stand food, the opening credits of *Snow White* began to play.

"Wow, they're going old-school," Daniel murmured.

Snow White. I hadn't seen that cartoon in ages. Lila and I used to watch the DVD all the time when we were little. Practically drove our mom nuts from our daily watching during one summer. We both had loved the way the animals would clean the small cottage with Snow White. Lila, wearing her fanciest dress, would stand up and sing along with a feather duster in her hand every time we hit that scene.

I swallowed the chocolate down my suddenly tight and dry throat, my hand shaking just a touch. I put my spork back in its wrapper, appetite gone.

"What food do you hate?" Daniel asked.

"What?" The question was so out of left field that it momentarily jarred me out of my sad memories.

"I hate coconut. Loathe it. If a food has coconut in it, I refuse to eat it."

"Even German chocolate cake?" I loved that dessert, with layers of chocolate, the frosting . . . all so good. Great comfort food.

He nodded and gave a fake shiver. "That food product is made by the devil."

"Well, I hate ketchup," I admitted.

"How can you hate ketchup? That's un-American. I don't think we can be friends." He pointed to the door, his forehead marred by a deep frown. "You need to walk home now, sorry."

I snorted and crossed my arms over my chest. "Come on, ketchup just masks the food's natural flavor."

"Ketchup enhances everything that's good in a meal."

We sat in companionable silence for a while, watching Snow White flitter across the screen.

"What's your major?" he asked me.

So, Daniel was apparently one of those guys who got you to open up by playing Twenty Questions. I wasn't sure how to feel about it—people like that tended to get pushy. But the questions weren't threatening my privacy so far. I forced back my wariness and said, "Business. I'm going to get my MBA in a couple of years, after I get a job somewhere. You?"

He cocked his head to the side. "What in particular interests you about business?"

I paused. "Um, it's a steady field, and I'll be able to find a job pretty easily. I've already started scouting potential companies."

"But what interests you about business itself?" he pressed. "What makes you excited to work in that field?"

My cheeks burned. "It's not about being excited. It's about dependability. The security of knowing I can find a good job." I reached into my purse and pulled out my wallet. "I'm going to go get a drink. Would you like something?"

"How about a Coke?"

I almost ripped the door open in my effort to get out of the car, making myself walk steadily to the concession stand. What about that question put me on edge? I didn't need to be ashamed of myself. Just because I wasn't frittering away my college years on a fluffy major like underwater basket weaving or speaking Pig Latin didn't mean I wasn't fulfilled.

I snorted. Security *was* fulfilling. I had a plan.

And I didn't need to defend myself to him.

Him or anyone else.

Chapter 5

I ordered two Cokes and took the overbrimming large drinks back to the car, ignoring the movie as I walked. A twinge of guilt twisted my stomach. Maybe Daniel didn't realize how he'd come across. I might have overreacted a bit to his questions. Of course he wanted to know what I enjoyed. Something I'd learned quickly about him—Daniel was a very curious person.

He opened the door for me when I approached, and I slid into my seat, handing him his drink.

"Thanks," he told me with a wide grin. "All that melted chocolate was making me thirsty."

"So, what's your major?" I asked him after taking a sip of my drink. It was good and crisp and cold, helping me clear my head. The alcohol was almost worn off now, which made me feel more confident and in control. Less floating and flowing with feelings. This was my safe space.

"I'm majoring in English and minoring in art history."

"What are you going to do with that?" What an unusual major/minor combination. Didn't seem very practical to me.

"I really don't know," he admitted. "I was thinking of teaching, but right now I'm trying to just enjoy the process of learning. Living in the now instead of worrying so hard about planning for the future. It helps that I can work flexible hours at my dad's title company and make extra money whenever I need it."

Another silence lulled the conversation, but this one a little more comfortable than before. The movie played on, with Snow White running into the woods, fear etched clearly on her face. I wanted to look away, but I couldn't.

Lila used to dash around the living room in her dress during this part while I chased her. I closed my eyes and breathed slowly. Triggers came from everywhere, and there was no real way to avoid them sometimes; the key was to be ready for them. Still, I wished we'd gone to see something else.

"What do you do when you're bored?" I forced myself to ask Daniel. I needed to get my mind off the past and back in the present. And turning his questions game against him might be the way to do so.

"I'm never bored," he declared in a haughty tone.

I chuckled and looked at him, one eyebrow up.

"Okay, that was a lie." He sipped his Coke. "I run around Cleveland, finding all the free things I can do to entertain myself. There's a lot in this town you can do without spending money."

"Oh, so you're broke."

"No, I'm not, and don't change the subject," he teased, his eyes twinkling. He turned in his seat to face me. "Have you been to the Rock Hall?"

The Rock and Roll Hall of Fame, a staple of downtown Cleveland. "Not yet, but I've heard of it, of course. It's expensive, though, isn't it?"

"Yeah, but there are parts you can see for free. The store, the main lobby. I also like people-watching downtown and taking pictures. There are a lot of strange folks around there, if you can believe it."

"Who do you go with?" I found myself asking, turning slightly in my seat to face him as well.

He shrugged. "I go by myself."

"Isn't that lonely?" I thought about him wandering around downtown, camera in hand. Mingling in and out of the jostling crowds as he captured happy families on film. I could never do it. Part of the reason why I preferred to stay at home, working on music, when I wasn't deejaying. It was a solo activity I could lose myself in without feeling self-conscious or awkward.

"Not at all. I'm surrounded by people, studying everything around me. You can learn a lot when you let yourself into the flow of traffic. Listening to conversations, watching people around you talk." He paused, and his gaze drifted to the dashboard as a secret smile creased his face. "I saw a guy and a girl break up right in front of me, but somehow they kept themselves composed as they said good-bye. Another time, this woman tearfully told her boyfriend she was pregnant—and then he dropped to one knee and proposed right there, in the middle of the sidewalk. When she said yes and jumped into his arms, crying, everyone stopped and clapped. And on one memorable trip, there were two old women holding hands on a city park bench as they fed pigeons. There's a lot of good things out there in the world if you open your eyes to it."

His words were charismatic, passionate. I could almost see the images as he described them, and I felt a momentary strange stirring in me to do . . . something. Anything. Get out of my own skin, my own brain for a moment, and live life the way he did. I couldn't imagine how it would feel to be so unguarded, open to everything.

To never be afraid.

"What do you do to escape your everyday life?" he asked

me, and I startled for a second, wondering if somehow he'd read my mind.

"Music," I said on a soft breath. It was my everything. The bass was my steady heart beat, the compositions my lifeline that kept me floating above water most days. "I make songs."

"What inspires you?"

Hm. I hadn't really thought much about inspiration. "I mostly just sit down and . . . feel a song. I layer in different tones and music samples to see what fits. Usually by my mood." Wow. I couldn't believe I was talking so openly about music with him. But I got the feeling that he would understand.

His gaze shifted to my eyes, and my heart bounced up in my throat. At some point during our conversation he and I had shifted closer until we were just a foot or so apart. I could see the flecks of freckles across the bridge of his nose, highlighted from the bright glow of the movie screen.

A pulse fluttered at the base of his throat, and his eyes dropped to my mouth. I licked my lips, and I saw him exhale.

I wasn't buzzed anymore, had nothing to blame except my own rampant emotions. Somehow this strange and quirky and magnetic man had wormed his way beneath my skin, and I couldn't fight the pull right now.

"You are a passionate person," he said in a quiet voice. "I see it in your eyes. I can hear it when you talk about music."

I just stared at him and gave a small nod, willing my heart rate to slow down to a reasonable tempo. I needed to get myself under control.

A light tinkling sound filled the car as another song came onscreen. But I couldn't tear my gaze away from Daniel's bottomless green eyes. It was like I could see every emotion flickering through them. Curiosity. Respect. Passion.

He reached out and, with a slow, steady movement, stroked the top of my hand with one lean finger. The gesture was soft and sent a burst of tingles across my flesh. He moved to stroke the line between my index and middle finger. Then he flipped my hand over and ran his fingers across my palm in featherlight touches.

"You are a mystery," he said to me, a crooked grin on his face.

"An enigma," I offered.

"A cornucopia of mazelike tendencies."

I burst out a sharp laugh. "*Really?*"

He chuckled. "Okay, I ran out of good analogies."

As my smile eased away and we fell into a comfortable silence once again, suddenly there were a bunch of questions I wanted to ask him. Like, did he have any siblings? Where did he grow up? What was he like as a kid? But if I did, he'd likely turn those questions on me. And I wasn't ready to answer things about my past.

Nor did I know how to tell him those questions were off-limits without looking like a psycho.

I rummaged through my mind for something to ask him, anything that wouldn't be too personal but would keep the conversation going. I wished I'd paid more attention when people around me made small talk.

"Um," I started, mind whirling, "what . . . cereal do you like most?"

"Cinnamon Toast Crunch," he answered without batting an eye. "You?"

"Chex. Lots of fiber and nutritional value."

"Ah, so responsible of you, Casey. Even in your breakfast cereal choosings."

I knew he was teasing, but for some reason the comment stung. Mainly because he was right—I chose cereal like I did everything else, based on what was healthy, not fun. "You'll be jealous when you have no teeth in twenty years and I still have all of mine," I finally replied.

Lame. I wanted to smack my forehead. For a moment I actually wished I had another beer in hand. At least when I'd had a drink I didn't feel like I was so painfully awkward. And if I was, I could blame the alcohol.

"Probably so." He looked down at my mouth again, then back in my eyes, and his eyelids grew hooded. He leaned a fraction closer. "I have a confession."

My pulse kicked up just a notch. "Why?"

"Why . . . what?"

I swallowed, fought every instinct to stare at his mouth. His full lips, now only six inches from mine. My body began to respond to his nearness, and I dragged in a ragged breath of his cologne. He smelled fresh, like a soft breeze on a spring day at the lake. I wanted to inch closer. *No, stop it,* I ordered myself. This was dangerous, to let myself even be this close to him.

"Um, why are you confessing something to me?" I finally asked him.

"You ask me the most unusual questions." He gave a ghost of a smile. "Honestly, I don't know. But I feel like I want to talk to you all night. Which is why I wanted to confess that I haven't been able to get you off my mind."

I swallowed, let his words sink in, then swallowed again. His honesty was disarming me, chipping piece by piece at the careful shield I had around myself.

"Casey," he said on a soft breath. "You intrigue me."

He opened his mouth to speak again, but before he could get out another word, I pushed my head forward, past the last few inches separating us, and pressed my lips to his. Daniel froze in surprise for just a moment, then slipped a hand to my forearm, stroking down until his fingers met mine.

With his other hand he cupped the back of my head and teased my mouth open with his tongue, tilting so he could deepen the kiss. He tasted like chocolate and Coke and something purely male, a combination that intoxicated me more than the beer.

My heart thrummed in a wild, erratic beat as he drank from my mouth. I opened wider, our tongues slipping and sliding, my breaths falling into his mouth in little pants. I moved closer, breasts brushing his lean and firm chest. His hand tangled deeper in my hair, and his body heat flooded through my thin shirt into my torso.

I was dizzy, drunk on him, aching with a surge of something intangible coursing through my veins. My core tightened; my belly fluttered.

He pulled back for a moment with a small gasp of air, eyes nearly black as he peered down at me. Then he gave me a crooked smile and kissed me again. Took my mouth in a sensual move that fluttered my lower belly.

I cupped his shoulders with both hands. His muscles bunched and flexed beneath my fingers. Heat poured off him, thickened the air around us.

His fingers stroked my scalp as he tasted me. The thumb on his right hand brushed against my thigh then moved up my leg, to the crease between my thigh and torso. The sensation of him so close to my stomach gave me a brief pause.

When his hand moved aside the bottom of my shirt and the very tip of his fingers brushed my bare stomach, I jerked away, pulling back to the other side of the car. It was like a bucket of ice water had been poured over my head. I tugged my shirt down as low as it could go, heart jackhammering against my rib cage.

God, please tell me he didn't feel it, I prayed. I wasn't ready. I wasn't ready.

"Is everything okay?" he asked, sitting straight up and raking a hand through his wild hair.

I wrapped my arms around my torso and gave a short nod. "Yeah. Sorry. I just . . ." What the hell could I say? Frustration bubbled beneath my skin—at my fears, at my flaws, at how perfect he was and how messed up I was. I blinked rapidly. I was not going to cry. "Sorry," I muttered again.

How quickly I'd slipped into the moment. And then had been jarred right out of it.

The silent tension between us was heavy, awkward. Daniel faced forward in his seat for several long moments, his long fingers pressed against his jean-clad thighs.

"I didn't mean to push you," he finally said. Regret filled his tone. "I . . . I just got caught up in the moment. I'm sorry I made things uncomfortable."

But it wasn't his fault. It was mine. I'd come on to him then pulled away out of nowhere, for what he thought was no good reason. He had to be confused, if not a little irritated. And I couldn't blame him.

I shook my head and checked once more that my shirt was firmly down in place. "No, it's my fault. But I'm a little tired. Can you . . . can we—"

He started the car right up and put the speaker back on its stand. "Sure. No problem."

The ride back to my apartment was only punctuated with instructions telling him where in Berea I lived. I kept to my side and he kept to his. Though his body seemed deceptively relaxed, I could see a thread of tension in the lines around his mouth, between his brows. My stomach was a knotted tangle of guilt.

What was supposed to be a simple hangout had turned complicated and messy. And no doubt once he dropped me off he'd run for the hills. And who could blame him?

I pushed back those pessimistic thoughts, not wanting to hop on the shame spiral. It wasn't like Daniel and I were going to be serious, anyway. I didn't have time for a guy, couldn't open up enough to trust anyone like that. It was better this way.

But I couldn't help the small sting of regret in my heart when he pulled into our apartment complex's parking lot.

He shut the car off and turned to me. "We're here," he said, then rolled his eyes and chuckled under his breath. "As you probably have figured out by now."

I gave him the biggest smile I could muster. "Thanks for taking me away from the party. I would have just been miserable there." That much was true—despite how awkwardly the evening had ended, it had still been better than the one I'd been facing. And that kiss . . . that was going to haunt me for a long time. "And thanks for the ride home too."

"No problem." He moved to open his door.

"Oh, that's okay. I can see myself in," I rushed to say. Even having him walk me to the door would feel far too intimate. I needed to run into my room and decompress for a little while. Shake off this deep sadness that had taken its familiar place in the bottom of my chest.

He thinned his lips but merely nodded. His eyes flickered with the briefest flash of an emotion I couldn't quite name.

"Good night," I said on a small whisper.

"Good night."

I closed the door and made my way into the building, into the empty apartment—Megan was probably still out having fun, so I sent her a text to let her know I was home—and lay down on top of my bed. After a few minutes and several rounds of slow breathing, my heart rate finally dropped to normal speed.

Despite what Daniel probably thought of me now, I wasn't a scared virgin who didn't want to go past first base. About a year and a half ago, I'd had my first sexual encounter with a guy named Jacob. He was a nice person who'd been in English 102 with me. During that semester, we would study together, work on our research papers, cram for exams.

I lifted my shirt off my lower belly and rested my palms against my scar, finger swirling around the puckered flesh.

Yeah, Jacob and I had had sex, but I'd kept my shirt on the whole time. It was in the dark, on my bed.

It hadn't taken long.

And I hadn't seen him one-on-one since. He would see me around campus and offer a halfhearted hi, but that was it. Obviously Jacob had been just as disappointed about the whole thing as I'd been.

Not an experience I was keen on repeating. Especially with Daniel, a guy who I found strangely interesting, compelling. Someone I sensed would easily challenge me out of my carefully constructed plans and life.

But I wasn't ready for any of that.

With a sigh, I dropped my shirt back over my belly and continued to stare at the ceiling until well past two in the morning, when I finally heard Megan's giggling drunk-whisper as she clunked her way into our apartment. But even then I was unable to get Daniel's warm hands and tantalizing lips out of my mind.

Chapter 6

"I missed you so much," Grandma said as she squeezed me close. "You have to tell me everything that's happened since I saw you."

I breathed in her vanilla-cinnamon scent and smiled, hugging her fragile body gingerly in return. The soft puffs of her curly, white hair tickled the underside of my nose. "I was just here last Friday," I said with a chuckle. But it was nice to be missed, loved. I'd moved out of their house freshman year to live on campus, per their insistence, but I knew I always had a home here. Hell, Grandma still kept my bedroom ready any time I wanted to sleep over.

"I know. But a lot can change in a week." She pulled back and peered up at me. Her dark brown eyes were crinkled in the corners, paper-thin wrinkles highlighted in the soft glow of the living room's lamps. "Come in, come in. Granddad's been chomping at the bit for the last hour, waiting for you to arrive. He has something new to show you." I gave a good-natured eye roll, and Grandma swatted me on the arm. "That's enough of that. You know how he is."

Granddad, an avid World War II collector, had discovered online purchasing last summer when he saw me buying a few textbooks off Amazon. And that was it for him. Now he had packages coming in all the time, bearing WWII items—old helmets, army gear, propaganda brochures . . . anything he could get his hands on. His den looked like a museum. Grandma finally had given up trying to dust in there, saying if he wanted to keep cluttering her house, he'd clean that part himself.

I followed her inside to the kitchen. Granddad was mashing potatoes. His brow furrowed when he looked at me.

"You're too skinny," he declared. "Don't you eat at school?"

This time I rolled my eyes for real. "Seriously, all I do is eat, I promise." I knew he was worried about me, though it had been a long time since I'd had some food issues. My intestines had long since healed, and I was able to eat normally. Still, that didn't stop him from pushing food on me every week.

He handed me the potato masher. "Good. Then you can help Grandma whip up these mashed potatoes while I go show you my newest acquisition." He thundered out of the kitchen.

"You'd better not bring any of that dust into my kitchen," Grandma said, shooting him a warning glare. Granddad was a large man—tall and stout, he was built like a linebacker. But even he got a little intimidated when Grandma got that tone in her voice.

I finished mashing the potatoes and whipped in butter and milk, just as Grandma had taught me. The kitchen smelled warm and homey. Fresh bread was baking in the oven. There was a casserole on the stove top, wrapped in foil. Probably chicken and broccoli, which she knew was my favorite.

"So how was school this week?" Grandma asked as she grabbed silverware and set the kitchen table.

"Oh, fine. My business classes are challenging, in a good way. But philosophy is killer." I paused just a moment, thinking of Daniel—of our kiss—then resumed mixing up the potatoes.

"And what else?" Grandma said, suddenly right behind me.

I jumped a little, my face flushing in guilt, and kept my eyes fixed on the mashed potatoes bowl. I'd already decided I wasn't going to talk about Daniel with them. It was a nonissue anyway, and I didn't want them to think I was squandering my studying time by going to parties and such. "Nothing much else going on. You know, just classes and stuff. Regular things."

Wow, that was awkward. *Way to go, Casey,* I chastised myself. No way was Grandma going to misread that.

And she didn't. "What happened?" she asked, her tone deceptively soft.

I grabbed the bowl and took it to the table, eyeing the room for Granddad. Wasn't he supposed to come back with an artifact by now? "Not much. I'm so hungry—that casserole smells divine."

I heard Grandma take a breath to talk, but Granddad came barreling back into the kitchen, bearing a military-green helmet with a net on the top. "Look at this beauty," he proclaimed, moving to set it on the table.

"Don't even think about it," Grandma said, her voice threaded with steel. She put the napkins down on the doily place mats, then shot me a brief glance that let me know she wasn't done talking to me yet.

Granddad quickly tugged the helmet back and held it at eye level with me. "This baby comes with a mostly intact camo netting. But . . . we'll talk more about it later, after dinner." He darted to the living room and put it on the couch.

I scooped helpings of the casserole on the plates as Grandma got the bread out, and we made quick work of setting the table and sitting down.

The food was piping hot, but Grandma had her air conditioning cranked to negative fifty degrees, so I was comfortable in my thin, long-sleeved shirt and jeans. I took a bite and sighed in pleasure. "You made this for me, didn't you," I said with a smile.

She grinned in return. "You always did have a soft spot for this casserole."

"So, how is your semester going so far?" Granddad asked after taking a sip of milk.

Ugh. My stomach twinged a bit. "Fine," I said brightly. "Philosophy is hard, but everything else is great. I'm really enjoying my business classes this semester. Oh, you'd really like my English professor, I bet—he visits Greece every summer because his family still lives there." Maybe talking a lot would help throw Grandma off the scent.

"I can't believe it's your last year." Granddad gave me a sad smile, then took a bite of mashed potatoes. "The time has flown by fast. You were so little when you came to live with us. And now you're a beautiful young adult, strong and smart and ready to step into your own life."

I reached over and patted his meaty hand. It was gnarled with thick veins, and arthritis had curled his fingers into knobby trunks, but those hands had held me through all those dark nights of screaming and crying. "I wouldn't be here if it weren't for you two," I said, appreciation closing my throat and choking off my words. How could I ever express the love and gratitude I had for them?

They'd saved me from the nightmares. When my family had died, there hadn't been any discussion—they'd insisted I come live with them. Had dragged me to the store to decorate my bedroom, buy new clothes since I didn't want anything that was in the old house. They'd also bought me an iPod and loaded it with songs. Grandma loved music and had passed that love on to me.

After the hell that had happened when I was thirteen, they'd given me something to live for.

And that was exactly why I didn't have time to mess around and lose my focus at school. I was so close to being done. I'd make them proud, show them I was worth the investment.

"Are you really okay?" Grandma asked, her own eyes filling up with a couple of unshed tears. "I worry about you."

I swallowed and pushed my emotions back into place. "I'm fine, promise."

"Are you getting out and doing anything?"

"Other than going to classes?" I raised an eyebrow. "I'm not stripping for college money, if that's what you're asking."

She swatted my arm, laughter making the tears leak out a bit, but her face brightened. "You knock that off. I just mean, are you making friends?"

The same thing she'd asked when I'd moved here with them and started at a new middle school. New state. Completely new environment for a new life. It had taken me months to work my way up to even telling my teacher hello, much less other students. But eventually, people had stopped staring at me like the new-girl freak and started accepting my quiet nature.

A long road, but one I'd climbed every step of the way.

"I do have a couple of friends," I told her. Daniel's crooked, dimpled smile flashed in my mind, and that hot flush crept up my face again. I didn't want to think about him right now. I wanted to focus on this delicious meal, on my grandparents and their company. But my skin tingled from the ghostly feel of his fingers on mine.

His lips pressed to mine.

"Huh." Grandma's mouth curled into a knowing smile. "I know that look. Who is he?"

I wanted to say "who?" but I knew she'd just get pissed at me for playing dumb. "A guy in my philosophy class. But it's not a big deal—we just hung out a little bit."

"Is he a senior too?" Granddad asked, his brow furrowed. He shot a concerned look at Grandma. I knew exactly what he was thinking—*Is this boy gonna distract her? Is he worthy of her time and attention?*

In halting steps, I told them about philosophy class, how I'd met him deejaying, how he'd been at a college party (I judiciously left out the drunken frat festivities, including the wet T-shirt contest) and how we went to a drive-in to see *Snow White*. I also left out the kiss. That amazing, toe-curling, soul-stirring kiss that wouldn't let me go.

They remained quiet the whole time, giving me space to get it all out. After I finished, I poked at my casserole, growing colder by the second, and took a bite.

"He sounds interesting," Grandma finally said. "When are you two seeing each other again?"

I thinned my lips. "I doubt that's going to happen. Um, I . . . I think I scared him away by freaking out. Just . . . I wasn't ready . . ."

Her eyes grew warm as she peered at me. She put her fork down and took my hand in both of hers. "Honey. I'm so glad you're working so hard at school. You make us proud—not just because you're acing your classes but because you have a wonderful work ethic. But you need to make time for a social life too."

"I do," I said, suddenly defensive. I'd hung out at the lake with Megan once or twice back at the beginning of summer, not to mention the party last night. Plus I deejayed at the club every weekend.

"Work doesn't count, Casey," she said with a raised eyebrow. She knew me far too well. "You're not mingling with others when you're standing on the outside looking in. I worry about you. You stay holed up in your apartment all the time and don't give people a fair chance."

"I'm fine, I promise." I gave Granddad a desperate glance, hoping he'd intervene and get her off my back a bit.

He shrugged his shoulders in a *you're on your own* casual

way. Traitor. Then again, he was the one who still had to live with Grandma.

"Every time someone gets close to you, you push him or her away," Grandma continued. "I want you to give this boy a fair chance. He sounds nice. *And* I want you to bring him by here so we can meet him too."

I snorted a laugh. That was so not going to happen. "He isn't going to want to see me again anyway," I said in a dismissive tone. "So it really doesn't matter." I shoved down the pain in my heart at the thought.

"I have a feeling you'll be surprised about that one," she said shrewdly. "Boys don't give up on things that easily. Not the good ones anyway." She glanced at Granddad. "This man right here chased me for months before I'd even talk to him."

"It's true," he said gruffly. "Wouldn't give me the time of day."

They hadn't talked much about how they'd met, so I was intrigued. "What made you keep pursuing her then, knowing she was hard to get?"

He crooked a grin and stared at Grandma, who smiled back. "There was something in her eyes that wouldn't let go of me. I saw her laughing with her sister one day at school, and the sun shone on her face. Her smile was wide, teeth flashing, laugh rolling and unashamed. And I knew then that she was the one for me. It was worth it to take the time and convince her of the same."

Who knew Granddad was such a romantic? My heart squeezed in my chest. I couldn't imagine being with another person for over forty years. Through thick and thin. Good times and hard times—and there had been some *incredibly* terrible times, including what had happened with my family.

Despite my intense fears, despite everything that locked me into this paralyzing mind set that I'd never be fully healed from my past, I still held a smidgen of hope that I'd find that kind of love too. That someday I could shed this pain and be whole and happy.

Then I'd see my dad's face, his eerie eyes blazing, and I'd remember what happened when you let yourself love someone fully.

I cleared my throat and pushed my half-eaten plate away, struggling to ease the knot of tension between my shoulders. "I should get going. I have a bit of studying to do before I head to work tonight." My stomach hurt too badly to eat another bite anyway. But I didn't want them to worry more about me than they already did.

"You hardly ate anything on your plate," Granddad said. "Try to eat a little more, Casey."

I sighed.

Grandma stood and took my plate before I could move. She scraped the remains into the garbage, loaded the dishwasher, then looked at me. "I know this stuff is hard for you. But I'm proud of you for still trying, even if it is uncomfortable. That's the only way you can grow—to push yourself out of your comfort zone." She paused. "Bring that boy by. Let us meet him. Your granddad can show him the collection of rifles . . . that'll encourage him to treat you right."

I gave a relieved laugh. The talk was over, the pressure off for a little bit. "Okay, if I ever hear from him again, I promise to ask him." Pretty much not going to happen anyway, so it wasn't hard to make that promise to her. Plus, I didn't say *when* I'd ask.

I helped clear the rest of the table, loaded the dishwasher, then gave them both a big hug and kiss. "I'll see you guys next Friday," I said.

"Text me if you need anything," Grandma added, patting me on the back as she walked me to the door.

I chuckled as I headed to my car. The ride to my apartment

was quiet, with soft music floating in the background, but their words were loud in my head, insisting I listen.

Give him a chance.

Could I risk it? There was something so freeing about being with him. Yet getting caught in that could be dangerous. I barely knew the guy. And I'd blown hot and cold at the drive-in. I'd pushed him away.

There was no guarantee he'd do like Granddad and pursue me. But I couldn't help that a tiny, little fraction of my heart wanted him to try.

Chapter 7

My stomach was a mass of butterflies when I walked into Philosophy on Monday morning. Professor Wilkins wasn't there yet, and half the students were still missing. Of course, I was a little early. Partly to get into my seat before Daniel did, to avoid the awkward passing-by-him-and-brushing-his-body thing.

And partly to watch him as he entered the room. Pathetic, but I couldn't help it. I hadn't talked to him since the night we went to the drive-in, and I had no idea what was going to happen.

I straightened my flyaway hair and settled into my seat, pressing my lips together to see if my gloss was still on. When I saw Amanda teeter in on the highest cork-heeled wedges that had ever been created, clad in a tank top and almost-see-through skirt, I flushed. I wasn't much better than her—I'd taken extra care with my outfit and makeup this morning in the hopes of him noticing me. I'd purposely worn the shirt that flattered my curves the most, jeans that hugged my hips. And I donned my Chucks too.

Embarrassing.

Daniel came through the door, wearing a white T-shirt and a pair of faded jeans. His hair was damp on the ends, like he'd just come out of the shower, his bag flung carelessly over his right shoulder. I tore my gaze away and fixed my eyes on my notebook, staring at the blue lines, willing my heart rate to slow down.

He dropped into the seat in front of me, and I dared to look up. A drop of water slid down the back of his neck, catching at his collar. My throat tightened and I gripped my thighs.

"Hey," I whispered, wishing my voice didn't sound so throaty.

He turned around. His smile, while polite, wasn't filled with a lot of warmth. My heart sank. "Hi," he said.

"Daniel," Amanda said, crossing her legs so her skirt rode up her slender, bare thigh, "I'm a little confused about what our homework was supposed to be. Can I look at your assignment to make sure I did it right?"

He dug into his notebook, and she scooted her desk beside his, their dark heads bowed together while they talked. I sat in my seat, rigid, torn, and kicking myself. And I was confused—I didn't want him to pay *that* much attention to me, right? It was uncomfortable. His eyes saw too much, pushed me out of my familiar zone.

But watching him talk to Amanda, seeing his fingers brush across her paper and remembering those hands on me . . . it was killing me.

I was jealous.

Jealous and stupid, because I couldn't handle this emotion I was feeling right now. His face was the first I'd pictured when I'd woken up this morning. His lips and eyes and the way he laughed and his doofy, nerdy comments. How he'd tried to make me feel at ease at the party, in his car. The brush of his fingertips across mine. The intensity as he'd talked about what he saw, how he felt. Something was so compelling about this man. It wouldn't let me go.

And now I was too late. Amanda was going to brainwash him with her huge eyes and tiny feet and tons of dimples, and he'd fall for her cute, spunky charm. Which I admit irritated me too—that he could go right from kissing me to turning all his attention to her. I smothered a groan. God, I knew I was being irrational and unfair, but it was how I felt. He was respecting my wishes, leaving me alone, but now that I was faced with it I realized that wasn't what I wanted at all.

Ugh. I needed to get out of my brain for a while.

Thankfully, Professor Wilkins strolled in right then, wearing an old white shirt and a pair of wide-legged pants made from lace and scraps of patchwork fabric. Her wiry braid was flung over her shoulder, and she plopped her massive bag on the corner of the desk. "Folks, let's get to work. We have a lot to cover today."

I tried my best to focus for the whole class. I dutifully wrote notes as she scrawled across the chalkboard, flinging chalk dust all over the floor. I even mostly kept my attention off Daniel's lean, muscled back, hardly peeked at the way his triceps flexed while he wrote. His fingers running absently through his hair as he pondered today's subject matter.

I sighed and dropped my pencil on my paper. I was beyond ridiculous. I wasn't going to think about him anymore. He was out of my mind, starting right now. Opening the textbook, I pored over the words, read and reread paragraphs, trying to wrap my mind around what the hell it all meant.

But focus was just not there today. And I knew exactly why.

The reason was two feet in front of me.

The clock ticked slowly, crawled minute by minute. I gnawed on the end of my pencil, stared at the board, did my best to not think about Daniel and that amazing kiss. Or the way I'd totally ruined the evening. I wish I could go back and fix it—but how?

Professor Wilkins cleared her throat, drawing my attention back to her face. Her brow was pinched as she looked at our row. "Been very quiet in here today," she drawled. "Are we distracted already? We're hardly even into this semester."

My cheeks burned; I could feel the heat of her gaze on me.

She huffed and waved her hands to the whole class. "Go. Don't forget to read the next chapter in your textbook. I *am* at liberty to give you a quiz any time I desire."

Everyone exhaled in relief and jumped to their feet, gathering their belongings and getting the hell out of there. I shuffled out of my seat and tucked my book and notebook into my small bag. I refused to look at Daniel, who was still sitting down; awkwardness made my chest constrict until I could barely breathe.

I shoved my way down the aisle and just made it past him when a gentle hand on my upper arm stopped me in place.

"Hey, hold on a sec," he said.

I swallowed and turned to face him as he stood. His green eyes were much warmer than they had been earlier, though I still couldn't quite tell what he was thinking. I tugged my bag higher on my shoulder and gave a small nod. My pulse raced in my ears, an ocean roar that I struggled to control.

"I'm sorry again about Thursday night," he started.

"No, no, please don't be," I interrupted, waving my hand in dismissal of his apology. "It wasn't your fault. It was just . . . I just . . ."

"Are you—" He cleared his throat, and I swore I could detect the faintest hint of a flush on his cheeks. "Are you busy this Friday night?"

"Um, no." I licked my lips. I deejayed most Fridays and every Saturday, alternating with another DJ who could only work weekends sporadically, and this was his week.

Was Daniel asking me out?

He released my arm, tucked the hand into his jeans and said, "I snagged two tickets to see an electro-house concert with a DJ I just learned about a few weeks ago. He's a local guy getting a lot of buzz. It could be a lot of fun. And I wanted to know if you wanted to come with me."

A date.

My stomach twisted in excitement, tinged with a healthy dollop of fear. He wanted to see me again. Despite what had happened last time. And he was tempting me with music—my weakness, my passion.

I couldn't say no to the concert.

I couldn't say no to him either. Because despite it all, I wanted to spend more time with Daniel.

"Sounds fun," I made myself say, proud of the way my voice didn't shake. Didn't give away the army of nerves fluttering in my abdomen.

His eyelids dropped a fraction and he looked down at me, the corner of his mouth crooking in that devilish grin I was coming to recognize. "Great. What time should I pick you up? Wanna do dinner beforehand?"

Oh, crud. I had a standing date with my grandparents on Friday, and I couldn't ditch them. I also wasn't quite ready to invite him over to meet them, despite my promise to them. "Um, can we just meet there right before the concert? I have some stuff to do earlier in the evening," I said.

"Sure." His eyes wouldn't let me go, and despite the next class's students pouring into the room, I couldn't look away. "I'm looking forward to it."

"Me too," I whispered.

I still couldn't focus.

The week had crawled at an impossibly slow pace. Yesterday evening—Thursday—I'd spent an embarrassing amount of time staring into my closet, wondering what I was going to wear tonight. For my date.

My date with Daniel.

Actually, I couldn't remember the last date I'd been on. As I walked out of my business finance class into the bright sunshine, crossing campus to head to Coffee Baby for a pick-me-up, I ran through my mental calendar. Jacob and I had hung out all the time that fall semester of my sophomore year, but we'd gone on a real date only once or twice. Grabbing pizza or going to a movie, that sort of thing.

Nothing like this. Sharing music with someone seemed so oddly intimate.

I padded across the plush grass. Students were grouped in clusters around me, girls poured into tiny clothes and precarious high heels. Laughing and shoving each other as they cracked jokes about teachers, fellow students, bad hangovers. For a moment my heart lightened as I overheard snippets of conversations, and I smiled.

Right now, strangely enough, I felt like one of them. Filled with that nervous hum of anticipation, the thrill and fear of my forthcoming night's festivities sizzling just beneath my skin. For once I was going to be on the other side of the DJ booth. Sharing the experience, the intensity of the music, with Daniel.

I tucked my books higher on my hip and headed down the sidewalk to the coffee shop.

When I arrived, stepping into the cool, refreshing air of the café, I blinked in an attempt to make my eyes quickly adjust to the dimmer lighting. There were students nestled around tables, animated conversations lilting and dancing along coffee-scented air toward me.

I headed to the back, where it looked a little less chaotic, and found a seat at a mostly empty table. Two lithe, very attractive black guys huddled close on the far end were too busy staring into each other's eyes and sharing the same heated breaths to pay any attention to me. I turned my attention to my notebook in order to give them privacy and flipped to my notes from business finance.

Before I could get up to place my coffee order, I heard an excited voice just a few feet away. "I thought that was you!" Megan came bounding toward me, her hair coiled into adorable little puffs on the side of her head. She was clad in a pair of low skinny jeans and a dark blue scoop-necked tee. She bore a huge cup of coffee. For the thousandth time I envied her casual beauty, how she lit up a room just by walking in with her big smile.

Megan was always happy, always having fun. Effortless grace. Maybe I could learn something from her so I wouldn't be painfully awkward tonight. Maybe she could give me some tips for my date.

My throat tightened as she slipped into the seat beside me. If I told her, she'd never let it go, would press me to bare every single detail. Was I ready to open up to her like that? Start letting her into my life, knowing what I was doing?

"I'm so glad it's Friday," she said, taking a sip and blanching. "Damn, that's hot!" She peeled the lid off and fanned it over her steaming cup. "You working this weekend? I wanna come hang at the club if you're deejaying."

"I have tonight off, but I'm working tomorrow night." I pressed my sweaty palms against my legs and tried to rub them dry. I was suddenly nervous to talk to her, my throat tight and stomach pinching. How the hell had I forgotten how to connect with people? To open up and just tell them about my day, my thoughts and feelings?

I used to all the time as a little kid. *Before.*

"You okay?" she asked, her brow furrowed. She put her coffee cup down. "You seem upset."

"I'm just a little nervous," I made myself say. "I'm . . . going out tonight. With a guy."

Her eyes widened so big, I thought they might pop out of

her head. She pressed the back of her hand to her forehead, then grinned. "Just wanted to make sure I'm not feverish and hallucinating. So why are you anxious? And who is it?"

My heart battered against my rib cage. If I was this nervous to talk to her, how was I going to be tonight, hanging out with him? "It's Daniel. The guy I was talking to at the party. He's in philosophy with me."

Her smile turned soft, and she reached a hand out to rub my upper arm. "It'll be okay," she said in a gentle voice. "He likes you. I could tell by the way he looked at you at the party. It's going to go fine, and you'll have fun."

Some of the fluttering in my chest eased up a touch. I drew in slow breaths. I was not going to panic about this. I was in control. He and I weren't getting married—it was just an evening out. I could do this. "Thank you," I told her with a small but earnest smile.

"So, what are you guys doing?"

I filled her in on the details. She nodded and "um-hmm"ed as I spoke, her face hiding none of her excitement for me. I had to admit, talking to her about it kind of made me a little more excited too. I hadn't heard of this DJ before, so it was a great opportunity not just for fun but for my music. To get the chance to see what other DJs were doing, how they were mixing and composing. I might get inspired for my own music.

"Okay." She eyed me closely. "I'm not going out until later tonight, so I'll help fix your hair and pick you out something sexy to wear."

"Nothing crazy," I said quickly. After all, I would have to get made up before going to Grandma and Granddad's for dinner, since I was leaving from there to go to the concert.

She lifted a hand, three fingers up. "Scout's honor."

"You were a scout?"

"Hell, no. I hate everything about the outdoors." She snorted. "But I thought that sounded more official."

I chuckled. My back muscles eased up their tension. "I'm going to get a coffee. Need anything?"

"I'm good. I'll wait here with your stuff," she offered.

I made my way to the line, glancing back at Megan. The conversation hadn't been nearly as difficult as I thought it would be. I'd been certain she was going to hound me to the point of discomfort, but instead she'd sat back and let me talk about Daniel without being too pushy.

Maybe I'd misjudged her, been a little harsh in my perception of her. Guilt flamed anew, heating my face.

I was so quick to make assumptions lately. Sure, it made my life safer, but it didn't make me that much happier. Just talking to her had lifted a weight off my shoulders. She was right—surely tonight would be fine. Daniel wasn't going to push me beyond my comfort zone; I'd made it very clear how far I was willing to go, and he had still asked me out.

I grabbed a coffee and made my way back to the table to talk with Megan about how I was going to get through the evening without being a nervous wreck.

Chapter 8

The music reached me even out on the street a couple of blocks away. It hummed and sang down the sidewalk, thrummed beneath my skin. I couldn't help the smile that turned up the corners of my mouth.

Daniel had said he'd meet me out front of the building. It was downtown, and I'd found a parking spot on the street, luckily. The club was small, but people moved in and out and milled around, laughing and talking. Punks, preps, hipsters—all mingled without care. It was almost surreal.

The warm evening air caressed my bare arms. I'd worn a sparkling tank top and a pair of jeans. Megan had given me a big frowny face for not dressing up, but I'd been adamant about it. So she'd taken a lot of pleasure doing my makeup and hair. I looked a bit like a pinup model, with twists and curls, my eyes highlighted with light eye shadow and black eyeliner. My lips were bright red; she'd loaned me her favorite shade to reapply after dinner. I tried to hold on to my feeling of confidence.

I strolled across the sidewalk in my black flats and looked

for Daniel's familiar form. It took me a minute but I spotted him, leaning against a brick wall. He had on relaxed jeans and a slim-fit black dress shirt with the sleeves rolled up, showing off the muscles in his forearms. The neck was unbuttoned, and I could see the line of his throat, the V at the base. His hair was appropriately mussed; the yellow glow of lights gave him a halo.

When he saw me, his grin widened and he shoved away from the brick wall. "You look amazing," he said. I could barely hear his throaty words over the throbbing beat from inside the club. He took in my whole outfit, his eyes growing slightly hooded.

My heart rate picked up, stuttered, and I gave what I hoped was a casual nod. "Thanks. You too."

Megan had advised me to just keep it casual tonight in our communication. To let Daniel pursue me—don't push him away but don't make it easy for him either. Apparently, guys liked the chase. I wasn't sure how readily I believed that. Then again, it had certainly been true with my granddad.

At any rate, I was supposed to play it cool and slowly show my interest throughout the night if I was feeling it. This I could totally do—I had distance down to an art form.

He whipped the tickets out from his back pocket with a dramatic flourish and handed me mine. "It's standing room only, of course. This is the opening act—some local band. Can't remember their name."

I nodded and fought the urge to smooth my hand over my hair. Megan had also told me I needed to appear self-assured, in my outfit, my hair, my makeup. To know that I looked good. That was going to be much harder. But I could fake it at least.

I hoped.

He stepped beside me; the fresh scent of his cologne filled my nostrils, made me a little heady. For one impulsive second I wanted to press close to him again, breathe him in deeply. He put his hand on the small of my back, and tiny fissures of pleasure snaked out across my skin from the unassuming touch. Even through my tank I felt the pressure of his warm fingers.

If I was reacting this strongly to him based on his cologne and an innocent touch, how was I going to get through this night without embarrassing myself?

I could feel the firm line of his body right behind me as we made our way into the line. People jostled and laughed, waving arms and talking loudly over the loud beat of the music. I got bumped into a few times, with one elbow pressing against the left side of my belly. A twinge of phantom pain made me pause. My chest tightened a fraction, and I drew in a few slow breaths.

Instantly I pushed back on that panic, made myself relax and focus on the moment. *Not here.* I was fine. I was healed and not in physical pain anymore, and nothing was wrong with me.

"Sorry about the crowd," Daniel whispered in my ear from behind me. "It's pretty crazy." His warm strength surrounded me, cocooned me from the crowd, and I clung to his scent and his words and his presence, let them fill me and distract me.

It worked. My chest finally eased up, and I gave him a grateful smile. We made it to the front of the line and handed our tickets over, and then we were shown inside.

The crowd was huge. Bigger than any of the ones I'd seen at my club. It was intimidating, wholly maddening for a few minutes. Daniel must have sensed my fear, because he skirted me along the outer edges to a free spot along the brick wall, where there were only a few people. I drew in a relieved breath.

"I'm going to get us something to drink," he said. His hand brushed against my elbow, and I felt a shiver of longing skitter across my flesh. I gave a mute nod and watched him saunter away.

I couldn't tear my eyes off him until he disappeared into the crowed. The air was thick and heavy but not as overbearing as I'd feared; small pockets of cool air streamed from vents in the ceiling. I glanced around for the first time and really made myself take it all in. I saw lots of smiles and laughs, people dancing sexy, dancing goofy, doing the robot.

The band was decent. Some kind of techno style with a guy singing, a guy working percussion and another running the digital sounds in the background off a unit. The lyrics were simple but catchy, and I found myself starting to sway in place.

No one was looking at me. I was just another face in the building, another lover of music. The tension unwound in my torso, seeped from my limbs as I let myself feel the melody.

A few minutes later, Daniel showed up, a beer in one hand and a plastic cup of ice water—with lemon—in the other. He handed it to me. "Here ya go."

He remembered. A small thing, but it made something in my heart twinge in response. I swallowed a big, refreshing gulp. "This is perfect. Thank you."

We stood side by side for a while, drinking, absorbing the atmosphere. It was a comfortable silence between us, woven together with the music, a brief comment here or there about whatever song was currently on.

The band played their last song, and electronic dance music filled the loudspeakers as the headlining DJ worked on getting his equipment up and running.

"Are you enjoying it so far?" Daniel asked me.

I leaned in close; I could barely hear him because the music was so loud. "I am!" I shouted. I knew there was a huge grin on my face, partly because I was actually liking the atmosphere. And partly because of him.

Okay, mostly because of him.

"So, what made you choose Smythe-Davis to go to school?" he asked, taking a long draw from his bottle.

"It's fairly close to where my grandparents live," I admitted, hoping that didn't sound lame. But that was a key factor. "I also got some academic scholarship money, which helped too."

He nodded. "My family lives a little south of the Cleveland area. I like being close enough to visit them when I want but far enough away that I can make my own life. I really enjoy Northeast Ohio."

"Taken any interesting pictures lately?" I asked, remembering our conversation in the car. And then our kiss. My cheeks burned.

His lips parted just slightly as he looked down at my mouth, and I licked my own in a nervous response. Obviously he was remembering it too. My pulse picked up again.

"Well, this weekend I hung out around University Circle, near the art museum. I also went to the cultural gardens," he said. "I saw a few little kids dancing in a dirty water puddle—they were muddy as hell, caked up to their eyeballs, and didn't care. It was cute."

Part of me was relieved he hadn't commented on our kiss. And part of me had been hoping he would. God, I was all over the place. What was with me? I wanted it, I didn't want it. I was driving myself insane with this confusion.

"I'll show you some pictures later if you want," he continued. "Several are on my phone."

The music shut off, and we turned our attention to the stage. "Ladies and gentlemen!" a deep voice cried out from behind the DJ booth. "I'm DJ Enrique. Let's get this shit going!"

The crowd roared, and hands went immediately in the air. Apparently DJ Enrique had quite a following. I turned my attention to him, watching how he interacted with the crowd. He was engaging, magnetic. His hair was cropped close, and I could see his thick slash of eyebrows even from here. The headphones were cupped around his neck, one pressed to his ear as he started.

A seductive, heavy bass throbbed through the speakers, and the crowd began to dance. He layered several electronic instrumentals over it but let the bass be the main line. I liked it instantly.

"This song is great!" Daniel said, taking another swig of his drink. He finished the last of his beer and tossed it in a nearby garbage can. Then he took the empty cup out of my hand, propped it on a small table littered with empty bottles and slipped his hand into mine. "Let's dance."

My heart stuttered. "Oh, no, I really couldn't—"

"Just one," he said, leaning so close I could smell him again, that rich scent interweaving with the music, with the heat in the room.

My body began to throb in response to his proximity, to the erotic undertones of the song. I'd never danced in front of other people—at least, not since I was a little kid, uncaring about where my limbs went flying or how I looked.

The corner of his mouth turned up, and that damned dimple made an appearance "One dance," he repeated.

For whatever reason, I found myself nodding. I let him pull me to the very edge of the dancing crowd; at least he didn't force me into the middle, where I'd be way too nervous. He loosely rested a hand around the curve of my right hip and started moving. I stood for a second, then began to sway too.

So awkward. I felt like I was all limbs, stiff and robotic. My throat tightened up and I stopped.

"Close your eyes," he said to me, warmth pouring from his face. "You're overthinking it—I can see it in your eyes. Close 'em. Just feel it."

I raised an eyebrow.

"Trust me."

The words were simple, but I knew he was right. I sighed and did as he suggested, shutting everyone else out. For several long moments I focused on the heavy beat, Daniel's scent, the slight pressure of his hand on my hip.

The world faded from me, and I started to sway. Music wove itself into me, into that blissful place where I escaped, into those moments that made me the happiest. I found my arms starting to raise over my head as I got caught up in the blind sensations I was experiencing.

Before I knew it, the heat from Daniel's body poured toward mine as we moved closer together, a fraction at a time. My nipples brushed against his chest, my pelvis bumping his. I resolutely kept my eyes closed, though my body instantly responded with a telltale tightening, tingling. He didn't push me, though, didn't try to tug me closer. He let it be. His fingers squeezed ever so slightly on my hip, and something deep in my core intensified in response.

I inched toward him and peeked open my eyes to find his locked on my face, his pupils so wide his eyes were nearly black.

My lips parted; my heart slammed against my rib cage. I let one arm fall to my side and the other drape over his shoulder, which drew us even closer together. His hand slid to my lower back, but still he didn't pull me against him. Neither of us spoke, but our shared silence was potent with emotions.

He was letting me dictate the terms, decide how fast I wanted us to proceed. A heady rush of power swept through me. I could see in his eyes, in the erratic flutter of his throat, that he wanted me. And my own pulse beat in time with his. Music poured between and around and through us. My breath became ragged.

I rested my hand on his hip so that our bodies were flush. He swallowed, then dropped his mouth to press a sweet kiss against my forehead. The gesture was so strangely tender that I found my throat closing again.

Someone bumped into my back, then moved away with a muffled apology. I'd been so wrapped up in him that I'd hardly noticed anything around me. But now I realized we'd moved deeper into the crowd, submerged fully now. It was liberating to just get wrapped up in the moment.

I lived my life on the other end of the DJ booth, watching but never a part of it. Controlling the music while I worked but never letting it sink beneath my skin.

The music suddenly dropped into a heavy beat. Daniel smiled and threw his hands up, and I did the same. Arms shot up all around us as people ground and danced with abandon to the song.

And I got it.

Now that I was inside it, among the writhing masses . . . I could suddenly see why people love going to The Mask to dance. What made them come back for more, let down their hair and give everything they had into the song. There was something wildly intoxicating about letting myself fall into the music this way, surrounded by others doing the same. A group madness, one I had craved without even realizing it.

Our bodies moved against each other, and a languid swell of sensuality filled me. I was fluid, light-headed, pulsing with a dark desire to be closer to him. He wrapped both hands around my waist and brushed his lips against my brow, the shell of my ear, the curve of my throat. I arched against him, rubbing my thumbs along the waistband of his jeans.

I *ached.*

His mouth moved down to lick the sweat-tinged flesh of my shoulder, and I bit back a moan. My lower belly thrummed in response. He gave a muffled groan and looked at me, piercing me with his stare. Desire was etched clearly in his face. I knew it was in mine too.

My heart raced hard, fast, tapping a beat that throbbed in my limbs, roared in my ears. I felt the length of his arousal pressed against me, and for one wicked moment I wanted to touch him there. To see how hard he could get for me. How hard *I* could make him.

I sucked in a ragged breath and shook my head. This was moving too fast. I was going to drown in these emotions if I didn't pull back. God, I was so tempted by him. Tempted and yet also petrified. I couldn't let my desire make me lose my focus.

I remembered what had happened the last time I'd gotten carried away with him, his fingers so perilously close to my terrible secret.

I pulled back and wiped at the sweat slicking my brow. "I'm . . . warm. I'm going to step outside."

He froze, his hands stopping their soft caress of my back through my tank. "Are you okay?"

"Oh, yes. Fine. I'm fine, thanks." I was stumbling over my words. The weight of the music, the crowd pressed in on me, and I struggled to draw in a fresh breath of air. "I just . . . I'm sorry." I pushed through the crowd and made my way to the door.

The air was warm but not tinged with sweat; I drew in a deep breath as I made my way to the sidewalk, where no one else was standing. Another. My skin was coated in perspiration, built up from the steaminess of the room, the body heat. My own stupid arousal for Daniel.

How the hell had I let my defenses down so easily?

Somehow I lost my mind around him. It scared me how quickly I would drop my guard, let him get close.

"Casey?" His quiet voice came from behind me. The music didn't reach us a lot over here, so he didn't have to speak loud.

I reined in my rampant emotions and turned to face him, a polite smile plastered on my face. "Sorry. I'm sorry—I just, it was hot, and the crowd . . ." And my own feelings had overwhelmed me. . . .

"Do you like me?" he suddenly asked.

I blinked. I hadn't expected that. "Um, what?"

He stepped closer, though he maintained space between us. Not pushing me, again. Being thoughtful, again. A pinch of shame twisted my heart.

"I'm getting mixed signals from you and I can't quite tell how you feel," he said. "Sometimes I feel like you don't want to be anywhere near me. Especially when things start getting a little . . ." He paused. "Hot."

My face flushed. I opened my mouth to speak, but he kept going.

"But sometimes . . . when you just let go and let us happen, it seems like you feel the same way I do. And I just wanted to know, wanted to hear it from your own mouth."

Chapter 9

Daniel's intense gaze ripped me down to the core. In that moment I knew he saw the entirety of me, my fears and desire and self-loathing and fakeness at pretending like everything was just fine. And it totally wasn't. Not even close to it.

All my tension, my sexual fearfulness and panic, churned in my gut. I blurted out, "Yes, I do like you. But I don't want to." Instantly I wished I could take those words back. Because that wasn't quite what I meant—at least, not the way I wanted to say it.

His face fell just a touch, but I saw his eyes dim. The corners of his mouth turn down. "Why don't you want to like me?" There wasn't self-pity in his voice, despite the look on his face. Just genuine curiosity.

A group of girls walked by, giggling. Two of them slid their gazes to Daniel, running up and down his physique. My chest squeezed with that tic of jealousy again. I knew what I was feeling and I couldn't deny it. I wanted him and didn't *want* to want him. But I didn't want anyone else to have him. Ugh.

He ignored the girls, keeping his attention fixed on me.

Daniel wanted to know why I was so nervous about liking him. But right now *I* wanted to know why he was still here. Why wasn't he backing away, running into the night to escape the jacked-up girl who blew hot and cold with him? Spending his time with someone a little more whole and normal?

Daniel chuckled, and the tension in his upper torso leaked away as he shook his head. I flinched in surprise at the sound, shocked once again by his reaction. "Look, I don't want to ruin this awesome night," he finally said, reaching over to take my hand. His thumb caressed my thin skin, and shivers of excitement skittered across my flesh. "I've had a lot of fun with you tonight. Let's just go inside and chill. We can dance or just people-watch, whatever you want. No pressure, no promises."

The tightness in my torso leaked away and I drew in my first real breath since I'd panicked on the dance floor. Did he mean it? What was with the change of heart? "Are you sure?" I asked, hesitation clear in my voice.

"I just wanna have fun and spend time with you. That's all." He stepped a few inches closer, studying my eyes to see my reaction. He seemed sincere.

I swallowed. Finally nodded. He'd been a true gentleman, not making me feel ashamed for my freak-outs. Okay, I could see something deep inside him wanted to push me a bit more, to make me talk to him about whatever the hell was wrong with me. But perhaps he knew this wasn't the right time. Regardless of the reason, I was relieved at the reprieve.

Daniel led me back inside.

The rest of the night was not as awkward as I'd been afraid it might be. The DJ kept the tunes going. Daniel and I stuck to the periphery of the crowd, doing that standing-dance thing as I drank more water and he had another beer. He didn't press me to talk or dance, though I did catch him looking at me out of the corner of his eye a couple of times.

Words were right there on the tip of his tongue, I could tell, but he bit them back.

It was well after two in the morning when the concert ended. While I'd had a lot of fun, I was exhausted. The emotions, the sexual tension, everything had drained me, and I was ready to shower, slip into bed and go to sleep.

Daniel walked me to my car. "Is it okay if I follow you home? I . . ." A slight blush crawled up his throat as he swallowed. "I just wanna make sure you get there okay. It's late."

His awkwardness was endearing. I couldn't speak, so I just nodded my response. Emotion closed my windpipe. I stood in front of my car door and reached a hand up, caressing his cheek for the briefest of moments before dropping my hand.

Daniel followed me back to my place. When I pulled into the lot, I stepped out of my car. He pulled in a few spots down, his car engine clicking as he strolled toward me. His smile was wide and genuine. "Thanks for going with me," he said.

A cooler breeze ruffled his hair, cooled the last lingering sweat on the back of my throat, the small of my back and between my breasts. "Thank you for inviting me."

Daniel reached a hand out and touched one of my curls. His mouth turned up at the corners. "I like your hair like this," he murmured. Then he stepped closer and cupped my face in his hands, like I was made of porcelain. His movements were slow, measured; he was probably making sure of my feelings.

Then his soft lips brushed against mine. I sighed, and his tongue slipped along the seam of my mouth, the corners of my lips. I pressed a fraction closer, let him open my mouth a little more. His hands remained light, his kiss far too brief. He pulled back, stroked a thumb across my cheekbone, then stepped away.

"Good night, Casey," he said. Then he turned and walked to his car. As he drove off, he gave me one last wave.

I stood there for a couple of minutes. I could still feel his hands on my face, his lips on mine. It was a gentlemanly kiss, not having any of that heat that our earlier dancing had shown between us. Yet somehow it had blown me away even more.

I brushed my fingertips against my lower lip. Then I headed to my apartment, unlocking the door. Megan's purse was on the side table, so she was obviously home. I gave a quiet chuckle—for once, I was out later than she was. She would be so proud of me when we talked about it tomorrow.

As I tossed my keys and purse on the table, I paused. Huh. The thought of talking to her about my date had just cropped up, and I hadn't even flinched about it.

I made my way into the shower, rinsing under the cool water. It was refreshing after being so hot and sweaty in the club. My soapy fingers brushed against my puckered scars. It was crazy how quickly he'd turned me on while we were dancing. I was a little scared, yes. But underneath that fear was another emotion, something that bubbled in my chest whenever I thought of him. Saw him. Touched him.

There was a craving for him I couldn't deny.

I rinsed and toweled off, slipped on a tank and sleep shorts and lay on top of my bed.

My head was still spinning; I couldn't get Daniel off my mind. His bluntness, his eyes, those wicked fingers caressing my back. His hot mouth on my skin.

Like me, Daniel was full of contradictions—he pressed me, then backed away. One thing was for sure. The guy kept me on my toes.

My lips stayed curved into a tiny smile until I fell asleep.

I was totally going to throw up.

Megan walked out of her bedroom in her lacy swimsuit cover-up and eyed me, one perfectly arched brow raised. "Don't you dare vomit on this rug," she demanded. "Seriously, it'll be fine. He'll be here any minute. And then we can go have a ton of fun." She gave a wide grin. "I have on my sexiest bikini. It's basically just strategically placed bright green string. Bobby's gonna shit his pants when he sees how fabulous my boobs look in it."

Obviously my nervousness was evident all over my face. I tugged at the neckline of my T-shirt and gave a weak laugh. "Please. You look fabulous in everything."

She sat down beside me and took my clammy hands in hers. "Hey," she said, her smile fading away. "You okay?"

My nod was jerky, despite my attempt to smother my fears. Why the hell was I so nervous? Probably because I'd put myself out there yesterday and impulsively asked Daniel to come with us.

Megan's family lived in a lakefront house, with its own private beach on Lake Erie, and apparently every year they had a massive grill-out for her dad's birthday. Earlier this summer she'd invited me to spend a weekend with her at their place and meet her folks, but I'd passed on going. Instead, I'd spent that time locked away in my room, reading a book and eating far too much Chinese takeout.

This time I couldn't make myself say no to her invitation. She'd pleaded with me with those big, brown eyes, reminding me how much fun I was having lately, getting out of the house and living. After a few minutes, I'd caved.

While bathing suit shopping yesterday in Target, a few hours before my Saturday night deejaying shift at The Mask, I'd grabbed my phone and fired out the world's lamest text to Daniel, asking if he wanted to come with me. Knowing it was super last minute and he'd likely be busy but unable to deny to myself that I wanted to see him again.

A few minutes later he'd replied that he was in.

So now here I was, sweaty yet strangely clammy in my one-piece navy blue swimsuit, a pair of cutoff jean shorts and a T-shirt. Hoping against hope that I didn't make a total idiot of myself in front of him today. I was nervous about going to the party, being surrounded by all of Megan's family and friends. I'd wanted someone on my side.

The first person—the *only* person—I'd thought of was him.

Plus, I knew that since Bobby was going to meet us there, he and Megan would be sucking face the whole time, and I didn't want to watch it.

The doorbell rang.

Megan jumped up and gave me a broad wink. "Ooh, I bet that's Daniel!" She flung the door open. "Come in! She's right here, on the couch." She waved in my direction.

Daniel stepped inside and peeked around, teeth flashing from his bold grin. This was his first time in our apartment, and he eyed the artwork, the furniture, the bookshelves. I'd spent the morning cleaning up to make sure it was presentable. Megan had laughed her ass off when she saw me scrubbing the floor a couple of hours ago, declaring Daniel wouldn't give two shits about how sparkling the tile was.

I stood and wiped my palms on my shorts. My smile was wobbly but genuine. He had on board shorts with a faded gray T-shirt. His eyes glowed, his dark hair wind-tossed. He looked devastating.

My stomach fluttered.

"You guys ready to go?" Megan asked, flinging her bag over her shoulder. She reached for the small cooler by the door, but Daniel took it right out of her hands with a smile.

I grabbed my purse and keys. Daniel followed right behind me as we locked up and made our way to my car. I'd offered to drive—one, because I knew Megan would want to party, and no way was I riding in a car if she drunk drove. And two, if I needed to bolt for whatever reason, I wouldn't be stranded there.

But I was going to challenge myself to not run away this time. I'd talked to Grandma about it yesterday, and she'd been thrilled I was going. She suggested I take small breaks away from the crowd, find a few minutes to be by myself every hour or two so I wouldn't get overwhelmed and panic. It was good advice.

I could do this.

The ride to the party was filled with Megan singing along to the radio. Daniel stayed quiet in his spot on the passenger side as I drove. Megan occasionally popped her head between us and sang loudly in our ears, slightly out of tune but enthusiastic. I couldn't help but laugh—it was good to see her so happy.

When we arrived, we had to park a bit down the street, since there were cars lined up for a couple of blocks in each direction. My breath started to come in small pants. So many people. Could I really do this?

Daniel casually reached over and rested his hand on my thigh. Not sexually. Just a comforting gesture. I shot him a grateful smile. He knew how I was feeling, had picked up on it instantly. It scared me a little how he was starting to read me so fast.

But right now, that was exactly what I needed. His silent support. I reached down to give his hand a small squeeze, then parallel parked the car.

We headed toward Megan's parents' house. The sun was bright, hot. As we got closer I heard the sounds of people talking and laughing.

Megan darted around us and opened the side door, welcoming us in. Cold air blasted me instantly, chilling my skin, and I erupted in goose bumps. The kitchen bustled with even more people, teens gathered in one corner, laughing. A few adult women were near the fridge, pulling out covered plates. God, this party was huge.

But everyone was smiling. No one was staring at us wondering why I was here. My tension seeped out bit by bit.

A tall black woman came over, her hair swept off her neck in a graceful ponytail. Had to be Megan's mom; the two of them had similar features. I could see where Megan got her good looks from—she was gorgeous. Didn't look old enough to be in her forties, actually. When she smiled, a few lines crinkled around her dark golden eyes. "Hello, honey." She kissed Megan's cheek, then looked at me and Daniel.

"Mom, this is my roomie, Casey," Megan said as Daniel put the cooler on the countertop. "And her . . . friend." There was a wide grin on her face as she said that, and I wanted to punch her in the shoulder for that telling pause. Awkward.

"Glad you two are here! I'm so happy you could come." Her mom clapped her hands, jangling the silver bracelet hoops around her wrist. She had on a dark purple one-piece suit with a thin red and yellow scarf skirt tied at her waist. "Help yourself to whatever we have. There's beer, wine, juice, water . . . and food everywhere."

Megan grabbed her mom's arm and they walked off, leaving me and Daniel standing there. I peeked up at him to see the smile in his eyes.

"What?" I asked him.

"I'm just happy to be here with you." The words were so simple, so . . . Daniel. I found myself melting from the heat of his stare. He grabbed two bottles of water from the fridge and handed one to me. "Wanna go outside? Probably a little less crowded."

A woman jostled into his side and apologized, and he shot me a knowing look.

I chuckled and followed him through the sliding glass doors into the bright green expanse of grass. More people were out here. We walked to the edge of the fenced-in grass and just stared out at the rich beauty of Lake Erie. The sun glinted off the dark blue waters, and boats were skating across the waves, leaving ribbons of white wake trailing behind them. It was windier out here, and my hair flitted about in my ponytail; a few strands tugged free and tickled my face.

"It's so pretty," I said after I sipped my water. I balanced my bag higher on my shoulder.

My mom would have loved it. The whirling air, the hot sun, the endless body of water stretching out far as the eye could see. She'd always wanted to live on the lakefront, had asked my dad to take us on vacation somewhere along Lake Erie several times that last summer. My heart painfully twisted, and for a rare moment I gave in to the emotion, remembering her gap-toothed grin and perpetually sunburned nose.

It hurt so much to miss her. But strangely enough, it hurt even more to not think about her. Or my sister.

Daniel interrupted my bittersweet thoughts. "My family and I used to go to Vermillion every summer when I was a kid—rented a cottage right on Lake Erie for the week." He cupped a hand over his brow and peered out across the lake, down to the beach waiting below.

"How many siblings do you have?" I found myself asking. My heart raced, and for a second I wished I could take it back. Knowing I was opening myself up to questioning now. Then I remembered how he'd backed off Friday night, had let me have space. He'd done the same at the drive-in too.

If I was going to try to be more social, I needed to get used to talking to people. Despite the intense discomfort.

"I have three younger sisters," he said, shaking his head with a laugh. "God, they are a handful. Growing up, I never had hot water for showers."

"I couldn't even imagine," I said. Before he could ask me anything in return, I asked, "Wanna go down to the beach?"

"Sure."

I strolled behind him down the sun-warmed wooden stairs. When my feet hit the bottom plank, almost entirely covered with sand, I sighed and stepped forward to dig my toes into the gritty warmth. There was nothing that could compare to that sensation.

This truly was a heavenly moment.

"So, do you have any brothers or sisters?" he asked innocently.

The moment soured, and my stomach flipped. I stepped past him and willed my heart to slow down its erratic slam in my rib cage. "No."

Daniel stiffened, and I saw the questions in his eyes.

Not now, please, I mentally pleaded. Today I just wanted to pretend to be a normal girl—or at least as close to normal as I could get. Not damaged or awkward or struck with a permanent case of foot-in-mouthitis.

"Casey!" a light voice hollered from above us. I turned and saw Megan waving down at me, her other arm wrapped around Bobby's bare torso. "We're on our way down!"

Never had I been more relieved to see her.

Saved from the questions I'd been eager to avoid. I just hoped my bluntness hadn't done any damage to the fragile threads binding him and me together.

Chapter 10

The elephant sitting on my chest finally lumbered off, freeing up the oxygen in my lungs, and I waved back at Megan. She would distract us all with her fun. And I could try to keep to my mantra of enjoying the day like everyone else.

As she made her way down the stairs, I saw she carried her cooler. She ran over and hugged me, then whispered in my ear, "My *God*, Bobby is smokin' hot today. Look at that washboard stomach. I want to lick him all over."

I rolled my eyes. "Somehow I doubt he'd complain too hard about that."

She pointed to the cooler. "So, I snagged some refreshments for us. And I decided we should take my dad's boat and go have some fun. Get out of this crowded party for a while. What do you say?"

On the one hand, salvation sounded perfect. I could have quiet time to relax with my roommate in a less overwhelming setting. But that would most likely involve Daniel and me watching her and Bobby clawing all over each other.

Still, having her around would keep our conversation light enough that I could hopefully avoid any triggers.

"Sounds great," I finally said and glanced over at Daniel. "What do you think?"

He gave me a wide smile and with the tips of his fingers just brushed the soft hairs on my lower arm. The touch was feather-light, barely discernable, yet my skin seemed to tingle even before the contact. "Can't wait."

It was ridiculous how aware I was of him. Always. He did something to me, something I'd never experienced before.

He made me crave.

And I was going to be trapped on a boat with him, out on the water. God, I hoped I was ready for this.

Megan whooped and grabbed Bobby's hand. We all followed our fearless leader to her dad's dock, where a small white boat sat bobbing in the water. It was comfortable enough to fit four. She tossed the cooler in, slathered on a little sunscreen and handed the bottle to me.

"You'll burn, pale girl," she said with a wink.

She was right—I barely lingered in the sunshine, and when I did I was sunscreened to the max. I put it on my exposed flesh, then handed the bottle to Daniel, trying to not swallow as he lifted his shirt to bare the lower half of his stomach. A small, light trail of hair led down into his shorts. He wasn't as cut as Bobby, but he was toned, tight. I clenched my hands into fists and pressed them to my sides.

I wanted to touch him, feel his sun-warmed skin against mine. Press my lips to his.

I tore my gaze away before he could catch me staring and got into the boat behind Megan. The guys followed us. Daniel took the seat beside me, on the bench in the back of the boat, while Bobby was in the passenger seat beside Megan.

"Hold on!" she cried out, then started the boat up and pulled it away from the dock.

Warm air shoved at me from all angles as we flew along the water, but it was tinged with small sprays, which refreshed my heated skin. Daniel's presence poured onto my right side. His knee brushed against mine, and I bit my lower lip. He'd dropped his shirt back down, but I couldn't get the image out of my mind. His stomach was tan, something I hadn't expected. Like he did yard work or was outside shirtless a lot.

I fumbled for the water bottle in my bag and took another swig. It was hard keeping my attention off him. Trying to act casual when every little bob over the water would send his knee bouncing against mine.

I could close my eyes, be spun in circles for a full minute and still know exactly where he was. My traitorous body had become hypertuned to his.

"Hot out here," Daniel said, and I raised an eyebrow about his banal remark, only to find a smart-aleck grin on his face.

"The sun does that to people," I replied.

His smile faded a bit as his face grew serious. "It also brings out all the highlights in your hair. It's such a pretty shade." He reached a hand up and toyed with a strand of hair in my ponytail.

My heart skipped a couple of beats, then stuttered along. I swallowed; my body started to sway toward him, like a magnet to strong metal, and I made myself jerk back into place.

"You two are awfully quiet back there," Megan declared, head turned over her shoulder as she peered at us. Her eyes were slit in mock suspicion, and her hands clenched the boat's steering wheel.

"We're just talking philosophy," I said in a droll tone. "And keep your eyes forward so we don't crash, please." Daniel still was stroking the lock of my hair, and based on how close we were right now, she'd know it was a flat-out lie.

"Huh. Looked more like chemistry to me," she said but turned forward again.

Bobby snorted in response.

Ugh. I rolled my eyes at Daniel. He dropped my hair and moved back a fraction, laughing. But I felt his absence when he pulled away.

When we reached a spot where the house was just a small blip on the distant coastline, Megan stopped the boat. We lulled gently along the water, a soothing rhythm that made me smile.

Bobby stood, winked at Megan then dove into the lake. She squealed when water splashed us all. Daniel laughed and wiped his arms.

Bobby's head bobbed above the water. He wrapped a firm hand on the side of the boat, eyeing Megan like she was a three-tiered chocolate cake. "It's refreshing in here," he said in a low voice. "You should come . . . in."

I bit back a sarcastic groan. Really? That was the best he had? Megan, however, almost ripped her clothes off in an effort to strip down to her tiny bikini. She jumped in and squealed even louder when she hit the water. More drops splashed onto my heated skin.

"Do you like to swim?" Daniel asked me. He stripped off his shirt in one smooth move, dug around in the cooler for a Gatorade and twisted the cap off. When he tilted his head back, his Adam's apple bobbed just a bit; I turned my attention to my water bottle, hanging in my limp hands. *Don't stare,* I ordered myself.

"I can pretty much keep myself alive," I said with a shrug and took a swig of lukewarm water. "I like floating more than anything else."

Megan and Bobby were clinging to each other and pushing away, giggling a lot, doing that flirt-shove thing that gives you an excuse to touch the other person every three seconds.

Daniel remained silent until I dared to glance at him. The

sun glowed across his skin, the crown of his mop of hair, the defined muscles along his shoulder and collarbone. My core pulsed in response. There was no denying to myself how much he heated me up. Even just looking at him made me throb. My fingers itched to touch his bare flesh.

"Wanna go float?" he asked me, the corner of his mouth crooked in that smile that dared me to let go of my inhibitions.

I couldn't deny I wanted to. Besides, even if the water made my shirt bob up, I was wearing a one-piece that covered me fully. I nodded.

He dropped his recapped drink inside the cooler and slipped into the water on the opposite side of the boat from Megan and Bobby, like he'd been born in the lake. When he rose from beneath the surface, he shook his head and laughed. "It's brisk," he admitted.

I drank the sight of him in, droplets sliding down his throat, where I wanted to press my lips. My heart raced madly. Maybe a dip in the water would help cool me off. Help me regain my senses.

My cheeks burned in awkwardness as Daniel watched me slip my shorts off. He wasn't leering, just . . . keeping his gaze on me. Like he was afraid if he blinked, I'd back out and change my mind. Could I blame him for that? My heart squeezed, and I dropped the shorts to my seat and stretched my legs over the side of the boat, then just plunged in.

I was submerged, the water chilly and pulsing all around me in one long, quiet moment. I floated back up to the surface and shoved my hair away from my face. Daniel trod water in front of me, his powerful arms working across the rippling waves.

The boat floated along, and my body eventually warmed. We were on one side, blocked from seeing Megan and Bobby, who had gotten suspiciously quiet on the other side of the boat. Better that I couldn't see whatever they were up to.

"When I was a kid I would stay in the pool for hours until I wrinkled," Daniel said. Somehow while we treaded water he'd moved closer to me, and I could feel the moving water beneath the surface pulsing against my own legs. "In fact, in elementary school I wanted to be an Olympic diver. I had no fear."

"I can just imagine." A tiny Daniel, diving into the pool, his scrawny body plunging the surface as he practiced relentlessly. "What made you change your mind?"

"I look terrible in Speedos." His grin widened and he gave a cheeky laugh.

I laughed in response. "I used to pretend I was a mermaid. I'd sit on the bottom of the pool and press my legs together and make believe they were a tail." How many hours my sister and I had lived in our neighborhood's pool. She'd refused to go in without her goggles and nose guard, uncaring if it made her look goofy.

I paused my thoughts, waiting for the sting of memory to sweep over me. But here in the quiet lake, with no one else around but Daniel, who smiled patiently at me, there was only a small, bittersweet ping. Maybe I was starting to heal a little. Maybe eventually I could get to the point where I didn't hurt at all.

You haven't even told him about her, a tiny voice spoke in the back of my mind. *Or about what happened.*

That made the smile fall from my face.

Daniel dunked underwater, then popped up only a few inches from me, and I startled backward, jarred out of my melancholy. "Boo."

"You scared me," I admitted.

"I know." His face turned serious. "I really want to kiss you again."

I swallowed, my pulse buzzing in my veins. Right now I wanted him to kiss me again too. In this place of light and sun and water and warmth and happy things. To ground me in the moment.

He snaked an arm out and brushed the side of my hip, his thumb caressing my naked thigh. My breath panted in response, and I let my leg kicks slow to a leisurely pace, just enough to help me float without sinking. I needed that hand of his on me.

"I want that too." My voice was so soft, a breath above a whisper, that I almost wondered if I'd said it out loud at all.

Daniel reached a hand over, grasped the side of the boat for stability and wrapped the other one under my ass to press me flush against him. It was instinct to wrap my thighs around his waist, to slide my hands along his damp flesh, tangle my fingers in the locks at his neck.

His body was burning hot between my legs, and I was suddenly very, very aware that the only things separating us right now down there were two thin scraps of fabric. His pupils enlarged, and I could barely see his irises. He swallowed, tilted his head closer to me.

I met him halfway with my mouth. Water throbbed against us, pushed and pulled at our bodies. But Daniel was my anchor, keeping me safe, keeping me floating.

My legs tugged him even closer, almost against my conscious thought. He was hard and ripe and straining against his swim trunks, and a delicate shudder of arousal made its way across me as I opened my mouth to welcome him deeper in. His tongue plunged right inside, swept along my lips and teeth and tangled with my own tongue. I dug my fingers into his hair and breathed him, *inhaled* him.

We bobbed together in the water. His chest rose and fell with small pants against mine that made me even hungrier for him. My nipples were pebbled from arousal and the cool water. I ached everywhere, forgot everything, knew nothing but him in this moment.

"Hell, yeah!" a light voice said from behind me with a saucy giggle. "Casey, you dirty little girl!"

Shit. I disentangled myself from Daniel and pulled back,

mortified at being caught making out. Right here when Megan and Bobby were apparently back in the boat, both of them peering down at us, swigging a beer and watching us like we were a TV show.

Bobby winked at me, and I swallowed, straightened my shirt. Daniel's hand pressed on my lower back, on top of my T-shirt—not pushing but not letting me forget about his presence either.

He helped boost me back into the boat, and I slipped but found my seat again. How quickly I'd forgotten everything around me. I grabbed my water bottle and swigged, desperate for something to focus on other than the scorching memory of Daniel's body. Of me wrapped around him like that.

Megan went to open her mouth, but I lifted a hand.

"Not a word," I warned her in a hushed whisper, right as Daniel pulled himself into the boat.

She frowned, and I shook my head. I didn't need to be laughed at, teased about this. The emotions coursing through me right now were too heavy and volatile.

Bobby shrugged and swilled the last of his beer, tossing the bottle at his feet. He grabbed another, burped as he popped the top off and chugged more. He winked at Megan when he reached the end of the bottle.

"Those are some lips you have there!" she said with a laugh.

"You just wait," he teased in return.

Ugh. Maybe I should be having a beer to make it through this awkwardness. But my water would do fine. Besides, my stomach was unsettled. And it didn't help that Daniel was silently peeking over at me every few moments.

I finally gave in and glanced at him. His eyes twinkled, and he reached a hand out toward me. I bit back a nervous sigh and touched his hand.

He pulled me closer to him. I was still slicked with water, so I moved easily. A breeze brushed across us, hardening my nipples. His eyes darted down for a split second, then he looked back up into my eyes. "I'm not sorry," he said. "I'm not sorry I kissed you. Though I don't want you to be uncomfortable with me about it all. We can just hang out on here if you want. No pressure."

Tension leaked from my limbs, my back. He wrapped his arm around my back, his fingers brushing my opposite upper arm. The flesh tightened in response.

Megan and Bobby were chugging beers. She swayed in her seat and laughed, giving a delicate burp behind her hand. "Holy shit," she said. "I think I'm buzzed."

Daniel raised an eyebrow at me, silent solidarity, and I quirked one back.

"I hope you can drive a boat," I whispered.

"We'll figure it out," he promised.

Megan stood and faced us, her dark brown skin almost entirely naked except for her scrap of bikini. A few water droplets snaked down her flesh. She was beautiful in her assurance, and for a moment I wished I could be like her. So self-confident. Comfortable. "You're wearing too many clothes," she told me, wagging a finger near my face. "You should take that shirt off."

Bobby's hand smacked her butt, and she jerked a little, then laughed. "And you should take that bikini off," he said with a low growl.

"I'm fine," I told her. Despite the fact that my bathing suit covered my scars, I still didn't want to take it off. Thin layer or not, it protected me from feeling so . . . naked. So exposed to Daniel or anyone else.

"C'mon," she pleaded, thrusting a hand on her hip. "You're gorgeous. Look, I'm wearing just my suit. You should too." She bent down and grabbed another beer, probably her third in twenty minutes.

Yeah, she was buzzed. A low hum started in my head, discomfort wrapping around me. "No, thanks," I told her, my voice getting a slight edge of frostiness. "I want to leave it on."

Daniel's fingers stopped stroking my arm; I barely noticed.

She snorted and rolled her eyes. "It's just the four of us. What's the big deal? These two guys are wearing only trunks. I have on a suit. You're dressed like a nun." She stepped toward me and reached for my shirt hem, but I backed away, my legs pressing against the seats behind me. No way was she going to take it off.

My jaw ticked, and I held the hem down. "Stop it."

Bobby tugged at her hand, but she shook him off, turning her slightly unfocused eyes to me. She swayed as a small wave knocked the boat on the side, gripping a rail. "God, why do you have to be such a prude? What, do you think I'm a slut or something for not covering up like you? What exactly are you trying to prove here—how much better you are than everyone else?"

"Seriously? That's *so* not fair." This was not happening. I didn't know how to deal with drunk and angry Megan, a side of her I'd never seen before. If I could, I'd swim my ass back to shore right now and leave her here.

She trembled with visible anger. "You know what's not fair? How uptight you are and how you make everyone else feel like sinners because we *like* to have fun." She spun around and plopped herself on Bobby's lap.

My eyes burned, and I blinked, blinked again. I was not going to cry. *Screw* that. Where had all of this anger come from, and why was it suddenly directed at me? I hadn't done anything to deserve it. I crossed my arms in front of my chest and drew in several ragged breaths.

Daniel tugged me closer and stroked my hair away from my face. "Hey," he whispered. "She's drunk and not thinking straight. Try to shake it off."

"I just wanna go home," I whispered hotly. My eyes were filling with tears, and I swiped at them. I didn't want to lose it right now. And I didn't want to watch Megan anymore, hear her talk to me like this.

All that vitriol in her voice about me. Trying to force me to be more like her. But she didn't know me, not really. She didn't know what I'd been through, the depths I'd crawled out of to even be here today. Screw her.

Daniel squeezed my hand. There was so much understanding in his eyes that it hurt my heart even more, and I had to look away from him. He didn't understand either. No one knew, and that was my curse to bear.

He slipped into the driver's side of the boat and after a few fumbling attempts, got it turned around and driving back to Megan's parents' house. We sailed across the water, bouncing and bobbing along waves, but our earlier levity was gone.

Back to the party and the lightness and the people who knew how to have fun.

Back to people completely unlike me.

Chapter 11

This movie sucked.

I leaned back on the couch and dug into my Häagen-Dazs ice cream. Well, at least it was good. Bananas Foster, one of my go-to flavors whenever I was blue. The heroine in the made-for-TV movie stared up into the hero's eyes, and they slowly kissed. I shoveled another bite.

Megan hadn't returned to our apartment last night after Daniel and I had immediately left the party—I hadn't heard one peep out of her, but I assumed she was crashing at her folks' house. Despite my anxiety, I'd somehow gotten through today's classes. It helped that Daniel was a quiet source of strength, distracting me with questions about philosophy after class.

Now I was home, alone, and it was quiet. Uneasy.

A few minutes later I heard a key scrape in the door, and my body tensed instantly. She was home. I plopped the carton of ice cream on a coaster on the table and tucked my feet under me, hugging a pillow to my stomach. I had on pajama pants and a T-shirt, my comfiest night clothes, since it was already after ten on a Monday night.

Megan came inside and dropped her bag and the cooler beside the door. She glanced over at me, her face unreadable. "Hey," she said in a low tone.

I nodded and turned my attention back to whatever this dumb movie was. All of my emotions from yesterday afternoon came welling back up in my stomach, which pitched violently from nerves. But I wasn't going to drop that protective wall and show her how badly she'd hurt me. I'd be damned if I did.

She shuffled over to the kitchen, picked through the fridge. I kept my gaze firmly on the TV. I heard a sigh, and then she sat down on the chair adjacent to the couch, a Diet Coke in hand. It cracked open and she took a long drag. "That was really shitty of me," she said, shame pouring into her voice. She pressed the can to her forehead, rolled it.

I wasn't going to speak, had planned to just sit here in stony silence so she knew how angry I was. But the words bubbled out before I could stop them. "Why would you say those things to me?"

Megan put her drink down on the end table with a thud, and a few sprinkles plopped out on the wood surface. "I overreacted. Way overreacted. I'd had too much to drink, and I was nervous about Bobby and trying to impress him, and . . ." She paused. "You know, I could give you a litany of excuses about why, but what does that matter? The point is, I was flat-out wrong. And I'm ashamed of myself for what I said. The way I treated you. You didn't deserve it." These last words were delivered with a slight tremble that made my heart wobble in response.

I tried my best to hold on to my righteous anger, to not let myself feel. But the swell of tears stung my eyes again, despite my best efforts. I hugged the pillow closer to me, swallowed hard. This was why I didn't like to open up to people. Because people could hurt you badly when you dropped your guard.

She sighed, shifted in the seat. "I just . . . I feel like you're not being honest with me about stuff. Like you're always hiding things. And I don't understand why. I was trying to force you to stop hiding, but it was the wrong way to go about it. I should have just sat you down and talked about my concerns instead."

I blinked. "What concerns?" Yeah, I wore a T-shirt when swimming, but that wasn't *that* weird, right?

"There are big, black holes when it comes to you. I feel like maybe something awful happened in your past, but I'm afraid to ask because it'll seem like I'm prying into your business." She kept her earnest gaze locked on me, and I wanted to look away but I couldn't. "I don't understand you. You've never once undressed around me or worn anything less than a tank top and shorts. When you leave the bathroom you're already fully dressed. It makes me feel awkward, like you're uncomfortable in your own body." She shrugged. "Obviously I'm not uncomfortable with my physique at all, and I know you're not like me. But it's just . . . so different."

I cleared my throat and loosened my death grip on the pillow. I wasn't ready to talk about any of this. I just wanted to move forward with my life, but my past kept dragging me back into the darkness.

"Look, I'm not saying you have to walk around naked, but I just don't—"

"I have a couple of bad scars on my abdomen," I blurted, attention focused on the delicate threads woven on top of the pillow. Green, pink, purple, blue. Small flowers and paisleys, rows of them. "I was badly injured when I was thirteen. It took a lot of surgery to fix me, and I don't like looking at them. So I keep them covered." My cheeks and throat burned so badly it was like I had a sunburn. I swallowed more and counted the flowers on the pillow.

"What happened?"

I shook my head. Not going down that road right now. The memory—*nightmare*—was locked away in a small, hidden recess in my head. The downside was that in order for me to move forward, I had to lock away *everything*, including all those good times in my childhood that hurt too much to think about.

When I'd first moved in with my grandparents, Grandma had tried to get me to talk with her and Granddad about my parents, about my sister. She'd finally stopped prying when I gave in and said I'd talk about it with my therapist. But every once in a while I still saw her slant me a sad look. Like she knew what a Herculean effort it was to pretend I'd been born at age thirteen. Like tragedy hadn't swept its cruel hand through my life and destroyed everything.

Megan sighed, and the sound drew my attention back to her face. That same sadness was pouring from her eyes. "I'm sorry," she whispered. "I don't know what's going on with you, but I didn't mean to hurt you. I hope you can forgive me."

I couldn't help but see how earnest she was. She still was trying to reach out to me, even though I kept pushing her away, kept her at arm's length for my own comfort. I couldn't give everything back to her that she wanted, but I could accept her apology. "Thanks," I finally said.

"If you ever want to talk, I'm here."

I nodded.

"Casey? Does it . . ." She paused, seemed to search for the right words. "Does it have to do with your parents? You never talk about them, and I'm guessing . . . they died or something? Were you guys in an accident, and that's why you have scars?"

My chest squeezed tight, and my head got a little dizzy. I

tossed the pillow aside and stood, drew in slow breaths through my nose and exhaled through my mouth. Megan jumped up and rubbed a few soothing circles on my back. Part of me wanted to shove her away—her pushing was why I was having the panic attack right now. But another strange part was craving her closeness, wanting to take comfort in the gesture.

When the symptoms finally eased up I gave an embarrassed chuckle and backed away. "I'm fine, sorry," I blustered.

Her eyes were so despondent they almost made me want to cry. "I just wanted to help. To find out why you're so . . ."

"Messed up?" This time my laugh was mirthless, bitter.

"Sad."

"Yes, my parents died," I told her, and looked away. The ice cream was melting in the container. The couple on the TV were fighting, with the heroine starting to cry. But my chest grew numb, and the coldness spread to my limbs. I was almost happy for the pain to stop. At least I could function this way. Fake it until I felt better. "I'm going to my room now."

I could feel the weight of Megan's gaze on my back as I put the ice cream back in the freezer, then closed the bedroom door quietly behind me. I stretched out on top of the bed, pressed my fingers to my scars. Dipped my pointer finger along the puckered ridge, the deep groove.

I'd been a breath away from death. Stared it right in the face. Watched my family die right in front of me. I'd gone through that and yet somehow still woke up every day. Went to classes, went to work.

But this conversation with Megan tonight, having my past hanging unspoken right there between us, put a guilty twinge in my heart. Yes, it was easier on me to pretend none of it had happened. Yet it had, and I was starting to forget the small things about them. Stuff it hurt to remember but would kill me to forget.

My hand shook as I reached to my bedside drawer and

pulled out a worn photograph. I stared at my mom's and sister's faces, glowing in the sunshine. The park's lush, green grass and trees were behind them. Lila was perched on Mom's back, soft tendrils of hair caressing the sides of her face and brushing the very top of Mom's forehead. They looked so damn happy.

I stroked my thumb across their brows, a bittersweet pain stabbing me in the chest, stealing my breath. Then I flipped the photo over and, grabbing a ballpoint pen, found a small, empty spot in the top corner.

Lila loved peanut butter and bananas, I wrote in tiny block letters. *Mom's favorite snack was strawberries dipped in honey.*

I put my pen down and ran my gaze over the phrases, words, sentences jotted on the back of the image. Snippets of memories I couldn't bear to forget, captured here, where they would be safe. There were a few other photos of them in the drawer that looked the same, packed with memories on the backs of them.

I turned the image back over and brushed a small kiss on their faces. Hot tears slid down my cheeks. It was supposed to get easier with time, the pain. What a lie. What a horrible, horrible lie.

My hands didn't shake as badly when I put the photo back in its spot. Somehow, the ritual of writing those things down about them eased the ache just a touch. Eased the guilt—of living, of moving forward, of wanting so desperately to let go.

I swiped my eyes and lay back down. Megan didn't push me as hard as she could have. But I'd revealed more than I'd planned to. I knew all about her family and she knew nothing about mine, except small snippets about Grandma and Granddad. It was better that way for me.

Something in my head told me, though, that now that I'd given her an inch, Megan would press me hard until she got more out of me. Until then, I'd do my best to cram these feelings back inside and try to pretend like I wasn't slowly cracking apart.

"I like your hair."

Daniel's soft words, whispered as I walked past him on Friday to exit class, stopped me in my tracks. I gave a self-conscious laugh and patted the back. "Oh, it was really hot this morning so I just tossed it up."

Total lie. I'd spent a good twenty minutes twisting and pinning my locks so the updo looked casual, effortless. Because I'd wanted him to notice me. And he did. The intensity in his eye, the heated interest, stirred me to my toes.

Something about this man kept calling me closer. Though I tried to keep a cool head, keep a cool heart, he warmed my blood. He'd walked with me after class on Monday and Wednesday, talking about nothing important—the weather, the school's sports team, a random newspaper clipping he'd read. But it didn't matter what the subject was. My ears had tuned in to the frequency of his dulcet tones, the soft sway of his words, the easy cadence of his consonants and vowels. He was a siren's song, a fishing lure on a hook, and I took the bait every time.

"Casey, I want to hang out with you again." Daniel stood, stared down at me. The liquid desire in his gaze almost knocked me off my feet. "When are you free?"

"Um, what did you want to do?" Wow, what a stupid question. Did it even matter? Whether we went to dinner, hung out at the coffee shop or studied, I knew I was going to enjoy the time with him. I had so far this week.

Wednesday night we'd studied philosophy together. He'd sat so close to me at my kitchen table that I could almost share his breaths. His thigh had been pressed against mine, a constant overload of sensation.

Needless to say, I'd been distracted. Trying my best to not

think about those hands on my skin, cupping my ass to draw me against him in the water. Apparently he'd been thinking about it too, because his gaze had fixed on my lips and he'd brushed the softest of kisses on my mouth.

Unfortunately, that had ended all too soon because Megan had come barging into the apartment. I'd jumped away, not wanting to be caught again making out like horny young teens, and resolved to turn my focus back on studying, where it belonged.

It didn't help things that I couldn't get the physical memory of him pressed between my legs, hot and hard and hungry, off my mind. How I'd wanted him closer, had had a burst of desire to feel our naked bodies sliding together. It would be so easy, so dangerously easy, to lose myself in this.

"Hm. Maybe we can work some more on our philosophy paper," Daniel offered, stepping closer. "It is due next week, after all. And I still have a few more pages to write and revise before it's ready to be turned in."

Students for the next class started pouring in, and I grabbed my bag. My heart hammered against my rib cage, nervous tingles skittering along my veins. In that moment I wanted to just *be* with him, even if only studying. "Want to come over later this afternoon for a couple of hours then?" The words sounded effortless, casual. I was proud of myself. "I have time before going to my grandparents' tonight."

"Sounds great. Send me a text when you're free."

I nodded. I was going to Grandma's house for dinner, and then off to work afterward. But I couldn't resist the opportunity to squeeze in time with him. He was like a bright flame, illuminating the edges of my dull world and setting me on fire with every hot look in his eyes.

His lips parted in an easy smile, and he brushed a thumb along my cheek. The green in his eyes was almost swallowed whole by his pupils, and there was a promise of something in his gaze that kept me transfixed in place. "See you at two."

I watched him walk away, taking a moment to compose myself before exiting the room. I walked out into a warm, humid gust of air. It was going to storm later today; I could feel the crackle of tension in the air.

The same crackle between me and Daniel.

I was losing myself, my steady life, bit by bit. Instead of seeking the solace of privacy, I was starting to discover the heady rush of Daniel's company.

It frightened the hell out of me.

It also made me ache for more.

Chapter 12

Studying went well. Okay, there wasn't much studying that happened. Daniel showed up just after two, and as soon as he stepped into the apartment, I lost all desire to crack open a book. Outside the window I could hear the ambient sounds of the storm; it was far too cozy being holed up in here with him.

"Um, we can sit here," I suggested, pointing at the table.

We spread all our papers and books out and began to slip into that strange, comfortable silence. I tried valiantly to pretend for a good half hour that I was going to keep my attention on philosophy, but dead philosophers couldn't explain to me why I was feeling this way. Why every time he was around me, I lost all the oxygen in my lungs and became filled up with something new, became buoyant and tingling and alive.

He opened his mouth to ask me a question, then stopped. Instead, he just looked at me—*in* me. Some sort of emotion flickered across his face, but before I could decipher it, he slipped his fingers along the back of my neck and took my mouth in a kiss.

This wasn't the gentle brush he'd given me on Wednesday.

This kiss filled my pores, slipped into my bloodstream like heroin. I was drugged, drinking his mouth, taking, wanting. My body came alive instantly as I tasted his maleness and detected a slight minty flavor.

I moaned, and my core twinged. My breasts became heavy, full, nipples hardening and pressing against the thin fabric of my cotton bra. It took everything I had to not arch and slide my chest along his torso.

"I can't get enough of tasting you," he murmured against my mouth. Our breaths panted, and his fingers tightened on my neck as he pressed his forehead to mine.

He wanted more and I wanted more, but I was too damn scared to run past first base. With a sigh I pulled back.

"What are you doing tomorrow, around lunchtime?" he suddenly asked. His lips were slightly plump from our kissing, a little moist, and it made me want to take his mouth again.

I steadied myself. "Um, nothing."

"Want to come to lunch with me?"

I nodded.

He smiled. "Good. Because I want you to meet my family."

I couldn't believe I'd agreed to it. But after saying I would go, he wouldn't take no for an answer or let me back out. I'd finally caved when he'd promised we wouldn't be at his family's house for long. Just lunch.

I stared into my closet. What the hell did one wear to go meet the family of my . . . what? What exactly were Daniel and I?

It didn't matter, I told myself. I was good with whatever we had right now, even without a label. Because being his actual girlfriend would bring a pressure I wasn't ready for. I would have to tell him things I didn't want to think about.

I decided on a nice pale pink shirt and jeans with flats. Simple. After all, I didn't actually need to impress them—we were going to have lunch there, since he'd promised his mom, then go to the park. It was more of a quick interlude with his family, really, not even an official "thing."

And if I kept telling myself that over and over for the next half hour, maybe I'd even start to believe it. I scoffed at myself, slipped into my clothes, grabbed my purse and ran out the door before I could fuss over my appearance anymore. Daniel was going to meet me in the parking lot in a few minutes.

Was it possible for a heart to explode from extreme nervousness? I waited underneath a nearby tree. The air was thick and hot, and sweat beaded on my brow, my upper lip. Good thing I hadn't fussed with makeup beyond lip gloss and a coat of mascara, because it would be sliding down my face right now.

My phone vibrated in my pocket. I pulled it out.

Have fun today, and just be yourself. They will love you, promise. And eat all the food on your plate—you're too skinny. Oh, and PS—I expect to meet this boy at Friday dinner VERY SOON. XO Grandma

Tension seeped out of my tight lungs, and I laughed. Leave it to Grandma to know when I needed to hear from her.

I'll eat two full plates if you stop signing your texts, I wrote back, still chuckling. I figured she did it to tease me now.

Daniel's dark red car pulled up to the curb, and he turned off the engine and opened the driver's door. He stepped out, his hair mildly tamed down, wearing a bright white shirt and jeans. My pulse picked up.

The car made a strange clacking sound under the hood.

He laughed. "Yeah, I know she sounds bad," he said, waving to his car, "but she still works."

"She?" I raised an eyebrow.

"Well, her name is Go-Cart, but she gets mad when I call her that." He gave an adorable shrug and patted the top of her hood. "My parents gave her to me when I turned sixteen. She's been chugging along nicely for me ever since."

"My grandparents helped me get my car," I said as I walked over to the passenger side.

He cranked the car back on; sweet air-conditioning hit me, and my skin got goose bumps instantly. "Tell me about them. Are you guys close?"

"Very." I forced my body language to stay neutral as we drove down the road. This was veering toward dangerous territory. "They've helped put me through college," I say as a way to deflect to a more current history. "Granddad loves it when I tell him historical nuggets I learn in class. He's a history buff, especially with World War Two."

"I took a Euro history class last semester," he says. "It was engaging and frightening at the same time."

"That's basically how he feels about it too. He collects a lot of memorabilia, feels it's important for us to remember the past so we don't repeat it." Whereas I preferred to bury the past and not let it drag me back down into the mire.

Daniel drove us on the highway, humming along to some old song on the radio. "So, I want to warn you. My family is . . . rather rambunctious. I have all sisters, as I think I mentioned before, and they are just as vocal as me." He glanced over and grinned.

My palms began to sweat, despite the blast of air on my face. I rubbed them on my thighs. How pushy would they be? Were they going to insist I talk about my family, about my life?

My lips started to tingle. I closed my eyes and drew in a few short breaths through my nose, exhaled out my mouth. This was not the time to panic. I would just deflect. We would only be there for an hour, max. I could make it through.

A firm hand wrapped around mine, and I startled, my eyes flying open. Daniel gave me a sideways glance, his other hand parked on the steering wheel. "Hey, I promise they won't bite. They're nice people." He paused. "I know there are things you don't want to talk about. I can see it in your eyes. But . . . you have to let people in sometime, Casey. Shutting yourself off hurts you more than you realize."

I knew he meant well. I could see it in the kindness of his gaze. But I resented being preached at. Like I didn't know that stuff already. Like Grandma and Granddad and the therapist hadn't already told me the same damn things. "I'm fine," I said.

His hand stilled. "I know you are. I'm just trying to help."

I didn't want help. I wanted to just live and breathe in the now. But I also didn't want to get into a fight with him before we spent the day together. "Thanks." I hoped it sounded genuine, even if I wasn't feeling it.

I thought I heard him give a soft sigh, but with the air blasting as hard as it was, I could have been mistaken. Nevertheless, he kept his hand on mine and resumed the thumb-stroking. I wanted to dig my phone out of my pocket and listen to music, one of my favorite ways to de-stress, but that would be rude. So I sang songs in my head until the tension leaked from my muscles.

The drive was over far too fast. We pulled up in front of a two-story colonial home on the corner of a nice neighborhood street. The front door was open, and a big, hairy dog sat behind the screen door, staring at our car.

When Daniel got out, the dog stood, tail thumping, tongue lolling.

He opened my car door and led me up the sidewalk. "That's Frankenstein," he said. "We don't know what kind of dog he is, but he slobbers a lot. Just to warn you."

"Who named him?" I asked.

We stepped up to the stoop. Frankenstein's whole body was wagging in excitement at this point.

"My oldest sister. She went through a . . . weird phase when we got the dog. Was mildly obsessed with old horror movies." He chuckled and opened the screen door, and the dog jumped up and planted two huge paws on Daniel's chest, giving a little howl. "Hey, buddy," he crooned, rubbing his hands over the dog's face. Sure enough, Frankenstein's tongue slathered his chin. "Come on," he said with a laugh, pushing the dog back down.

Frankenstein stopped and stared at me for a long moment, and I could swear his eyebrow was raised. His fur was mostly gray around his face; he was older than I'd expected. Must have been in their family for a while.

I reached out a hand under his nose so he could smell me. We used to have a dog a long, long time ago, back when I was in kindergarten, and though I hadn't been around many pets since then, I still remembered how fun they could be.

He sniffed my hand, then thrust his head under my fingers. I skritched his fur, and his tail began thumping again. I even saw his back leg begin to twitch as I hit just the right spot above his ear.

"He likes you," Daniel said. I could hear the smile in his tone.

"Daniel? Is that you?" a light but masculine voice called from a room out of view.

That started my heart racing again. But I guess I couldn't just stand here in the doorway for an hour, playing with the dog.

Daniel took my hand and led me through a tiled hallway. My heart galloped as hard as the dog's feet behind us. The hallway opened into the kitchen, with a large, open-floor family room extending beyond. There was a fireplace on the right, and a tall, lean man perched on the edge of a fluffy, cream-colored L-shaped couch.

He stood, and I could see Daniel's eyes, the curve of his lips on this man. Had to be his dad. "Glad to meet you," he said as he stepped toward me, hand extended. "We've heard a lot about you."

Frankenstein planted himself right beside the man and stared at us all.

I shook Daniel's dad's hand and tried to not panic that Daniel had obviously been talking about me with his family. What had he said? I forced a smile to my face. "He's talked about you guys too."

"Please, come in and have a seat." His dad led me to the living room, and I settled back on a plush seat. Daniel took the one beside me.

A thunder of feet clamored above me, then down the staircase, through the hallway, into the family room. Three tall girls, ranging from young teen to just freshly adult, stared at me with open curiosity. And they all looked exactly the same—dark mop of hair, bright green eyes. Just like Daniel, but their features were softer, feminine to his strong masculine lines.

"So, you're Casey," the youngest one declared. She thrust her hand on her jean-clad hip and eyed me, lips pursed just a touch.

"Miranda," Daniel warned.

She held up her hands in a universal gesture of innocence. "Just stating the facts, bro."

I couldn't help but laugh, which helped ease some of my awkwardness. "It's true. I'm Casey." I looked at the other two.

The middle one, who couldn't be more than sixteen, gave me a shy smile. Her fingers twiddled in front of her stomach. She had on a simple blue dress and flats. "I'm Francine."

"And I'm Parker," the oldest girl said with a wide grin. Her dark brown hair was tossed up in a haphazard bun, and her golden skin glowed in her sleeveless glittery tank top and short shorts. "Can I get you something to drink?"

"Um. Water or a soft drink? Anything is fine."

She scrambled off to the kitchen. A short, redheaded woman with curvy hips dusted off her hands and extended one to me. Her gray eyes were wide, friendly. She wasn't pretty in the traditional sense, but so much warmth poured from her that I couldn't help but stare at her. "Hi. I'm Daniel's mom. We're so glad to have you here."

I glanced from her to Daniel. They looked nothing alike.

She laughed. "Yeah. Every single one of these kids got their looks from their dad." Striking a pose, she fluffed her mop of red hair. "Too bad for them."

I couldn't help but like her. I smiled in response.

Parker brought me a Dr Pepper, which I sipped. We all made our way to the large dining room, the dog trailing a few feet behind. On the sideboard there was an assortment of lunch meat, bread, cheese, and every topping you could ever want on a sandwich.

"We eat buffet style for lunch," Daniel whispered, pressing his strong hand to my lower back. "Help yourself, please."

I made my sandwich as quickly as possible so everyone didn't have to wait a long time for me. Dr Pepper in one hand, plate in the other, I watched Daniel with his family. He laughed and nudged his sisters, tugging on Miranda's braid, elbowing Francine in the side to get her to smile bigger.

It was clear his sisters adored him.

We all settled in at the table. Daniel sat on my left, Parker on my right. The noise increased as the girls happily chattered. They talked about nothing in particular, the dreariness of early morning classes, how bad school food tasted, Parker's first year of college—she was attending Marshall College, another local school with a stellar reputation.

It was a lot of stimulation. I was used to quiet days in my room or with my grandparents.

Daniel seemed to sense my growing tension. He squeezed my knee under the table, then stroked his thumb along the outer flesh of my kneecap. A ripple of delight spread from the warm contact. I shot him a surprised glance.

"How are classes going, honey?" Daniel's mom asked him. "Are your professors nice? Any funny stories about your first weeks of school?"

He chuckled. "Well, our philosophy prof—Casey's in the

class with me—is a bit of a relic. She actually wants us to hand-write our next homework assignment instead of typing it." He described Wilkins, from her quirky mannerisms to her hard stares in class as she talked.

Miranda snorted. "My handwriting is terrible. I'd hate that."

"That's true," he said. "I seem to remember you barely passed handwriting in elementary school."

I studied the dimples in the corners of Daniel's mouth as he grinned. I couldn't stop staring at him, despite my efforts to keep my attention on my delicious sandwich. I was sure my emotions about Daniel were written all over my face.

I was content to sit quietly and observe them all. His family was engaged, asking a few more questions about his teachers, the coursework. Just like my grandparents.

Every few minutes, one of them would ask me a question about school, my grandparents, what I was going to do after graduation. Safe topics. It made me wonder if Daniel had schooled them to not push me on anything else. The thought both bothered me and relieved me.

His youngest sister, from her seat across the table, blurted out, "Are you two boyfriend and girlfriend?"

My face burned. I cleared my throat. "Um."

Francine shot Miranda a disapproving look; she didn't say much, but her face was very expressive. "We just met her. We shouldn't ask personal questions like that," she said in a low whisper. "It's not polite."

"Sorry," Miranda mumbled. She stared sullenly at her plate.

"It's okay," I said, not wanting her to be down. "We're really good friends." Okay, more than friends, but I didn't want to be put on the spot to label it. He and I hadn't even discussed it yet.

Daniel's hand squeezed my knee once more, and I shot him a grateful look then dropped my own hand to cover his own.

It felt right resting there.

Crazy—the more time I spent with Daniel, the more I saw

these different sides to him. The impassioned artist, photographing the world through his unique point of view. The scholarly student, intent on learning for the sake of learning.

The subtle but sexy seducer, who made everything in my body flutter. Who set my skin on fire with the lightest touch. His kiss spun my senses, turned everything upside down. Made me ache and crave.

With a hot flush, I turned my attention to my almost empty plate. I knew what was happening to me. I was falling for Daniel, despite my efforts to keep cool and not get in over my head. Something about him made me want to drop my walls a little at a time. To invite him in and share more of myself, learn everything about him. To explore this chemistry between us.

But only where it was safe. Because I wasn't ready to feel the pain I worked so hard to bury. And I didn't think that would be enough for Daniel. I suspected that with his gentle yet persistent ways, he'd eventually push me to open up until I laid myself bare before him, no guard, no hope of saving myself from the risk.

When lunch was over—I had to admit, while I was looking forward to the quiet, I also couldn't help but want to spend more time with his family—we cleared our plates. Everyone gave me a hug good-bye. That part made me uncomfortable, but I couldn't be rude, so I tried to keep my body as relaxed as possible.

They followed us to the door.

"Come back soon," his mom said. "Our door is always open."

I believed it. I shoved aside my awkwardness and squeezed her hand. "Thanks."

When we got back into Daniel's car, I buckled up and settled into the seat, ready for the rest of our date. And in the back of my mind, I couldn't help but think that my mom would have loved his family.

Chapter 13

I pressed my back against the outside of my door, staring into Daniel's shaded eyes. The light in our hallway wasn't very bright, so the angles of his face stood out in strong relief. My heart thudded almost painfully in anticipation of . . . something.

"I had a lot of fun," I said. And it was true. We'd spent the afternoon in the bright sunshine at a local park. Daniel had brought snacks, drinks and a Frisbee. We'd spent hours just laughing, talking and running across the bright summer grass.

I was pretty sure my face was burnt to a pink crisp, but I couldn't remember the last time I'd laughed so much. Daniel had told me about all of the shenanigans he and his sisters had gotten into when they were younger.

"I had fun too," he said, stepping closer. His soft breath huffed against my cheeks, my mouth. He leaned forward and brushed his lips against mine—just a light touch, but enough to make my stomach flutter.

"Come in," I said in a rush. I didn't want him to go. I

wanted to stretch this moment on and live in this space, like sustaining a single perfect note in a violin solo. "I'll make pizza."

"You had me at 'make,' " he said with a chuckle. "I can't cook most meals worth a damn."

The apartment was dark; Megan was probably out with her friends already, getting her Saturday night partying on. I flicked on the light switch. "You're giving me a lot of credit. I'm just going to pop in a frozen pizza."

He followed me inside and closed the door behind him. The lamps on the end tables cast a warm, honeyed glow on his skin. Suddenly I was nervous. We were here by ourselves. In my apartment. Where anything could happen.

I cleared my throat. "Um. Can I get you something to drink?" I made my way into the kitchen and flung the door open.

"Coke, if you have one," he said from the living room.

"Megan can't live without caffeine," I said drolly. "We're always stocked." I grabbed two and headed to the couch. He was already sitting down, so I took a spot beside him, hoping he couldn't see the tremble in my hands as I gave him a can.

Our silence was easy, peaceful. Our knees touched, since we were angled toward each other. As we drank, I marveled at the changes in me even in such a short time. Instead of freaking out and hiding in my room, I was sitting on my couch with a guy I was wildly attracted to. Had kissed him, touched him—let myself get absorbed in the moment.

A strange sensation filled my chest. Pride. In myself. *Baby steps,* I told myself, peeking at him from beneath my eyelashes. My cheeks flushed, and a wave of shyness hit me. Daniel was so striking, the way his dark hair flopped over his brow. The intensity that practically poured off him. I couldn't resist him, and I didn't want to.

I'd never felt this way about a man before. Somehow I'd

gone through my life not realizing what I'd been missing. Existing but not really . . . living. But Daniel made me feel things that scared me. Exhilarated me.

"Where are you right now?" he asked me with a smile. He put his drink down and leaned back on the couch. "Your face looks like you're deep in thought."

My throat tightened. Busted. "Oh, just . . . flitting all over the place."

His mouth slid into a knowing grin. "Uh-huh."

I licked my lips. "It's quiet in here. We need some music." With fumbling fingers I found the TV remote and turned it to a music station.

"So, let's pick our game back up," he said, mercifully letting it go. Daniel had started a game back at the park while we'd been throwing the Frisbee. We'd toss goofy questions back and forth and answer them as fast as we could. It was surprisingly hard to throw straight while scrabbling in your brain for the response.

"Favorite movie," I said quickly, tucking a pillow over my lap and folding my legs underneath me.

"Like I can name just one." He furrowed his brow. "I guess . . . *Rear Window*. Favorite—"

"What's that one?" I interrupted.

His eyes widened. "A brilliant movie by Alfred Hitchcock. It's a classic in the American film canon. You've never seen it?"

I shook my head.

"Never even heard of it? Oh, that's it—I'm going to make you watch it."

"Is it black and white?" I groaned.

Daniel's eyes slit. "There's a rule in our house about movies. You're not allowed to judge them until you've seen them. I'm enforcing that ground rule here."

"It's my apartment." I jutted my chin and stared at him in mock defiance.

He inched closer. "I bet I can make you."

My pulse thrummed on the side of my throat. With those eyes and that delicious mouth, he probably could make me do almost anything he asked. "What . . . were you going to ask me?"

His brow arched. He didn't move back from me. "Favorite crayon color."

"Burnt sienna."

He barked out a laugh. "You answered that surprisingly fast."

I shrugged. "Favorite brand of underwear." Oh my God, where had that question come from? "Oh, wait, I didn't mean—"

"Hanes. Boxer briefs, in case you're curious." He winked. "You're a saucy minx, Casey. Never would have guessed."

I took a swig of my drink, letting the bubbles burn my throat. That was flat-out flirting, plain and simple. I was awkward and uncomfortable, but Daniel still rolled with the punches and didn't make me feel bad.

"Favorite childhood memory," he asked.

I froze. My heart gave a painful, irregular thud. With robotic movements I put my can down on a coaster.

"I don't understand why you never talk about your past," he said in a soft tone. Like he was trying to soothe a wild animal or something. "You have to know I'm curious about you—about everything. I've opened up and shared with you. I just want a little of the same in return. I feel like something bad must have happened—you've never mentioned your parents."

I knew this was coming. I hugged the pillow to my stomach. A weak shield, but it made me feel protected. "It's not something I like to talk about," I finally managed to say. "I prefer to live in the now. Live for the future."

"I keep trying to not pressure you. But it's like there's this huge chunk of your life that's off-limits for discussion. How can we move forward—*live for the future*—if you hide yourself and your past?"

I could feel his hot gaze on the top of my head, but my eyes were fixed on my thumbnails. On the ridges and plains of my knuckles. There was a quiet roar echoing in my ears, the edge of panic starting to creep in my senses.

My stomach churned. Some strangely self-destructive part of me just wanted to blurt out the whole truth. Throw it in his face and watch him look horrified, then pitied, then walk out the door, leaving me and my drama behind. Too much mess to put back together the way I used to be.

I felt like I deserved that pain. Because I was alive to actually experience it—a fluke, a miracle, a shock. I was alive, and my dad and my mom and my sister were rotting in graves, and I had to deal with that knowledge every day of my life.

And besides my grandparents and a handful of relatives in my extended family, no one else was inside my world.

"It's not hiding." My voice sounded far too scratchy, a patch painfully dry in the back of my throat. I swallowed and tried again. "Not hiding. Just trying to keep going." I paused, stayed quiet for a really long time. The music filled our silence, but it didn't put me at ease. "My parents . . . they died. Along with my younger sister. It was really horrific, and I don't like to talk about it." I didn't even like to *think* about it.

I finally dared to glance up at Daniel. His eyes were steady and fixed on me—not pitying, not horrified. Just . . . open. Tinged with a hint of sadness for my pain, but more empathetic than anything. It was like I could see right into his soul, feel the way he wanted to wrap his arms around me and ease my ache.

"I'm very sorry," he finally said. His voice was hushed. "I've never had anything like that happen to me. I can't imagine how it feels."

The words were simple but sincere. A small piece chipped away at the protective coating around my heart. I nodded, unable to speak past the lump in my throat.

He looked to the left, at the open door of my bedroom, and

his face softened. "Hey, is that where you make the magic happen?"

My jaw dropped, and I blinked, startled out of the somber moment. "Um, excuse me?"

He gasped when he realized what he'd said and how it had sounded. "Oh. Shit. That came out all wrong." A streak of red crawled up his throat and covered his cheeks. "I saw your computer set up on your desk with some equipment there. I meant deejaying. Not . . . that. *Shit.*" He smacked his forehead.

I laughed so hard my throat hurt. Oh God, that did me good. It helped me shake off the lingering sadness from our conversation. "Do you want to see it?"

"Can I?" Suddenly he looked shy, and another piece of my heart's armor chipped off and fell away.

I nodded and stood, holding out my hand to him. "Come on. I'll show you how the stuff works."

It was so strange, leading him into my room. My private zone. Granted, I didn't have much personal stuff up, but it was intimate. He pulled a chair from the corner of the room up to my desk, and I sat down in front of the computer and fired up the program. It took everything I had to not focus on how he filled the empty space in my room with his larger-than-life presence. "Sometimes I use this program to help me make special mixes of songs that are out there. Like a special DJ remix."

"Do you ever make your own?"

His rich, warm scent rolled off his skin, and I bit back a groan. Oh God, I wanted to bury my face in his neck and breathe him in. Having him this close to me, the intensity of the chemistry crackling between us, watching how he moved, how he looked at me . . . it was too much.

I forced my mind back to his question. "Um, yes. I have made some songs in the past."

"Can I hear one? If you're working on any right now?"

I thought about the haunted song I'd finished composing. It

just needed an hour or two of work to be completely done, but for some reason I wasn't quite ready to share it yet. Maybe because it was so personal and heavy. "It's . . . not ready," I hedged. I scrolled through and got a blank template loaded up. "But tell you what. Let's make one together."

His face lit up. "Tell me what to do."

I walked him through the basics, showed him my folders of music clips. We started with a thrumming bass line, a sick beat that got us grooving quickly. I set it on loop in its track, and we flipped through some more sounds.

When we got to a weird plopping sample, he laughed. "Seriously?"

I shrugged, stifling the urge to giggle. "You never know when you need a plop."

"Maybe if you're doing a diarrhea commercial jingle."

I slugged his arm, and he grimaced, rubbing the spot. "Gross."

Over the next couple of hours, we worked our way through my samples. Daniel had a surprisingly good ear for music. I'd never composed a song with another person before—but it helped that we weren't worried about being fancy or intricate, so the pressure was off. We just layered in and spliced pieces and had fun with it. The end result was actually not too bad. I even burned him a copy on a disc so he could take our "masterpiece" home with him.

When eight rolled around, I grimaced. My stomach gave a large grumbling groan. "Crap, I'm sorry. I forgot to make us something. And I have to head to work soon." There would be times when I got so caught up in my music that I didn't eat until hours after mealtime. But I couldn't afford to be late to The Mask, despite the effort it took to drag myself away from Daniel's company.

His face was mock solemn. "And here you promised me artisan pizza. Straight from the freezers of Italy."

I gave him a smarmy smirk. “I’m sorry I’ve let you down.” I stood, stretched the kinks in my neck.

“So when do we cut a record deal?” he asked. “This song is suh-weet.”

I laughed. “Yeah, I’ll get right on it.” But secretly, the thought tingled something in my head. It would be so fun to do a record—even indie. To make my own music and share it with others.

And it would also cost an arm and a leg. Plus take away from my school and work time. Not in the cards for me.

Daniel stood, and his hand reached up to cup the back of my head. His thumb caressed the base of my skull, sending cascades of pleasure across my flesh. I couldn’t help but melt against him. “I know you have to work, but I don’t want to go. I’ve had a great time with you today, and it’s so hard to drag myself away.”

The raw honesty in his voice undid me. I’d never had a man so blatantly honest, so straightforward with me before. It disarmed me, tore down my usual defenses. I spent my life building my walls. Protecting myself. But with his steady words, his hot kisses, he was stripping me bare.

He leaned down and took my mouth in a heated, possessive kiss. His other hand snaked around my waist and tugged me close. I opened my mouth and breathed him in. He tasted faintly of Coke, faintly of him. His cologne wrapped around me, and every sense went into overload.

I gripped his shirt, filled with a grinding, aching need for him. I desired Daniel, wanted to strip him and lick the divots on the sides of his hips where his thighs met his torso. I’d seen that spot at the lake from his low-slung shorts. I wanted him right now.

And he wanted me too. He was hard, pressed against my belly. His arousal was strong and evident. I rubbed into it, and he groaned in my mouth. His breath was warm and damp, and it sent spirals of fire coursing through my chest, down to my aching lower belly.

"Oh God, Casey," he breathed. "You're driving me crazy." His hand threaded in my hair, and he tilted my head so he could take my mouth deeper. His tongue thrust in, slid along mine, and I rubbed my breasts on his firm chest, nipples beading, my sex swelling and throbbing in response.

I didn't know how long we stood there in my room, kissing and touching. Though his firm hand on my back slid down to cup my ass, to draw me closer to his rock-hard erection, he didn't push it any further. Eventually we drew apart, panting, eyes glazed and mouths swollen. His hand was still threaded in my hair, fingers massaging my scalp.

He pressed his forehead to mine. "You mix me all up inside," he finally said, then gave a weak laugh. "And I never saw you coming."

"Me neither," I admitted.

If I were completely honest with myself, I was glad he'd come into my life. More than glad—honored, even. Daniel saw something in me no one else saw, made me want to feel vibrant. Made me want to just . . . be.

I walked him to the door. With a final parting kiss—this one sweet and soft—he left. I closed it behind him and kept my back to it a long time, unable to drive away the wide grin on my face.

Chapter 14

I groaned. "This poem is the creepiest thing I've ever read."

Daniel tucked his pencil behind his ear, grabbed the table and tugged his chair right beside mine. "Whatcha readin'?"

I shoved the textbook toward him. "It's for Brit Lit, my other elective class this semester. We're in the poetry section of the course." I pointed at "Porphyria's Lover" by Robert Browning. Soft light from the large library windows spilled across the table, splashed on the page and illuminated the haunting words.

Daniel read it to himself. He blinked, then said, "Wow. So the guy choked her."

"With her own hair." I shivered. Who thought of those kinds of things? And why was our prof making us read them? "Why would he do that?" Our class was supposed to write a short essay about why the narrator killed the woman.

We sat in silence for a moment, mulling it over.

"It's apparent in the beginning of the poem that she came to him despite whatever was keeping them apart—like class issues." Daniel turned his eyes to me.

I lost myself in them for a moment, and his smile widened.

"Um." I cleared my throat. *Focus.* "So maybe the narrator was just desperate to keep her there so she wouldn't leave him again."

"He really seems to believe she loves him." The words, spoken softly, ignited something in my belly.

"Thanks. That gives me a starting point."

Daniel slipped his hand over and squeezed my fingers, enveloping my hand in his warmth. "Glad to help."

We remained clasping each other as he read from a history text and I studied the poem once more, through the viewpoint of a desperate lover who would stop at nothing to keep his love with him. But after a moment, my thoughts began to wander. The background noise of the midday library crowd faded away.

Daniel and I had been spending a lot of time together over the last couple of weeks. It was technically fall now, my favorite season, and though late summer temperatures had clung tenaciously to the last few days, the days were growing shorter.

I couldn't help my anticipation. Something about fall felt like new beginnings to me, as strange as it sounded. Crisp air, sweaters, apple cider, pumpkin spice, brightly colored leaves. I was excited to share all of those things with Daniel.

The soft, regular puffs of his breath reached my ears. He was completely focused on his book, which gave me a chance to open my senses to him, breathe in his ocean scent. Hear the scratching of his pen as he took notes with his other hand—for once, being a leftie came in handy, as we could both hold hands and still write.

The more time I spent with him, the more time I wanted to be around him. Studying. Watching a goofy movie. Strolling around campus. Drinking coffee. Talking about philosophy or which candy tasted the worst or whatever. Didn't matter, so long as he was around.

I cared about Daniel. Really cared.

The thought made my cheeks flush, and I fought the telltale stiffening in my body. It wasn't that I was ashamed of my feelings, because strangely enough, I'd grown . . . used to it. Comfortable, even.

But I was keeping secrets from him, big secrets about myself. And that gap was getting wider every day. I felt an ever-increasing sense of guilt mingling in on the fringes of my conversations. Daniel thought he knew me, but he didn't. How could he when I had basically severed the first thirteen years of my life from my history?

I knew *him*, though. I knew that when he was in deep concentration mode, like now, he'd tap the bottom of his pencil on the table in cycles of threes. And he'd nibble on his lip and sometimes mumble under his breath.

Daniel loved water. He was afraid of clowns, funny enough. He couldn't get enough lunchmeat piled on his sandwiches and always asked for double on subs.

He made my heart flutter like mad whenever he walked in a room.

Oh, I was falling for this man. I could tell myself it was a fun, tiny crush as much as I wanted, but he had slipped inside my veins before I'd even realized it. He'd become a part of me, and I needed him.

"Still having trouble?" he suddenly asked.

"Huh?" I glanced over at him, hoping my raw emotions weren't written all over my face.

"You've been staring blankly at that page for several minutes now." He shoved his shoulder against mine in a chummy gesture. "Not *that* hard to understand, is it?"

"Oh." I chuckled weakly. "No. It's creepy, but I'm getting it now."

He dropped his pencil in the seam of his book and reached a hand up to cup my face. "In this light, I feel like I can see right into you." His own eyes were so open and honest with me. Genuine openness as opposed to my fakeness.

Shame filled my belly, hot and uncomfortable. I knew him

so well, yet he knew nothing about me. Not the things that had messed me up until I was just a shell of a person. "Daniel," I whispered. "I'm not—I mean, I don't know how to—"

"Look, I know you're . . . reserved." He paused, and the smile slid from his face. But he didn't release his hold on my face. His thumb stroked the apple of my cheek. "You're still a mystery. But I learn more about you every day."

I wanted him to. Oh, I did. But I also feared the hell out of it. Yes, the day would come where he'd eventually learn everything. And somehow I knew that once he did, that would be the beginning of the end. Because every conversation would become more and more stilted until there was nothing left for us to discuss. Daniel would censor himself, careful to not mention parents, or suicide, or alcohol, or mentally ill people. Eventually he'd stop talking to me at all.

And that would finish us for good. We'd dissolve like a handful of salt in a pool, scattering and fading into nothingness.

It had happened to me already with the rest of my extended family. I was the person they were afraid to come to now, had been for years. They were afraid my darkness would rub off on their small, comfortable corners. That somehow, if they cracked my chest open and really peered inside, they'd see . . . themselves in there.

My personal hell could happen to anyone. And that scared the shit out of *everyone*.

Which was why I always kept my damn mouth shut.

I pulled out of his grip. A frown knitted his brows, and he dropped his hand.

"I wish you'd open up to me," he said. Though I could tell he tried to keep his words steady, there was a thread of pain in there. Pain mingled with growing frustration.

"I'm not ready yet," I said. My words were quiet but steady, and I was proud of myself for not breaking down, though the hard knot forming in my chest wouldn't go away.

I wanted him. I was afraid of him.

But somehow I knew Daniel wasn't going anywhere. All I could do was hold on and try to enjoy these sweet moments with him while they lasted. Before everything changed on us.

I closed my book, then closed his and stood. I reached my hand out toward him. "It's stuffy in here," I declared, lifting my chin and giving him the biggest smile I could muster. "I'm done studying for the day." Probably a mistake—I really needed to work on this essay—but I'd do it tonight.

Not now. Not when I could drop my shackles for a few hours and feel free with Daniel.

After a moment he took my hand and though there was a lingering edge of wariness in his eyes, he stood too. I released a lungful of breath I hadn't realized I'd been holding. "Where do you want to go?" he asked.

I gave a casual shrug. "Anywhere. Oh, I know. Let's get some ice cream while it's still nice enough outside to enjoy it."

Blessedly, warmth came back to his face, and his smile melted the edges of my deep-seated fear away. "Ice cream sounds amazing right now."

We gathered our things and headed out of the library. Our pinkies brushed against each other and he took my hand, winding his fingers through mine. It felt so right; our hands fit perfectly.

I leaned my body closer to his, and as we strolled across the campus grounds in the midafternoon sun, I stood taller. However long this lasted, I could take comfort that at least now, for a while, this man wanted to be with me. He found something in me no one else had seen.

And though he might not know it, I could sense my barriers cracking apart every day.

"I can't possibly eat one more bite of potato salad. Oh my God." Daniel moaned and lay back on the blanket, cupping his hands over his still-flat belly, despite his grumbles. "I'm so full, my pants are literally going to explode off of me."

"As my English prof would point out, you mean figuratively," I said in a prim tone. "If your pants literally exploded, we'd be in a world of legal trouble, since this is a public park. And as punishment for your grammar error, I'm making you eat the rest of this potato salad." I scooped a heaping spoonful out of our bowl and shoved it toward his face.

He sat up and mock glared at me. Dappled sunlight from the setting sun spilled across the dark mop of his head, hit his deep green irises. Before I could react, he grabbed the spoon and flung it, loaded potato salad and all, across the park. "Oh, crap. Sorry, it slipped."

"Litterer!" I cried out, looking around like I was seeking a police officer. Not that there was anyone else around us except for a couple of young kids playing on the swing set nearby.

Daniel tackled me to the ground and dug his fingers against my right side, where I was superticklish. "Narc!" he said, laughing hysterically.

"You jerk!" I swatted up at him and scrambled to get away. I stood and wiped the bottom of my shorts with a huff. "That was a perfectly good spoon."

He raised an eyebrow. "I'll buy you another."

"It was part of a set." I tugged my tank top down to make sure my abdomen was covered. Thankfully, Daniel had stayed away from my scarred side.

"I'll buy you six, then."

"You have an answer for everything, don't you." I chuckled.

He stood, peering down at me. His eyes were light and dancing, and my heart hadn't felt this light in a couple of days—not since my moodiness back in the library. His hand slid along my unscarred side again, but instead of torture-tickling me, his fingers slipped and danced over my tank top. The warmth of his touch still seared me, despite the barrier.

"Not everything," he murmured, his attention turning to my mouth. His fingers tightened incrementally on my hip. Something shifted then, sexual tension crackling in the air between us.

I automatically licked my lips, and his eyes flared. I stepped closer. I needed to taste his mouth, right now.

"Ooooooooh!" a high-pitched kid's voice said from behind me. "They're gonna kiss!"

I closed my eyes as a light flush stole over my cheeks.

Daniel's mouth hovered close enough to me that I could feel his breath huffing against my skin. "I need to kiss you," he said, and the raw edge in his tone had my eyes flying open.

Yes, the need was right there, unmasked, unashamed, completely bared to me. I felt my body respond, my core tightening, heart thudding, hands trembling.

I nodded, leaned my face up. My mouth already hungered for his.

He brushed his mouth against mine, a butterfly touch that didn't satisfy the growing pulse in me. "Not here," he said, his words barely a whisper. "I want you alone."

Alone. The ache I heard in that one word sent shivers of anticipation across my skin. My flesh burst into thousands of vibrant tingles. I gave a mute nod. I wanted it too.

We packed up our picnic and stuck the remains into the bags. My fingers fumbled, and I just started cramming everything in. His words echoed in my head.

I didn't know what was going to happen, but I knew I had to be alone with this man. Had to feel him better. Maybe touch *his* bare skin, taste him.

Our ride back toward campus was quiet. The air hummed with unspoken desire, flowing and thickening with every passing mile.

"My place," I said in a husky whisper. Wow, I was almost embarrassed by how much longing was in my voice. "Um, Megan's out tonight." There was another Thursday night frat party she was attending with Bobby. So the place would be ours for hours.

Alone.

Daniel shot me a side glance and nodded. His hand reached over and stroked my bare thigh. Heat exploded in my lower belly as something unfurled in me. Though I knew it wasn't ever going to happen, suddenly I wanted his hands everywhere on me. Every stroke of his fingers across my inner thigh was making me throb, my panties dampening. It was ridiculous how he drew this longing out of me.

Daniel pulled into the parking lot, and we made our way to the apartment, our pace a little faster than usual. I keyed the door, and once I was in the dark room, him right on my heels, he closed it behind me, then nudged my back to the nearest wall. One hand wrapped around my lower back and the other cupped my neck.

He tilted my head and possessed my mouth in a kiss that scorched me to my bones. I gasped and gripped his shoulders, drawing him deeper, inhaling him fully into my lungs, into every cell of my body.

"You taste so good," he breathed out, tongue swiping against mine. "I just want to kiss you for hours."

His lean torso pressed against my curves, my breasts pressing hard to his chest. My nipples beaded into tight, almost painful nubs, and I groaned. I rubbed against him; his erection was evident as he pinned me tight against the wall.

Daniel's mouth slid down my throat, nipping and licking and sucking flesh. Tingles cascaded across me in growing waves. I grew wetter, my breasts full and heavy. His hand slid up my back. He paused, pulled away from me. His thumb was resting against the underside of my right breast.

I nodded.

Then his hand cupped me, kneaded me, and he rained kisses down my upper chest. His open lips were a wet heat that dampened my tank top, my bra, right to the upper curves of my breast.

The boiling heat that was building in my core kicked into high gear. I arched my back, nudging my breast closer to his mouth. With one hand I cupped his head and silently urged him to do it.

His hot mouth suckled my nipple through my clothes, and I groaned as pleasure spiked in my pelvis.

"Oh God, that feels so good," I said on a breathy sigh.

He sucked my nipple in deeper, and I caressed his soft hair, stroked his neck.

I wanted more. I wanted to touch him.

"Bedroom," I managed to grind out.

He paused, pulled back. "Are you sure?"

I knew what he was asking. My heart was racing so hard I was sure he could hear it. I was scared and excited and I craved him with a feeling I'd never experienced before. But was I ready to have sex with him?

If we did, he'd see me.

But maybe we could keep our clothes on and kiss in the dark. Kissing was good, right?

"I want to lay down and kiss you," I finally said. It was as honest as I could be in this moment.

He took my mouth again in a quick, possessive kiss. Then he grasped my hand and led me to the bedroom. After closing the door behind us, we made it to my bed and nudged our shoes off, our mouths pressing together again. We fell together, limbs wrapped, bodies so close there was no space between them.

I tugged Daniel's shirt off. I needed to feel his muscles under my fingers. His torso was like a furnace. I urged him onto his back and hovered above him. There were small slits of light coming from the window.

My breath stuck in my throat as I looked down at his body. Even in the dim light, I could see every muscle, every plane. I was filled with an almost painful urge to rub my naked breasts against him.

Daniel remained silent, staring up at me. I knew he was letting me dictate the terms. Since that first night, he'd kept his hands above my clothes. But right now, that wasn't satisfying me. I ached for more, even as I feared it.

I was torn between my hunger for him and my debilitating concern of what he'd think if he saw me naked. But I knew there was no real way to win this battle—I'd have to be brave and let him see me, or be content with just kissing.

"What's wrong?" he said in a quiet whisper. "Do you want to stop?"

I sat back, pulse roaring in my ears. I could put everything on hold right now. I could stay safe and keep my secrets for longer. "No." The word ripped out of me, though my head screamed for me to stop. "I don't. But before it goes any further"—I swallowed—"there's something I need to talk about."

Chapter 15

Daniel sat up in bed and flicked on the table light. He scooted back and looked at me. "What do you need to talk about?"

As much as I wanted to run away from this conversation, I made myself stare right in his eyes. My brain scrabbled for the perfect words, how to explain everything churning around inside me right now.

He paused, and his eyes flickered with an inscrutable expression. "Are you a virgin? Because you know we don't have to—"

"Oh. No, that's not it." My face burned a bit. "I've . . . had sex before. It just—" It was awful, and I hadn't felt anywhere near the intensity I did with him. My entire body was still thrumming, right on the edge. "I have a hard time being comfortable with this kind of intimacy." Boy, could this conversation make me sound any more awkward?

Daniel reached over and stroked his thumb along my palm. The gesture was meant to be comforting, but it kept my arousal brewing. "I understand. We don't have to go any further than you feel comfortable with." His eyes were perfectly clear and honest; I could tell he meant every word. If I only wanted to kiss him, he'd keep it at that.

But how long would that really satisfy either one of us? He wanted me, and I wanted him so desperately. I could feel my own arousal, and his was evident too.

Daniel shifted like he was going to stand, reaching for his shirt to put it back on. *No,* I wanted to cry out. He was leaving my bed, leaving the intimacy of this room, and every cell in my body was screaming for him to stay here with me.

"Wait," I said, resting a hand on his still-bare lower back. "Wait."

He paused, his head angled so I couldn't see his eyes clearly. He slipped the shirt on. "I . . . figured that meant you wanted this to stop. Our interactions so far have had a clear pattern of me pushing you somehow, stepping on a landmine I don't even know about. Then you run away. I don't want to keep doing that. Not here. Not right now."

"It's just . . . I have scars," I told him. I pressed my hand over the area where my familiar abdominal scar tissue rested; emotion welled in my chest, though I fought it off as best as I could. "And I don't want you to see it." A bubble filled my throat and I bit back a frustrated sob. "They're ugly. Deep. I don't even like to look at myself naked in the shower."

Shame heated my face. It was hard, making myself so vulnerable to this man who was beautiful and perfect. He could be carved out of marble, his skin flawless, his muscles lean and sculpted. He didn't understand what it felt like, knowing I would be physically damaged for the rest of my life.

"I'm . . ." I paused, drew in a shallow breath. "I'm afraid you'll be grossed out if you see them, and it just might break me if you are." My last words faded into the silence stretching between us.

Daniel stood, not looking at me. My heart started to splinter. I stood too; I was going to scrape together my pride, walk him to the door and keep this emotion bottled up until he left.

But instead of leaving, he turned toward the bed, ripped the blanket off, then tossed it on the floor. Confusion filled me, and I stared dumbly at him. Then he tugged off the top sheet and threw it on the floor as well. He took my hand and stared into my eyes, through my eyes and into my heart. I saw a rapid pulse fluttering at the base of his throat.

"Casey." There was so much emotion in his voice; it poured over me like warm oil. "Trust me, please."

Could I? I swallowed, nodded.

An edge of the stress ticking the strong line of his jaw faded, and he nudged me to stretch out on the bed. He picked up the sheet and draped it over my top half so my legs and head were exposed. I lay there, wondering what was happening.

Then he raised my arms and, with the sheet still covering my torso, gently tugged the shirt over my head.

My heartbeat picked up again, danced a scattered beat. I was topless except for my bra. But I was still covered, my stomach scars out of sight.

Daniel flicked the light off; his breathing was soft and a little ragged. He sat on the edge of the bed and brushed his hands across my skin. "I want you to feel good. I don't want you to be ashamed of your body." His hands were like velvet on my flesh. I almost purred at the gentle strokes up and down my arms, across the very top of my chest. It was soothing and arousing at the same time.

After a few minutes of him quietly running his fingers across my flesh, I slipped into a more relaxed state. I felt like I was melting in the bed. And yet I also became extra-aware of him—the raspy edge of his breathing, the underlying remains of his cologne. The pads of his fingers. Everything surged into my senses.

His fingers brushed against the waistband of my shorts, then paused. "I promise you, any time you want to stop, I will, immediately. Just say the word." His voice was husky with his arousal, and I wished I could see his eyes. I knew they shone with intensity right now.

"Okay," I managed to say. I wanted to feel him do those same stroking motions on my legs too.

He adjusted the sheet so it covered me to midthigh, then tugged my shorts off too. I was left in panties and a bra. A flash of self-consciousness hit me, but he began moving his hands in one long, continuous motion down my thigh. His thumb swept under the bend of my knee, and I moaned at the erotic sizzle in my body from the touch.

"I love hearing the sounds you make when you're turned on," he said, his voice rolling over me like warm sunshine.

"You make me feel good," I admitted. He did, and not just physically. No one had ever gone through this kind of effort to help me relax. To nurture me.

When his hand came back up my leg, fingertips brushing my inner thigh, I arched toward him. Suddenly I needed more than just his hands on me. I reached over and slipped my fingers under his shirt, tugged it up just a bit, wordlessly asking for him to remove it. He quickly shucked it and tossed it at the foot of the bed. Then he crawled on the bed beside me.

Our bodies touched from toe to pelvis to chest. Then our mouths met, and I exploded with hunger, gripping him. His hands moved across my exposed thighs, skimmed my hips and waist over top of the sheet, moved to my breasts, where he lowered his mouth to one hard nipple and sucked through the thin fabric of my bra. Then he slipped the cup down and bared me.

When his mouth captured my bare nipple, my core grew damp and throbbing. I dug my fingers into his hair, urged him closer. He licked and swallowed and sucked my flesh. I rubbed my knee along his inner thigh, let my leg stroke him where he was hardest.

"God, I want you," he said. There was an edge of frantic need in his voice.

"I want you too," I managed to get out. "Please. *Please*." And I did. I knew it wasn't going to be enough to kiss like this. I needed, ached to feel him inside of me. I wanted us to connect in a way I'd never had before. I had to give him a piece of myself that would stay with him forever, and him with me.

I felt him fumble in his pocket, and then something rustled.

"Are you sure?" he asked. He pulled back and looked in my eyes. I could hardly see him in the dim light, but I caught the glint in his pupils. He was intense, his emotions brimming right there, unflinching. "I need to hear you say it, please. Because if . . . this . . . comes between us and you run from me again, it just might kill me."

"Please make love to me," I whispered. "I promise, I won't run." I trailed kisses along his jaw, filled with an overwhelming urge to show him how I felt.

Daniel had been an open book for me since day one. But I'd kept him at arm's length, had come close, then run away, again and again. He deserved better than that, and for tonight, I wanted to be that person. The one he deserved.

The one I deserved to be. A girl who didn't feel like she was beyond hope. A girl who felt . . . worshiped. Adored. Valued.

Daniel nuzzled his mouth against my throat and tugged off his shorts and boxer briefs. And then he was fully naked, hard and firm against me. A nervous flutter started in my belly. But not fear.

Anticipation. I *wanted* this.

One hand moved up the bottom of the sheet and cupped my apex, pouring heat into my already overheated body. Then he slipped a finger inside, and pleasure spiraled in a low hum. Every sense was exploding with detail, etching this moment into my mind.

"You amaze me," he said as he licked the flesh underneath my jaw. His breath sent warm, damp puffs against my throat. I ran my tongue along his skin.

My orgasm began to edge closer. My whole body was humming, singing, alive because of him. "I'm . . ." I tensed, arched. "I'm going to . . ."

His finger stroked the right spot at that moment, and I was enveloped in a blaze of sensations, sizzling from my core down my limbs. "Yes," he whispered, taking my mouth with his. His words were ragged and rough, and I clenched around him.

After several long moments, the furious explosion died down. I reached a hand up and stroked a lock of hair away from his brow. He kissed the tip of my nose, then paused as he slipped on the condom.

Daniel slid on top of me, arms bracketing my head, legs nudging my pliant thighs apart. I eagerly wrapped around him. A pause, and then he was in me, and we both groaned our pleasure.

"You . . . feel . . ." He rasped his words against my forehead, kissing my face, the fingers of one hand tangled in my messy hair. He pulled out, then pushed back in, and he was big and filled me in a way I'd never imagined. "You feel beautiful," he finally said.

Daniel stared down into my eyes, stroked a thumb across my mouth as we moved together, him thrusting and me rotating my hips to draw him in deeper. I saw all the way into him, and realization blinded me in that moment. I felt like all of my walls were shattered apart, and I didn't think I could resurrect them again.

I was falling in love with this man.

My heart stuttered, and I swallowed the surprised gasp that almost came out.

Our pace increased. Sweat made our bodies slippery, permeated the thin sheet between our torsos; the moment was intense and emotional, and I was almost overwhelmed with my feelings. His eyes were dark and full of life, full of desire for me. And with the sheet between us, my scars still hidden away, I didn't feel self-conscious. I felt sexy, caught up in the moment.

In *him*.

And he'd done this for *me*.

I couldn't stop touching Daniel's body. The fire had been ignited and was consuming everything in me; I burned for him. I dug my heels into his firm backside, urging him on. Our mingled breaths panted in time until we were breathing each other in. His limbs began to tense and he slammed into me harder, with a more erratic pace, stroking my inner walls with his impossibly hard length. I wanted him to feel good, as good as he'd made me feel; I arched beneath him, ground against him.

"Come for me, Daniel," I whispered. I nibbled on the shell of his ear, rubbed my bare breasts on his chest.

He gave a little shiver, and his breathing grew harsh and irregular. His pace sped up more, and our pleasure began to spiral toward that intense zone again.

"I'm—" His head jerked back and his whole body tensed. "Oh God . . ."

I clung to him, needing him to fill me. And with a beautiful shudder, he moaned my name. His hand tightened in my hair; the other gripped my hip, keeping us pinned together as Daniel orgasmed.

We grew still. He released the tight clench on me and withdrew. But before he moved from on top of me, he tilted my chin so our eyes locked.

"Thank you," he said. Simple words, but I could see the genuine affection behind them. He brushed a kiss on each corner of my mouth.

My throat closed up, and tears threatened to well. There was something so . . . humbling about this man who was thanking me for *our* pleasure. As if I'd given him a precious gift.

Could it be anywhere close to what he'd done for me?

He disposed of the condom, then came right back to my side. Our bodies touched along every curve, like we couldn't bear to be apart for a long time. He spooned against my backside, and one hand lazily played with the strands of my hair. The other arm lay on top of my sheet, stroking my hip.

I love you, Daniel.

The words wanted to crawl right out of my mouth, to my elation and horror. I had never had an experience that intensely pleasurable before, so maybe that was making me this emotional. I had never just let go and . . . felt. While I could allow myself to feel this love, there was no chance I was going to say it to him.

I still needed time to process this all. I wanted to be sure this was real, not just a product of sexual elation. Though even as I thought that, I scoffed at myself. I knew it wasn't that. My feelings for him had been growing for a while now. This had made them explode in front of me so vividly, I couldn't deny it anymore.

My fingers slipped over his and rested there. I stroked the lean digits, let myself memorize him by touch, piece by piece. I could feel his heart beating steady against my back. Our sweat-slicked skin made us even closer.

"Stay the night," I found myself saying. "Um. If you want to. You don't have to, but you can—"

"I'd love to," he said, and I heard a light chuckle. "But I'll have to swing my by place either tonight or tomorrow morning to get my things. Hopefully my roommates haven't destroyed the place." Daniel had three roommates who were all much wilder than he was. He didn't hang around them much since they were party animals, and I was fine with staying away from their apartment. Not my kind of people either.

Sleepy satisfaction kept me rooted in my spot. "Maybe we can take a little nap and then head over there," I offered. I smothered a yawn. "And find some dinner, too, while we're at it."

He fit so perfectly against me. How was that possible? Even as I thrilled at our growing connection, I knew it meant I was vulnerable to him now. That I was letting him in and he could very well crush me if this didn't work out between us. But I didn't want to focus on that right now.

For once, I wanted to live in this moment and let myself be happy.

"That sounds great." His breathing evened out, slowed down, became regular as he slipped into a quick sleep.

I took a bit longer to fall asleep, but when I did, the last sensation I felt before I went under was our fingers still linked.

Chapter 16

My heart was going to explode right out of my chest. I was sure of it.

Daniel reached over from his spot on the passenger's seat and squeezed my hand. He seemed to sense my sudden tension spike. Probably because I was as stiff as a board in the driver's seat.

I couldn't help it. We were heading to my grandparents for my usual Friday meal with them. Only this time, I'd brought Daniel. Late last night, while I'd waited in the car for Daniel to fetch his stuff—he'd brought a small bag with his belongings, plus his books for Friday morning classes—I'd impulsively called Grandma and asked if it would be okay.

She had not only insisted I bring him today, she'd put Granddad on the phone to make him insist it as well. Apparently, my calling to ask wasn't enough proof that I wanted him there. I'd laughed and promised them we'd come.

But now that we were actually on our way, I couldn't seem to keep my pulse under control. It was erratic to the point where I could feel it thrumming on the side of my neck; if I didn't calm myself down, I was going to have a stupid panic attack. I was so nervous about what would happen.

"Tell me a little more about them," Daniel asked as he headed onto the highway. He flicked the radio on and dug through my CD collection, then popped one in, an instrumental album with an old-fashioned feel.

"Okay." I blinked and forced myself to focus on our conversation, on the music, instead of on my building panic. To stay grounded in the moment instead of imagining complications. To trust that things would go okay.

This was what you did when you were dating someone, I told myself. And it was definitely a good step if you were secretly in love with that person and wanting to make sure the two most important people in your life would like him too.

"So, Grandma likes to cook. A lot. She was a stay-at-home wife and mom for many years while she raised her kids. My granddad is retired—he worked at the airport for a couple of decades, repairing airplanes."

He gave me a slow nod of approval. "That's pretty badass. My grandmother worked for Ford in their accounting department. She actually didn't retire until she was in her late sixties. She loved her job."

"And your grandfather? What did he do?"

He paused. "He passed away last year. He was really sick for a long time—cancer. But before that, he was in life insurance."

"I'm sorry." I squeezed his hand. "Were you guys close?"

"He was a cool man." His voice was light, but I could detect a thread of sadness in his tone. He was still upset by the death. "I miss him a lot. My sisters and I went to his house every summer. He was very outdoorsy."

It kind of surprised me Daniel hadn't talked about him before now. Then again, with all the secrets I was still carrying, I had no right to think anything of it. And if I let him unravel himself at his own pacing, then I could do the same without the guilt.

Though I knew when he found out the truth about my past—and he would at some time, though thankfully not tonight, since I'd made my grandparents swear to not bring it up—I didn't know how that would change things with us. Would he be mad at me for keeping it to myself for so long? Would he understand why I was hesitant to discuss what had happened?

It was hard enough to fight my instinct to retreat into myself all the time. It was hard enough knowing that despite the pain, I needed to keep my mom and sister alive in my memory. But to rip that vein open and pour it all out? I couldn't do it. Not yet.

I couldn't dump those burdens on him.

Yes, I had a right to my secrets. After all, at this point, he and I hadn't been together that long as a couple. But hurting him would make me feel horrible. I worried it could do real damage to us if he was offended and pulled away from me.

I shook off those dark thoughts, keeping my hand firmly locked in his, and drove to the house. Today was not about my past. It was about my present. I looked over at him and saw the way the air conditioning fluttered that one lock on his brow. That dimple that popped up whenever he thought of something that amused him. I wanted to commit everything to memory. Mentally photograph each moment we spent together.

"I can feel you staring at me," he said, eyes still facing forward. That dimple deepened. "Like what you see? I am quite the catch."

I snorted. "Your modesty is overwhelming."

"Eh, you don't love me for my modesty," he declared.

My breath hitched. I knew he was joking, but having it out there so easily made me freeze up. Maybe he already knew how I felt. If he did, why hadn't he said it, then? Was he waiting for me to do it?

Our arrival onto my grandparents' street interrupted my train wreck of thoughts. "We're here." I pulled into their driveway. *Pull yourself together!* I ordered myself. Good grief, falling in love was making me a neurotic mess. *It was a passing comment, nothing more. Stop reading into everything.* I pasted on a big smile and flung the door open.

He got out too but paused before closing his door, staring at me over the hood of the car. "You okay?"

"Oh. Yes. I'm fine," I said. My fake smile grew wider, and I tried to slow down my hammering heart.

He frowned. "Okay." He sounded skeptical.

The door opened, and my grandmother stepped out onto the porch. "Come in," she said, raising a hand over her eyes to shade them. Her other hand waved us closer. "It's hot out here—seems like this summer's never going to end. You're going to melt."

My smile was growing increasingly brittle as my hands began to shake. My stomach churned. Daniel and I walked over to her; he was at least a good foot taller than her, but he didn't try to look like he was towering.

"Grandma, this is Daniel."

He stuck out his hand. "I'm so pleased to meet you, Mrs. Mackintosh."

She raised a brow and shot me a glance as if to say, *Wow, a boy with manners—shocker!* "Pleased to meet you too. Come inside. I have some fresh lemonade ready, or iced tea if you prefer."

We followed her in. The air conditioning hit me hard and sent goose bumps along my bare arms. In all the fuss, I'd forgotten to wear long sleeves to her house. Crud. I rubbed my arms and moved into the living room, and we sat down on the couch.

With Daniel here, I eyed the house from a stranger's perspective. Furniture that was a bit old-fashioned but comfortable. Neutral beige carpet. Knickknacks on curio cabinets and shelves. Photos of me covering most of the back wall. My high school graduation picture on the fireplace mantel, with a red and black tassel hanging from the corner.

I finally dared to look over at him and saw him eyeing the room too.

He glanced at me. "She seems nice," he whispered.

"She is," I found myself whispering back. A little bit of tension drained from my shoulders.

Grandma returned with two glasses of lemonade. My mouth began to water just from thinking about it—there was something about her tart, sweet lemonade that I couldn't seem to replicate, no matter how often I tried.

She sat down on the edge of her chair and crossed her slender legs at the ankles. I noticed she'd taken care to put on blush and eye shadow today, and she was wearing the gold cross Granddad had bought her for her birthday last year. My heart swelled—I guessed she wanted to make a good impression too.

I wasn't the only one nervous. Of course, this was the first guy I'd ever brought home, so no wonder she and I were on edge. A little more tension seeped away.

"Granddad will be home any minute," she said. "He ran to the store to get more milk, since I used the last of it for mashed potatoes." She paused and set her hands on her lap. "Daniel, tell me about you. I understand you're an English major?"

He nodded. "Minoring in art history."

They spent the next few minutes talking about his classes. I sat in silence and just watched. He was easy and respectful with her, his laugh quiet but genuine as he explained his future aspirations. "So after weighing all of my options, I think I'll get my master's and then teach for a while," he concluded. "I really do love school. This seems the best way to stay in without having to keep racking up student loans."

"Casey's been working hard on her classes. We're proud of

her. She's been on the dean's list every semester since freshman year."

"Grandma," I said, trying to not roll my eyes. "It's not that big of a deal."

"Pish," she said with a wave of her hand. "You're too modest."

The door opened. "I have the milk," Granddad declared. He strolled into the living room and held out his free hand. His voice was even, but his eyes were serious. "Pleased to meet you, son."

I stifled a moan. So it was going to be that kind of night. Maybe we could eat fast and run.

Grandma stood, giving a slight groan as she pushed up from the couch. "Back's killing me today. Anyway, let's get the table set. It's time to eat."

Dinner wasn't nearly as painful as I'd been afraid it would be. For the most part, my grandparents didn't embarrass me by asking Daniel supernosy questions. Little by little, my uneasiness settled. I felt guilty for my earlier paranoia—I should have known they wouldn't push my comfort zone by being too aggressive with him. They were polite, and he responded in kind.

Even so, with all of that politeness, my heart was a riot of emotions on the inside. I kept a faint smile on my face and finished my dinner—fried chicken, green beans and mashed potatoes, another favorite meal—but I couldn't stop being aware of Daniel. Couldn't stop thinking about how important he'd become to me in just a few weeks. Crazy, but true.

His knee brushed against mine. On purpose? Accident?

I shifted in my seat so our legs would be just a touch closer. His knee reached over again, and it stayed there this time. A solid, steady pressure that warmed me. Definitely not an accident, then. I tried to suppress a huge smile that would give anything away.

"I understand from Casey that you collect World War Two memorabilia," Daniel said to Granddad. "I took a course last year that focused on modern wars of the twentieth century. It amazed me how fighting tactics changed so drastically with World War One. Rules no longer applied, and people struggled to adapt."

Granddad blinked. A genuine smile crept over his face, and his wrinkles deepened around the eyes. "That's true. I have some autobiographies by soldiers from World Wars One and Two, and they talk about how hard it was to adjust returning home after all the violence."

"Did you ever read *Unbroken*?" Daniel asked. "It's about an Olympic runner who was in the second war. His tale of survival was amazing."

They spent the next twenty minutes discussing the book. Granddad was in his zone—I could see him getting more and more worked up as Daniel shared thoughts and speculations about the wars. He was no longer simply being polite but was full-on engaging.

Seeing Daniel reach out to my granddad on something so important to him made emotion suddenly tighten my throat. I reached my hand under the table and rested it on his thigh.

He dropped his hand down and slipped it over mine, squeezing.

I'd never had a connection with someone like Daniel before—he challenged me, made me laugh, frustrated me, turned me on like nothing I'd felt in my life. Was it too much for me to hope this was real, that it would last? The pressure of his fingers on mine was very real, very concrete. His knee pressing against my knee.

The way he'd held me last night. Stroked my hair until I'd fallen asleep.

Real too.

All I knew was, I wanted to bring him back here with me

next week. I wanted to learn everything I could about him. I wanted us to have inside jokes we could laugh about before bed. To put my cold feet against his legs so he'd grumble. Watch hours of marathon movies together. Go on vacation to somewhere fun and take a hundred pictures we'd plaster all over Facebook.

Do things that regular couples did, things that wove them together.

My heart was aching, bursting with all my emotions for him. It was all too much, too much and yet not enough, because I wanted more. Did I have the courage to reach out for it and take it?

"Casey?" Grandma's voice penetrated my consciousness. She waved in front of my face. "Hey, are you listening?"

Crap. I'd been caught daydreaming. I gave an embarrassed smile. "Sorry. My mind just—"

"I was saying, let's clear the dinner plates, because I think your granddad wants to show Daniel some things in his den before you guys have to go. You do have work tonight, yes?"

I nodded.

"I can help clean up," Daniel offered.

"No, really, it's okay." I laughed. "I've seen his collection a hundred times. You're fresh meat—he won't let you get out of it that easily."

The two men walked away.

As Grandma stood, I noticed her reaching for her back. Her face twisted in a momentary flash of pain.

"You sit right there," I ordered. "I'll take care of this." Gave me something to focus on, anyway.

She sighed. "My old bones are growing older. I can tell the autumn cold's finally going to come on soon—I'm getting achy."

"Please. You're not that old," I said as I grabbed the plates and scraped them off. "You guys are barely in your seventies."

It kind of scared me to think about them getting older, so I tried to focus on dishes.

We were quiet for a few minutes as I worked. I loaded the dishwasher and turned it on.

"He's a sweet boy," Grandma said. Her voice was quiet, sincere. "Cares a lot about you too."

I turned around and pressed my back against the counter. "I really like him," I admitted to her. It was so strange, saying it out loud. But it was true. "Maybe even more than like." Okay, not just maybe, but I wasn't quite ready to admit my love yet. And when I did, I'd be telling him first.

Grandma gave me a small smile. She looked so tired. My chest squeezed. Had she always looked this wiped? Was she sick?

"What's wrong?" I asked. I couldn't help the nervous tremble in my voice. "Are you okay?"

"Healthy as a horse," she soothed. "I'm not going anywhere, honey. At least, I don't think so—not for a while. Just a little tired today. Most days are fine."

I dropped down into the seat beside her. I knew she wouldn't lie to me; if she was sick, she'd tell me. But this reminded me I needed to value our time together more. And do what I could to help take care of her.

She reached for my hand and clasped it between her palms. Hers were so tiny, so frail compared to mine. "I love you, and I'm glad you brought him here so we could meet him. But you need to tell him, Casey. Don't keep putting it off. I can see how it's eating away at you."

"I know." My stupid throat tightened again. I cast a guilty glance in the area of the den. "But . . . it'll change everything."

"If he's the right man, things will work out."

I gave a wordless nod.

She patted my hand and released it. "You'd better go find that boy before your granddad overwhelms him. You know how he likes to go on." She chuckled. "Though I gotta say, if he can survive Granddad, he can survive anything."

We said our good-byes; Daniel thanked them profusely for having him over. Granddad even gave him a hug before we left.

"Thank you for inviting me," Daniel said after we got in the car. "That was a lot of fun." He shot me a grin. "Now what?"

I glanced at the time on my phone. "Now I head home and get ready for work. You?" With a smile, I put the car in reverse and pulled out of the drive, onto the street.

"Oh, I'm just going to sit at home and think about a girl who's at work tonight. No big deal."

My cheeks flushed with pleasure. "Huh. Well, maybe if that gets boring, you could stop by. You know, to say hi or something."

Wow. I was flirting. Definitely flirting. And the more I did it with him, the less awkward it got.

I merged onto the highway.

He slid me a sideways glance, and there was a melting heat in that gaze, that crooked smile that curled my toes and made my lower belly hum in anticipation. "Maybe I will, Casey."

Chapter 17

The crowd was extra packed tonight at The Mask. Thankfully, Sal had finally repaired the air conditioner—after Justin and I had harassed him nonstop—so it wasn't superhot in the club. Which was good, since I'd taken extra care with my appearance today. Makeup, curled hair, even a tight-fitting tank top with my favorite jeans.

Megan had given me a loud, embarrassing whistle when I'd stepped out of my bedroom. I'd rolled my eyes but secretly, it was nice to feel attractive.

A guy walked up to the DJ booth. He was nice looking, with shaggy blond hair and huge brown eyes. His smile was wide and appreciative. "Hey, what was the name of that last song?"

I glanced down. "Um, it was a new song out by Paradise Found. 'Gutter Mom.' " I chuckled. "They have a way with titles, I guess."

He laughed. "Not what I'd been expecting, but thanks." He turned to go, then paused, looked back up at me. "Can I buy you a drink?"

Me? I blinked. "Um, I'm . . . good, but—"

"Gotta get hot up there in that booth," he cajoled. He took another step up until he was just a couple of feet away. His thick, tanned hand leaned casually against the rail of my booth. I could smell his body spray. "Sure I can't get ya something?"

"I got it covered," a familiar voice said from right behind him. Daniel squeezed by, holding a water and a beer, and pressed a soft kiss to my mouth. He put the water down and snaked an arm around my waist. "Sorry I'm so late. I meant to be here earlier."

The guy took in Daniel's possessive gesture, then gave a small nod. "Gotcha. Thanks."

"Thanks anyway," I said as he departed. I turned to look at Daniel. A small smile crooked on my face. "That was interesting."

"What?" he said as he grabbed his beer and took a sip.

I narrowed my eyes. "Were you jealous?"

He huffed. "Me? Jealous?" Then, "Okay, yes. Maybe a little."

"It's not normally like that," I said. I sipped my water, happy to relieve my parched throat. "No one pays any attention to me."

The song ended, and I changed to the next one.

"You think you're invisible, but you're not." Daniel's words were surprisingly serious. "You have no idea how attractive you are. And it's not just about looks. There's something about you—an intensity that makes people want to be one of the trusted ones. One of the people you drop your walls for and let in."

I swallowed, stared at him. No one had said anything like that to me before. For so long, I'd *wanted* to be the invisible girl, though. Having my family nightmare plastered all over the news for weeks as a young teen had scarred me for years.

And yet . . . I could sense something changing in me. When that guy had come up, I hadn't rebuffed him with a gruff word. I'd talked to him.

I hadn't even thought about my scars.

"I think you're attractive," I admitted to him. "And magnetic." I couldn't believe I was confessing it, but in the intimacy of the booth, with music throbbing around us, it felt right. This was the place I was most secure. Where my confidence could shine—music was my soul, my voice.

I spun around and flipped through my selections. Suddenly I wanted to put on just the right song for him. Let the music speak what I didn't dare say. I found a strange yet addictive little love song written by a no-name band I adored and made it load up next. There was a small tremble in my hands.

"I wanna pick one," he said from right behind me. The length of his body pressed against mine; his heat warmed my skin, and I fought the urge to lean back and let my building arousal take over.

"Um." I cleared my throat and stepped away, giving him a sheepish grin. He knew he was affecting me. "There's my book. You can flip through and see if there's anything you want to hear."

The next half hour flew by. Daniel had good taste in music—he picked eclectic songs that were a bit older but got the crowd excited. We had fun. Laughed. I finished the last of my water.

"I'll be back," he said as he scooped up my glass and his empty bottle.

"You don't have to—"

"Shush," he admonished. His eyes were stern. "Let me do this, please."

I gave a meek nod.

Daniel headed out of the booth and toward the bar. Justin darted over, and the two of them began talking.

I got the next song loaded and blended the songs so they faded seamlessly, the beats lining up. When the crowd got worked up like this, they liked songs to keep going for a while.

I looked over and saw two pretty girls talking to Daniel, their faces animated.

He was talking back with them, his head thrown back as he laughed at something the redhead said, and a stab of jealousy hit me in the gut. Wow, was I for real? Getting jealous because girls were trying to hit on him? This must have been how Daniel felt earlier when the guy had come up to my booth.

There was some strange, possessive streak in me that wanted to go down there and let them know he was mine. It was ridiculous, caveman-like, but there nonetheless. I'd tasted his body, had given him mine. Felt him inside me, seen the flash in his eyes right before he came. I had him—I didn't need to prove it to anyone.

Justin came over to their group and handed Daniel two waters. Daniel said a few parting words to the girls, then came back toward the booth, weaving along the edge of the dance floor. The girls stared at him as he left, whispering to each other, their gazes hot and hard on his ass.

My cell phone buzzed in my pocket. I took it out.

That one's a keeper. Perfect gentleman. Cool your jets, Miss Jealousy. He wants YOU.

I barked out a laugh, but my cheeks burned. Guess I needed to do a better job hiding my emotions if Justin could see it on my face from his spot behind the bar. I texted back an emoticon of a tongue sticking out and sent it to him, then crammed the phone back in my jeans pocket.

Daniel handed me my water. He filled our pockets of silence with observations about the crowd, pointing out who was hooking up, making up stories about people. We put on a run of songs that got the crowd writhing and dancing, moving as one to the throbbing bass. Like me, Daniel seemed caught up in the power of controlling the energy in the room.

"This is so cool," he said with an excited flush on his cheeks.

"I can see why you find this addictive. I'd dig having a job like this."

"I help people experience the passion in music that I feel. I love that so much." I smiled at him, and he took my hand in his. It was even better to share this moment, this emotion with him.

The rest of the evening flew by far too fast. It was the most fun I'd had at work in a long time.

Because of him.

When my shift ended and I shut down and packed away my portion of the equipment, he helped, so the process went much faster. Sometimes those pieces were large and unwieldy, and Justin usually gave me a hand.

I stood by my loaded-down car and wiped the dripping sweat off my brow. Moving cargo had made my face uncomfortably warm. "Thanks for your help," I told him.

He stepped close, and an altogether different kind of flush filled me from the inside out. His eyes were hooded. He reached out and brushed a stray strand of hair behind my ear. "My pleasure."

The way he said those words, low and full of promise, made me think about pleasure.

"I'd better head back to my place," he continued, regret clear on his face. "I have a huge paper due next week, and I haven't started it yet." His hand cupped my face, and he pulled me toward him with a gentle kiss.

I opened my mouth, drew him deeper in. We kissed for a good minute; my blood surged in my veins. I wanted him again, was filled with a deep longing. But I needed sleep. I was sweaty and sticky.

When we pulled away, I said, "Have a good evening." My voice was so throaty, I barely recognized it. I gave an awkward chuckle.

Daniel brushed his lips against my brow, slid his mouth to

my ear and whispered, "I'm looking forward to seeing you again."

He walked away toward his car, leaving me staring after him long after he got in and drove away.

As one song ended at The Mask the next night, I transitioned into a newer, more popular electronica release. The crowd screamed in pleasure and their dancing kicked up. I smiled. It was addictive, this job. A way for me to make people happy, to share something I loved so much.

My phone vibrated. I snagged it.

My roommates are gone all night. My paper is well under way. I miss you and want to see you. Tonight?

My heart gave a hard, aching thud in response, and I read the text another dozen times. I missed Daniel too. We'd both been busy today finishing up papers for other classes, studying for exams.

Not done until after 2. Have to drop equip at apt too, I texted back. God, I wanted to see him again. Not even twenty-four hours had passed, and I was already going through withdrawals. I'd seen him every day for the last few days. Funny how I had grown addicted to having him around.

It thrilled me that he felt the same way.

My phone buzzed. *That's okay. Can you come?*

Yes. My fingers trembled in anticipation as I sent the text.

I can't wait.

Three words that made my core pulse with need.

Unlike last night, the rest of tonight crawled. Probably because I kept looking at my clock every five minutes, willing the hours to pass. Even loving my job couldn't make me want to stay a second longer than I had to.

I pasted on a polite smile and took recommendations, kept the tunes going. But in my head I was already lying in bed with

Daniel, breathing in the scent of his skin, running my fingers along all those spots I wanted to explore. Tasting the hollow of this throat.

I almost missed switching songs. I chastised myself to pay better attention. Even though work was going well, I didn't want Sal to have any reason to doubt my competence.

One of Justin's bartending partners, William, was also handling the crowd at the bar, so Justin slipped away and brought me a water. Tonight he was wearing all black—skinny jeans, tight T-shirt, hair spiked in front.

"You looked thirsty," he declared as he thrust the glass at me. "Here."

"God bless you." I took a long drink.

"Everything okay? You seem a bit . . . off today." He raised a knowing eyebrow. "Like you're preoccupied. Maybe with the delicious body of a certain sexy guy?"

My cheeks flamed before I could fight the response. "Knock it off," I said, though my tone wasn't harsh. I rolled my eyes.

"You dirty little slut!" Justin laughed. "You know I'm going to make you tell me all the hot details. But I'd better get back to the bar before William throws a dagger in my back." He narrowed his eyes. "Hot details. I expect thorough text messages to fill me in."

"Use your imagination," I retorted.

He blinked, surprised at my sassy reply. Frankly, I was a little surprised too. This wasn't the normal me—the one who flirted, who joked about sex.

Being with Daniel was changing me.

Daniel wrapped a lean, naked leg over mine as he rolled onto his side and draped an arm over the top of my chest. He nuzzled his face against my neck, right under my ear. His breaths were warm and damp, a pleasant contrast to his slightly chilly bedroom.

"I'm exhausted," he whispered. Small kisses pressed against my earlobe, and I shivered in delight. "I vote we sleep in tomorrow."

"That can so happen," I agreed. I checked to make sure the sheet was draped across my stomach. My breasts were bared, as were my legs, but all of my scars were covered.

He sighed; heat radiated from his torso against the side of my body. I rested my hand on his forearm and listened in contented silence as his breathing slowed and evened out.

I was tired, but I couldn't quite fall asleep yet. I wanted to live in this moment for a little more before I did. The sex had been amazing—hot, frantic. Filled with needy kisses, grasping fingers, gasps and breathy sighs. He'd thrust in me, made me come. I was still riding high from it all.

I peered around his dimly lit room. The walls were covered in rock posters, pictures of his family and friends, various ticket stubs and newspaper clippings, and even pages from *National Geographic* magazine. His bedspread was bright blue with pinstripes of black, his sheets a crisp, soft white. Eclectic, interesting. I wouldn't have expected anything different, to be honest.

He mumbled something, his voice thick and slurred with sleep. A smile slipped across my face. I leaned just a little closer and allowed myself to just . . . feel. Let myself love him in the quiet darkness of his room, my heart burst wide open and exploding with those things I didn't dare whisper. Though I wanted to. God, for some stupid reason I wanted to wake him up and ask him if he loved me too. If he could possibly love me as much as I loved him.

The intensity of the way I felt scared me. I was overwhelmed. Drowning in it.

Tears welled into my eyes from a sudden surge of panic that Daniel was pushing right through my walls, breaking them and leaving the crumbled remains of my emotional protective barriers in his wake. My pulse fluttered in response, and that familiar tingle crept to my lips, my fingertips.

Don't do this right now, I whispered silently to myself. There was no need to panic. Everything was under control. I could keep my secret a little while longer, at least until I could be certain what was going to happen with us. There was still time. No need to rush. *Breathe.*

After a few minutes of deep breathing, my heart started slowing its nervous pace. Sleepiness finally, blessedly began to overtake me, and I let myself relax in his comforting embrace. I focused on the moment, as my therapist had recommended to me all those years ago. The sensation of his fingers resting on my bare skin. The soft tickle of his breath against my ear, fluttering my hair. The scent of our mingled sex.

Everything about him, about us, was a study in sensation.

My eyes slipped closed. I turned my face toward him, smelled the light scent of his shampoo. I could smell him on the pillow too. I tugged my sheet up to cover us, since I knew we'd get chilly soon.

As I drifted off into a state of deep drowsiness, I focused on the quiet, even puffs of Daniel's breath and let it lull me to sleep.

Chapter 18

"Casey," a soft voice whispered in my ear.

I groaned and rolled over. Morning light slanted in my eyes. "Too. Early."

"It's almost eleven," Daniel said with a laugh. I felt the side of the bed dip, and then a warm hand was stroking my hair.

Not a bad way to wake up. I stretched, then scooted up in bed, giving a sleepy smile as I wrapped the sheet tighter around my torso. "I can't believe I slept that late."

Even more amazing, I'd slept the entire night through. No nightmares. Just sweet, serene deep sleep. Such a rare occurrence. I felt like I'd conked out for a week.

"I made breakfast. You should eat something." He stood, then tossed me a clean T-shirt from his drawer. It was dark gray and supersoft.

I probably could have put my tank top on, but there was something intimate about wearing his clothing. Like a way to announce to the world that we were together. That we shared things with each other, had a real relationship.

I flushed. "Okay, I'll be there in a sec. I need to . . ." I glanced down at my topless self, my nipples beading under the thin sheet from awareness of his scrutiny.

He winked. "Take your time. After breakfast, you can take a shower if you like."

Daniel sauntered out the door and closed it behind him. I scrambled to toss on my bra, panties and jeans, then slipped on his shirt. It was a little big on me, but the fabric was soft. And it smelled like him, fresh and clean.

I padded into the kitchen. The scent of bacon and eggs wafted into the air. I smiled. "You really go all out." I hadn't had a real Sunday morning breakfast in ages.

"What can I say? I'm a great guy. Hopefully it's edible." He winked and went back to serving up the food on two large, white plates. He brought them to the table he'd already set with napkins, forks, knives and juice.

I settled in the chair across from him. We dug into our food with gusto, silent for a few moments. The eggs were cooked perfectly and even had a hint of cheese in them. Delicious.

I bit into a strip of crispy bacon. "You're not as bad at cooking as you led me to believe."

"It's only bacon and eggs. Hard to mess up. So, what do you normally do on Sundays?" he asked me.

I shrugged. "Not much. Homework, that kind of thing." On the rare occasion, Megan had made breakfast for her hookups and asked me to join them. I usually declined, hiding in my room.

"My parents make a huge breakfast every Sunday. It's a ritual for them—pancakes, eggs, bacon, sausage, the works. I always thought it was too much for us to eat, but somehow we managed to pack it away every time." He chuckled. "Did you have any kind of rituals with your family?"

My stomach turned. I put the bacon down.

Daniel sighed when he saw the expression on my face. "I just want us to know each other better, Casey. But there's a huge gap that we can't seem to bridge because you always clam up. Anything to do with your family, with your past, is off-limits."

"I'm not ready to talk about things yet," I said stiffly. My heart began to beat a rapid staccato.

"But when? *When* will you be?" I could hear the frustration in his voice. "Next week? A month from now? Five years? We're nowhere closer to you opening up to me than we were that first night, when you pushed me away without any explanation. I feel like I walk on eggshells all the time around you. Dance around topics that are even mildly personal so I don't offend you or make you run away."

My eyes stung. I swallowed, blinked. "That's not true. I have opened up to you. I took you to see my grandparents." The half-eaten breakfast didn't smell so good anymore, the bacon pungent and eggs unsavory. I nudged the plate away.

"And I took you to meet my family," he countered. "It's not a competition here."

My jaw clenched. "I didn't say it was. Don't put words in my mouth."

"Why can't you just open up and be honest with me?" He pushed his plate away as well, then raked a hand through his hair. "I'm an open book. Ask me any question, and I'll answer it."

"Well, not all of us are like you." My words were low but heated. "You know what? I don't want to talk about this." I stood to go. I wasn't going down this road with him today. My good feelings were all gone now, but I could stop the conversation before it damaged things in a very real way between us.

"Don't do this to me," he said, standing as well. He stared me down. "The moment you feel threatened, you always run away. Always. I back off and back off. I let things go. But—"

"You're pushing me too hard, Daniel. I don't want to talk," I interrupted. My voice was ice-cold, belying the mad flutter in my stomach. My hands started to tremble. I crammed them into my jeans pockets.

"What are you so afraid of? Why won't you just tell me what you're thinking and feeling?" A vein ticked on the side of his forehead. His nostrils flared as he narrowed his eyes, staring me down. I'd never seen Daniel this frustrated before. "I'm good enough to sleep with but not good enough for you to open up to?"

I reeled back from his raw comment like he'd struck me.

The room grew quiet, still. The only sound was our ragged, panting breaths.

"That's not fair," I finally whispered. My throat closed up, and I blinked back tears.

"No, it's not." His tone was quiet. His eyes grew anguished. "This is killing me, Casey. Stop shutting me out. I want to be there for you, but you're so damn stubborn. You throw up a wall every time I try to press you about anything. I'm not the enemy." He paused, and his tone flattened a touch in disappointment. "I've let you into my life. You've seen me—all of me. The good and the bad. I only get to see the pieces you *want* me to see. But that means I never really know you at all. Even after all this time, you still don't trust me."

My heart thundered in my chest. Guilt and anger roiled in my stomach. "You're making this about you, but it's not," I said, voice trembling. I stood in front of him and poked my finger on his chest. "Despite what you may think, this goes back *way* before you. There's a reason no one knows a thing about me, Daniel. Except that I'm jacked up, of course." I gave a bitter laugh. "Because that's the way I cope with things. That's how I keep going every day. But you . . . you think you can just swoop in and I'll drop everything and change who I am on your schedule? That's not how it works."

"For God's sake!" he scoffed. His brow furrowed. "Seriously? I never asked you to change. That's not fair." He flung my earlier words back at me.

"No. It really isn't." I crossed my arms, jutting out my jaw.

My anger swelled like a living thing in my belly, its companion that all-too-familiar pang of guilt. I knew this would happen some day. That this serenity between us wasn't going to last.

He stared at me in silence for several long moments. I refused to squirm under the scrutiny, though on the inside I could feel myself crumbling into pieces. How had everything gone so wrong? It had been a great start. A great evening. But like usual with me, it all went to shit.

"After everything we've been through so far," he said in a tone so low I could barely hear, "I would have thought I'd earned the respect of your honesty and openness."

"You want openness?" I blurted out. "You want honesty?" I tugged my shirt up and showed him my deepest shame. I kept my eyes fixed steadily on the ground. There was no way I wanted to see the flash of revulsion that would surely be on his face. "That's what I hide from you, from everyone."

My heart hammered against my rib cage so hard I was sure it would smash its way through.

I dropped the shirt but kept my gaze away from him. I looked at the floor, studied the patterns of the square tiles. "My dad was depressed. Bitter. Angry. A drunk. He was hardly ever a happy man. Hated taking his meds, said they 'numbed' him." I paused to suck in a shaky breath. "Mom tried to be patient with him. Encourage him. Smile and do everything that made him happy."

A sudden image of her smiling face hit me, and my throat closed up. How long had it been since I'd told anyone all of this?

I knew the next part of the story. Knew what was coming, but it still hurt for me to rip the words out of my tight throat. "One night Dad was in a particularly bad mood. He'd yelled at Mom, yelled about how miserable he was." So many cruel words about how he hated his life. It still killed me as much then as it had that night. "I was only thirteen. Lila, my little sister, was ten. We stayed in the living room with each other for a full hour while they argued, quietly listening."

Tears burned my eyes. I blinked. They multiplied, slid down my face. From the edges of my perspective I could see Daniel's feet, frozen in place. I still couldn't look up into his face. I was simultaneously here and back in our old home. I could smell the apple candles Mom loved so much, their scents wafting to us from the coffee table. I could hear a distant train rumbling on tracks. The neighbor's dog barking.

"Finally things got quiet. I took Lila upstairs after that. We got ready for bed and went to sleep." I couldn't breathe. I pressed my hand to my chest.

"Casey—" Daniel began in a tentative voice.

"I woke up when I heard the first shot," I said, talking right over him. The words tumbled out of me now like a gushing river; I couldn't stop it even if I wanted to. The story begged to be purged, come hell or high water. "I didn't know what it was. I thought someone had broken something, a thunderous crack from the direction of my parents' bedroom. I woke Lila up, and we stood in the middle of our room, holding hands, unsure what to do. Then our bedroom door opened . . . and there stood my dad, eyes dark and a little unfocused, a rifle in his hand."

"Oh God, Casey." His words bled with emotion.

My eyes blurred. I couldn't see anything anymore. "He shot my sister, right in front of me," I managed to squeak out. My chest began to throb from all the anxiety building beneath my rib cage. "He shot Lila, and she just . . . fell. And then he turned the rifle on me. It all happened so fast. I didn't do anything, just stood there, staring at him." I pressed a trembling hand to my mouth, and a sob ripped out.

It's okay. But you have to finish, I soothed myself. I pulled my rampant emotions back in.

My voice was a painful whisper as I pushed words past a closed throat. "I don't quite know why I survived. *How* I survived. I don't remember much about what happened after that. I have dreams about it, but I don't know if they're true or if my brain is just trying to give me answers. But in my dream, his hand twitched right before he shot me. The shot missed vital organs, though it did damage my intestines. Then he . . . he shot himself. One of our neighbors must have heard the commotion, because I woke up in a hospital. And when I did, I asked where everyone was. And they were all dead."

Dead because my father couldn't control himself, wouldn't take his medicine, could never seem to be happy.

Dead because he wanted to die and wanted us to die with him.

My knees gave out, and I gripped the edge of a nearby chair. Daniel rushed over, but I held up a hand. I didn't want him touching me right now. If he did, I'd shatter into a thousand pieces right here on the floor. I was barely hanging on, a scrap of ragged thread. "Just . . . give me a second."

Deep breaths. In and out. In and out. Grandma's voice soothed me. I followed her instructions, the same ones she'd said to me every night after every nightmare during the first year I'd moved in with her.

I steeled my spine. *Courage, Casey.* I finally looked up into Daniel's eyes. Hot tears had streaked down from his face, splashed on his dark shirt, leaving tiny puddles. The pain in his eyes was so vivid that I felt my own tears spring up again.

"I'm going to go home," I said in a whisper. I needed to curl under my sheets and sleep for a year. I'd tried so hard to keep this in my past. But Daniel couldn't be satisfied until he'd gutted me.

He wiped at his face. "We need to talk about this. I can't just let you go after . . ." He waved his hand. "After all of this."

"I'm going to go home," I repeated. I walked into his bedroom and with careful movements took off his T-shirt. I folded it and put it on the rumpled bed; with fastidious care I ignored the pillow creases where our heads had just rested together. I donned my tank top and dug under the bed to find my shoes.

"Please." His plea was so raw, it splintered me. "You have to stop running away from me. You just . . . opened up to me, and now you're going to leave. But we need to talk about this. Please. If we're going to work, we need to talk." He paused, his voice rich with an emotion that sounded dangerously close to pity. "I'm so sorry this happened to you, Casey. Not in a million years could I have guessed—"

I looked up at him. "I don't want pity. I'm a strong person. I've spent the last eight years building a new life for myself. But you needed to know the truth, no matter what. You pushed and pushed me. And I resent that, Daniel."

He reeled back, blinking. "Pity? It's not pity. It's empathy." He took a tentative step toward me. "I've never faced anything traumatic like this, I know. But it doesn't mean I can't share your pain. But you're so determined to be independent that you won't let anyone in." Frustration poured anew from his voice, even though I could see he was trying to rein it back.

"You can't share my pain," I said. I stood and grabbed my purse. "You have no idea how it feels to know your own father wanted to kill you. And even worse . . ." I sucked in a shaky breath, made myself continue. It was all out there now. Might as well rip off every bandage and show all my scars, physical and emotional. "Even worse, knowing there's a possibility of me becoming him. Losing control and snapping one day."

"You're not him." The words were hot, impassioned, and I could tell he believed it.

But how could he? Like he said, he didn't know me. I'd been fooling myself, thinking we could work. "You don't think so? I can't even think about my father because if I do, I want to rage. I miss my mom and my sister every day because he was a monster who stole them from me." I walked past him to the bedroom door, to the front door, flinging them both open.

Daniel was hot on my heels. "You can't drive like this."

"I'm fine." I didn't need him to parent me. I just wanted to run away, try to flee these dark, violent, scary emotions surging in me.

When I made it to the front of his apartment building, I fumbled in my purse for the keys. Where the hell were they? The panic in my chest spread to my lips, my fingertips. *Oh God, not here. Make it home. Not here.*

"Let me drive you at least. Please."

"No."

"Dammit, Casey!" He growled. "Stop doing this! Just let me help you."

I turned to him. "I want to be alone, Daniel. *Leave me alone.* Haven't you made me hurt enough today?" Anger made me say the words, but as soon as they came out, a part of me wanted to take them back. The pain in his eyes flared, and he stepped back.

I swallowed and dug once more for my keys, finding them tucked into a corner. Finally. I was just barely holding myself together. I jumped in my car, started it and pulled out of the lot. I could feel Daniel's damaged gaze still fixed on me, but I couldn't look back.

I fumbled for a random CD and popped it in, cranked the music up as loud as it could go. It was heavy and intense and throbbed in my cells with every beat. I let the bass-laden song fill my ears and head so I wouldn't have to think or feel.

My solace.

I drove around like that for an hour, just listening. The tears had dried into crusty streaks on my face. My hands clenched the steering wheel so tight my fingers ached. But the music finally did its work and eased the pain enough so I could face going home.

When I made it to my apartment, I rushed through the front door to my room, not stopping to talk to Megan, who was sitting on the couch. Shoes on, I curled up on my bed. My chest ached so badly, like someone had dug beneath my rib cage with a spoon. I was breaking apart, and I had no idea how to make the agony go away.

Chapter 19

My stomach was a tangle of knots as I got out of bed for philosophy on Monday morning. I wasn't ready to see Daniel. Not yet, not when I was still so devastated. I'd slept like shit last night, tossing and turning, reliving the nightmare over and over again each time I tried to close my eyes. Seeing my sister's body hit the floor, her eyes rolling toward me, blood gurgling from her wounds.

Instead of taking my shower and getting dressed, I lingered on the edge of the bed, trying to get myself under control. A half hour passed, with me no closer to getting ready than I'd been when I woke up. I felt like I was going to vomit. I wanted to kick myself for being so weak and overemotional, so under the mercy of my emotions, but it was what it was.

Daniel's face flashed in my mind, the harsh edge of his breathing as I explained my past. My chest tightened. I sat on the edge of my bed and made myself draw in slow breaths. My shaky fingers gripped my knees. No, I was not going to let this turn into a panic attack. I was in control of myself, my emotions. They did not control me.

I wasn't like my father. I wasn't going to fall into those dark places.

The mini pep talk finally took the edge off my panic, but it didn't resolve the situation with Daniel. I needed time and perspective. I was afraid to see him today, knowing there would be hurt and possibly anger in his eyes. Emotions that would be reflected in my own.

And when I did see him, what the hell could I say—*Hey, sorry I dumped all of my freakish past on your shoulders?*

Were things messed up with us for good? A hot flush burst on my cheeks. He'd pushed me to the point where I couldn't hold anything back. I'd lifted my shirt and so cavalierly showed him my scars. Like it was so easy, like it hadn't cost me everything to do that. He had to be repulsed.

My fingers slipped to the dimples and knots and thick, scarred tissue. I was used to them, but they still grossed me out sometimes. Especially when I looked at how perfect and smooth other girls' abdomens were. And I knew mine would never be like that. The doctors had saved my life; I was simultaneously relieved and guilty about it.

Guilty because I was alive.

Guilty because I hated being so damaged, permanently etched with a reminder about what had happened to me.

Ungrateful Casey, that was me.

A soft knock on the door startled me. I dropped my hand to my lap. "Yes?"

Megan peeked her head in. "Hey, you okay?" Her eyes were filled with concern as she took me in, still wearing the shorts and T-shirt I'd thrown on last night before bedtime. I'd stayed in my room all day yesterday, only coming out for bathroom breaks. Hopefully she hadn't heard my crying jags.

I blinked. "I'm . . . I don't know," I finally said. "I'm not feeling well." It was a bit of a lie, since I wasn't physically sick, but my soul still ached from yesterday's fight. And I didn't know how to make that any better.

My heart throbbed with a deep, resonant sorrow I couldn't shake off, and I was flat-out exhausted. I wanted to escape into sleep. I wanted to cry more. I wanted to scream and get out of my own head, even if just for an hour.

"Can I get you anything?" She stepped in my room. "Normally you're on your way to classes right now, so I figured something must be wrong. You're never late." She paused. "And . . . you seemed upset yesterday when you came home. I didn't want to pry. Not trying to be nosy. But . . . I'm here if you want to talk."

My throat tightened. She was trying to help me feel better, and I appreciated it, but I couldn't even begin to tell her everything that was wrong. I gave a short nod. "I think I'm going to stay home today. I don't feel like going out."

"Been there," she said as she gave me a small smile. "We have some cans of chicken noodle soup in the pantry. Sometimes comfort food and a little soap opera watching can get you back on the right track. Want me to stay with you?"

"No, that's okay," I said. If I was going to be a coward and not face him, I wasn't going to make anyone else do it with me. "I'm . . . just going to curl up here and take a day off. Maybe catch up on sleep."

I couldn't remember the last time I'd skipped classes. Probably not since I got that heinous flu going around campus my freshman year. Even then, I'd only missed a couple of days.

I was owed some time off.

"Rest up, girl," Megan said. "Oh, I have some melatonin on my bedside table if you need more sleep. They're not habit-forming . . . they just help you fall asleep. Take one if you want." Then she exited my room.

A moment later, the front door closed, and I was alone in the apartment. After a minute I ventured out, going to the bathroom to pee. I saw my reflection in the mirror—eyes swollen and red, hair a total mess. No wonder Megan had been so worried. I looked like an utter disaster.

My stomach was too upset to eat, but I did wrap up in a blanket and lay on the couch. I turned on the TV, needing the mindless noise to fill the spaces. Hoping it would help me escape the thoughts ramming across my head. Anger with Daniel. Fear about losing him. Guilt over hurting the people who cared about me. Anger. Fear. Guilt. A never-ending spiral.

I stretched out on the couch, tugged the blanket tighter around me and closed my eyes. They were gritty and heavy. My body hurt.

Eventually I fell asleep. I wasn't sure what time it was, but a gentle hand on my shoulder roused me from a deep sleep. I blinked heavy-lidded eyes and saw Megan, smiling down at me. The room was dark—someone had closed all the blinds, and the TV was shut off.

"I made you soup," she whispered. "It's there on the coffee table. Try to eat, okay? You haven't had anything since you came home yesterday morning. You need to stay hydrated if you're sick."

I swallowed. I wanted to tell her I wasn't sick, but she was being so sweet, trying to take care of me. Instead, I nodded and sat up. My head swam a bit from lightheadedness, and my mouth was all cotton. I sipped at the rich, warm soup, surprised to find myself hungry, and finished it in no time.

Megan came back from the kitchen, grabbed my bowl and spoon and whisked them off. She sat beside me and turned the TV back on, flicking to a rerun of some popular sitcom. "Nothing like a few laughs to get your mind off everything," she declared.

She was right. Halfway into the show I found myself chuckling along. It was nice, sitting here with her. The tightness in my chest eased a fraction.

The following day I went to all my classes. I didn't see Daniel anywhere on campus, which relieved me yet made me sad too. I skipped philosophy the rest of the week, though I went to my other classes. I saw my grandparents at Friday dinner and managed to fake my way through the meal, blaming my weirdness on just being super tired. I deejayed at the club, I did homework, I ate, I slept. All without Daniel.

And my heart wouldn't let me forget about it for one damn second.

Sunday morning, I sat on the couch in sleep shorts and a T-shirt, watching some stupid cartoon and eating a piece of toast. Megan hadn't come home last night, had sent me a text saying she was staying with Bobby—filled with exclamation points and lots of squealing—so the place was quiet.

There was a knock on the front door. I rose and answered it.

It was Daniel. The first thing I noticed was the deep fatigue in his eyes, the dark smudges underneath them. "Hey," he said, that familiar husky tone washing over me.

"Hey," I said back. My heart thundered in my chest. I felt so unbelievably awkward with this man who had held me, kissed me, been inside of me, made me feel special. I hated this.

He sighed, rubbed the back of his neck. "I . . ." Pause. "We need to talk about this more. I've—You haven't shown up for classes, and I . . ."

My chest squeezed. I'd never seen him this off-kilter before. Daniel always seemed so self-assured. But right now his dark green eyes were filled with anxiety. His brow was furrowed with deep lines. Mouth pinched, like he was afraid of speaking.

I swallowed and opened the door wider, trying my best to not devour him with my eyes. He was still so attractive, in spite of his obvious turmoil. "Come in and sit on the couch. Let me get dressed, okay?" My hands began to shake, and my stomach fluttered. I darted into my room and threw on a thin, red long-sleeved T-shirt and jeans. I pulled my hair back into a ponytail and slipped on my black flats.

When I returned, Daniel wasn't sitting. He was hovering near the doorway, and his face looked like he was torn about something. "Casey," he said. "Can we get out of here? I want to talk."

A waft of his ocean scent hit me, and I was filled with a sudden ache of missing him. God, I'd missed him this week. I had tried my best to not think about it, but he'd etched himself deep into my heart. Our fight hadn't made that fade, despite how much I'd tried to tell myself it had.

With a steadying breath, I grabbed my purse, then nodded and followed him out the door.

We got in his car and pulled out of the parking lot, then made our way to the highway. Silence was thick and tense between us. Daniel's hands gripped the steering wheel, and twice he rubbed his palms on his thighs. When I dared to glance at his stern profile, I could see a muscle twitch along the edge of his jaw.

Was he nervous about talking to me? I twisted my fingers in my lap. While I was glad I wasn't the only one filled with anxiety, it kind of broke my heart to see him so tangled up inside. Whatever he was thinking about was eating him apart; I could tell that much.

Maybe he was taking me out somewhere to tell me he didn't want to see me anymore. My heart gave a painful thud. But why not just do that back out at the apartment? Why drag me into his car then?

Daniel huffed a sigh. "I'm really nervous," he admitted. "Things went badly on Sunday. I have so many things I want to say, but I'm afraid to."

I gripped my fingers tighter. "You should just spit it out, whatever it is." If he was officially dumping me, I didn't want to sit in this car, wondering when the ax was going to fall. I wanted to go back home and scrape together whatever semblance of pride I could muster. To not fall apart until I was safely back in my room.

"I keep thinking about the things you told me. And a lot of things make sense now," he said. His tone was quiet, and it was almost hard to hear him over the soft rumble of the highway around us. "Why you keep yourself covered up. Why you're so self-reliant, so closed off sometimes. I don't mean that in a bad way," he rushed to say, shooting me a quick sidelong glance. "Just that you don't want to get hurt."

I sat in silence, listening.

"I'm sorry I pushed you so hard. I can't imagine the things you've gone through. My family life wasn't like that at all. But . . . Casey, I've seen how you've changed since we've been together, even if you don't realize it. You laugh and smile a lot more. You've been dropping your guard. And while I know it's hard for you to trust me, I think it's that trust that has been helping you start to heal. You're allowing yourself to open up and care about people."

Tears stung my eyes. I blinked, swallowed. He was right.

"It took a lot of courage for you to tell me all of that. And I don't want you to keep running away from me. I'm trying to help you, not hurt you. But you're still so raw. It's killing me to see you in this pain. Once you're able to let it go, I think you'll be amazed at how good you feel."

"Easier said than done," I replied. My pulse thrummed in my veins. "I don't know how to . . . stop feeling this way." I paused, surprised at myself. Despite the way things had gone, I was still confessing my secrets to him. Still opening up.

I could sense his hesitancy as he removed his right hand from the steering wheel and reached over to mine, curled in my lap. He rested his hand on top. My stomach fluttered in response to the soft, comforting sensation. Those damn tears welled back up again.

"I know. I'm proud of you for how hard you've worked. And . . . I think I have some ideas that might help you." He removed his hand to steer off the highway.

I peered around. Where were we going?

A few minutes later, my stomach tightened so badly I thought I was going to be sick. No, he couldn't possibly have known about this place we were about to drive right by. It was just a sick coincidence.

Daniel slowed the car, keeping his gaze steadily fixed ahead. He drove through the wide-open cemetery gates.

Into the place that held the bodies of my mother, sister and father.

"No," I said. Desperation made my tone wild. I hadn't been here since that one visit right after I got out of the hospital. They'd been buried for weeks by then. Grandma and Grandpa had held me up as I'd cried and begged to go to their home. It was a horrible experience.

I clawed for the door blindly, looking for a way to get out.

Daniel stopped the car, put a hand on my shoulder. "Stop. *Stop.* Listen to me," he said. "You have to trust me, okay? Just . . . hear me out, and if you want to go after that, we can go. But just listen."

Tears slid down my face. My stomach burned with anger and intense fear. I turned accusing eyes toward him. "I can't believe you. After what we went through, *this* is where you take me? Seriously?"

"You won't be able to heal until you let this go," he said. I could see the steel in his eyes, hear the determination in his voice. "You need to face your father, Casey. Tell him you hate him, you're angry—whatever. Get it out of you before it poisons you."

"What, so you're my therapist now?" I said, crossing my arms over my chest. I struggled to suck in breaths. "Am I a pet project for you to fix?"

"I care about you!" He clenched his jaw, ran a hand through his hair, leaving messy waves everywhere. "God, why can't you see that? It's not you against the world, Casey. I'm here for you! Let me help you, please!"

A swell of betrayal hit me as I took in once again where we were. Where he'd taken me. He'd obviously looked me up online, found all the articles blaring about it. Knew where my family was dead and rotting.

"I can't believe you." The car felt too small. I unlocked the door and escaped, breathing in the brisk air. It was getting colder outside as fall finally made its appearance; goose bumps scattered across my arms, peppered my torso. I kept my back to the car when I heard him get out and close his door. "I don't need healing. I'm doing fine."

"Yes, you're doing fine, Casey. You're making it through each day." His voice dropped, and the breeze carried his next words to my ears. "But when you face your father and purge all of these feelings, you'll be more than just 'fine.' You'll be able to start healing for real."

I knew he fervently believed what he was telling me. I also knew he crossed a line bringing me here—surprising me with this. My scoff rang out into the quiet cemetery. If he'd told me, he'd have known my answer would be no. Hence the secrecy. How could I trust him?

A layer of ice formed over my heart. My words were cold as I spat them out. "I'm going home. Either you're going to take me or I'll find a bus or hitchhike. But I'm not doing this here, and I'm not doing this with you."

"Casey—"

"No. I'm done listening to you. I'm done with you trying to fix me, change me, make things be the way you want them to be. If you cared about me, you'd accept me for who I am." And stop trying to cram my past in my face.

There was silence. A few birds chirped in a tree in the distance. I kept my gaze squarely on the ground, refusing to even look at my surroundings. Sunlight danced along the grit and rocks under my feet.

"I'll take you home," he finally said. I could tell he was frustrated. I so didn't care right now.

We got back in the car. The tension was almost unbearable. I kept my eyes straight ahead, watching to make sure he was taking me home as he'd promised.

When the car pulled into my parking lot, Daniel put it in park. "I was just trying to help," he said. "Not hurt you. I wish you could see that and believe in it."

My throat was so tight by now that I didn't think I could respond even if I wanted to. If I opened my mouth, I'd start bawling and never stop. With shaky fingers I fumbled for the door. I got out, closed it behind me, walked toward my apartment. Not looking back.

We were done. I knew that now. Done for good. The realization brought both pain and relief from pain, strangely enough. I couldn't deal with someone trying to fix me, with all the pushing. I didn't want to be fixed. I wanted to make it through life on my terms.

I keyed the door. The apartment was still empty. I sat down on the edge of the couch, and all emotions leeched out of my body, leaving me cold and numb.

In that moment, I wanted my life back the way it was. Before Daniel had come along and changed me forever, had shifted my expectations. Had made me fall for him, drop all my protective walls. Trust him.

Love him.

I wanted things to be safe and careful. Steady.

And I wasn't sure I was ever going to have that again.

Chapter 20

I spent that afternoon zoning out in front of the TV, trying my best to not think, not feel. If I gave myself even a minute to mull over everything that had happened, I was afraid I would go so far into the dark that I'd never come back out. It had taken everything I had to claw my way out of that blackness when I was thirteen. I wasn't sure I had the strength to go through it again.

My phone buzzed. My heart gave a sick thud, and with trembling fingers I dug the cell out of my pocket. But it wasn't Daniel.

Hope work went well last night. Love you! Grandma (yes, I signed it) :-P

That one simple message from her shattered my numb walls. My soul ached with an almost physical throb of pain. I needed to go home, absorb the safety and comfort of the people who were there for me when everything was bleak.

Can I come over? I sent the text.

My phone immediately buzzed back. *Granddad's helping a*

friend with house repairs, but I'm home. Meatloaf's in the oven and should be ready soon. Come over, honey. Love, Grandma

She knew, even without me saying anything about what was bothering me, had instinctively known I was craving her comfort. Appreciation and love filled my chest and bolstered me enough to get off the couch, grab my purse and head out the door.

The whole ride there, I held my focus on whatever song was on the radio station. Not listening to all those whirring thoughts in my brain. I needed to keep my shit together for a little while longer. Though Grandma was tiny, her thin arms had been strong enough to hold me through many rounds of tears. She and Granddad were my rocks.

When I got to her house, I knocked on the door. Grandma answered, her face filled with such warmth and love that my chest tightened in response. There was a knot of tension right under the center of my rib cage that almost hurt with its intensity. My shoulders ached with the effort of keeping myself stiff.

"Hey, honey," she said as she reached out to take my hand, drawing me into the living room. From the kitchen I could smell the meatloaf and the scent of freshly baked bread, probably warmed in a basket on top of the stove. "Come in. Can I get you something to drink?"

I shook my head. Suddenly I couldn't talk, though words ached to spill out of me.

Her brows knitted. She sat down on the couch beside me, her hand still holding mine. "I don't want to push you, but I can tell there's something wrong. And I'm worried about you. You've been very quiet this week, even a little off at dinner on Friday."

Guess I hadn't fooled her as well as I'd thought. A choked sob ripped out, and I popped my free hand over my mouth. *Control. Get yourself under control. You can't talk if you're a total mess.* The harsh words helped; the tightness in my chest eased up a fraction so I could at least speak. "It's been . . . a hard week," I finally managed to say. My eyes burned, though I tried to blink back the tears. I didn't want to get lost in my misery.

In halting words and phrases, I told Grandma the truth about everything. How I was falling for Daniel, how he'd made me open up, laugh, smile. Fall in love. The fight where I'd showed him my stomach scars and confessed about my past. Cutting classes this week, and then him showing up this morning. The cemetery.

As I talked, the emotions I'd been suppressing flooded me in hot waves of pain, and hot tears streaked down my face.

"I can't believe he did that to me," I said, knowing my voice was weak and thready but unable to keep my calm any longer. My palms throbbed; at some point, I must have released her hands because now my nails had dug so hard into the fleshy pads that there were angry imprints on them. I unclenched my fingers and pressed my open hands to my jean-clad thighs. "I trusted him, and he betrayed me."

"What makes you feel that was betrayal?" she asked. There wasn't a challenge in her voice, just genuine curiosity.

I cleared my throat, wiped my face. "He knew this was something that I struggle with, and he snuck me there without telling me that was where we were going." That anger rose again as I thought about it. Anger and hurt.

How could Daniel not have known it would kill me to go there?

"Oh, Casey. I know that had to be hard for you. I'm sorry." She reached over and hugged me. Her tiny hand stroked my hair, and I rested my head on her shoulder. "Sweetheart, what he did wasn't right—it wasn't fair to spring that on you out of the blue. I don't blame you for being upset about it." Her grip on me tightened a bit, like she knew her next words would hit me hard. "But he was right in one big thing: you have to let your past go if you're going to heal."

I froze; her grip tightened just a touch more. Not pinning me to her, but her silent way of asking me to not retreat from her. "If he cared about me," I whispered hotly, "he wouldn't be trying to change me. I can't help who I am."

She pressed a soft kiss to my brow. "I don't think he's trying to change you. He just wants you to be happy." She pulled me back and looked deep into my eyes. "I saw the way that boy was with you when he came to dinner. He cares about you. A lot. Yes, his method was wrong, but the core idea is worth thinking over anyway." She sighed. "I know this has to be hard for you. Facing a past like ours isn't easy for anyone."

Her eyes welled with her own sadness, and my heart about broke. Suddenly I felt selfish. Here I was, wrapped up in my own issues once again. Whining to her about how dejected and scared I was. But I knew she'd had her own sleepless nights over the years. That my father's madness had crushed a part of her heart too.

Sometimes as a teen, I would lie in bed, unable to sleep, and I'd hear her quiet sobs from their bedroom beside mine. Yes, I'd lost my family, but she had also lost hers. Had lost her son, her daughter-in-law, her beautiful granddaughter. Yet she didn't let it cripple her, hadn't hidden in bed forever or swallowed a bottle of pills or booze. She'd pulled it together and helped me through the worst period of my life.

"How did you do it?" I asked.

"Do what?" She tucked a strand of loose hair behind my ear.

"How did you forgive him and stop feeling so . . . angry about it?" Pain thickened in my chest. "I just can't, Grandma. Every time I even think about him, I want to scream. It's been eight years, and I still hate him just as much. He doesn't deserve my forgiveness." That old familiar emotion, bitter loathing, came rushing back to the surface.

Really, I didn't want to forgive him. Why should I? After all, he wasn't around to explain to me why he'd snapped. What had gone through his mind when he'd picked up a rifle and blew away his family, then himself. There was no possible way for me to understand that.

Nor did I want to. After all, if I could understand a murderer, what did that make me?

She gave me an understanding nod. "I know. It took me a long time of talking to the therapist and your granddad to let go of my anger and hurt. Even longer to start the process of forgiving him. I still work on it every day." Her sigh of pain shredded me. "I'll be honest. I still hurt, though. There's nothing like knowing your own son was in such horrible emotional pain that he'd go to those lengths to escape it. I couldn't help or save him."

I reached over and took her hand in mine. Our hurt swam between us, wrapped us in a thick layer. I wasn't alone in this—I never had been, though it had felt that way sometimes. "I'm sorry," I whispered.

"I had to learn how to start forgiving your father," she continued, and her wizened eyes fixed on me. "Not because he deserved it. Not because I was supposed to. But because if I didn't, I'd be bitter and angry all the time. And how could I move forward, take care of you and your granddad, if I was filled with so many negative emotions?"

I thought back on my past. How I'd shoved all of those overwhelming feelings about my family's death into a tiny box in the corner of my heart, not wanting to experience it ever again. Trying so hard to pretend I wasn't still deeply damaged from it. "I don't know how to forgive him," I admitted.

"It is a struggle." She nodded. "But I know you, Casey. This resonant sadness, it isn't the core of who you are, though it may feel like it sometimes. You were a happy child before this happened. And that incident swallowed up who you were, smothered that happiness down. But I'm seeing it in you again, honey. You smile and laugh so much more freely than you have in years, since you've met Daniel."

Those damn tears filled my eyes again. I squeezed her hand. "I'm trying," I whispered around a tight throat.

"I know you are—I can tell. And I know this will be hard for you to hear, but I'm going to say it anyway. Because if you're going to move forward, find real happiness, you need to remember a few things. Things I have to make myself remember too." Grandma paused and drew in a breath. "Your father did love you, in his own way. He loved Lila and your mom too. But he struggled with his demons, and they took over. He was too mentally ill to cope with them, but he refused to get help." Her eyes grew sad. "My personal burden to bear is that I saw this happening to him over the last several years of his life, saw him fighting off that darkness, but in the end it won. Maybe I could have stopped this from happening if I'd fought harder, had pushed him to check into a facility where he could have gotten the help he'd needed."

Wow, she'd never told me that before. I wasn't the only one with survivor's guilt. My heart hurt for her. "No," I said, my voice determined. "None of us could have. Dad was stubborn and he wouldn't have listened anyway." I paused, blinked, startled to realize it was true.

Grandma's gaze drifted over my shoulder. "I remember when you and your sister were little. You were in kindergarten, so Lila was around two. It was Halloween. Your father always loved that holiday—he would plan for weeks to make you guys the perfect outfits. That particular time, he'd made you fairy wings. You came back from trick-or-treating with a bag full of candy and flushed cheeks from all the compliments."

Oh, that was right. I vaguely remembered that now. Everyone had gushed over my outfit. My dad had held my hand as he'd dragged my sister behind us in the wagon. After that, we'd eaten so much candy my stomach had cramped. But it had been a great night.

I felt an uncomfortable pinch in my chest. I didn't want to remember the good things about him. I'd spent all these years struggling to maintain my memories of my innocent mom and sister. Yet now that Grandma had brought it up, those things I'd pushed aside were screaming in my head and rising to the surface.

Dad and I sharing cotton candy at a local fair.

Him coloring the tips of my hair blue because I'd seen it in a magazine and wanted the same look.

He and Lila drawing on the sidewalk in colored chalk, then racing around the front yard to color each other with streaks of pink, blue, green.

My breaths began to shorten, and I pressed a hand to my chest. The anger I'd felt earlier now mingled with a bone-aching sense of loss. I'd lost my sister and my mom. And the dad I'd loved as a little girl. The pain of it all stripped me

I reached over and hugged Grandma to me, breathing in her soft vanilla scent. Body-wracking sobs took over and I cried hard into her shoulder for several minutes. My throat grew raw, and my chest ached.

"Will this ever stop hurting?" I asked her, my tone begging for relief.

"Shhh," she whispered as she stroked my hair. She wrapped her arms around me a little tighter. "It's okay. Let it out—purge it, sweetheart."

In my head I knew all this anger and fear were poisonous, boiling in my blood, just waiting to kill me. I wanted to be rid of them. Yet I feared what would happen if they were gone. I'd been living like this for so long that now I didn't know any other way.

Her words sank into my consciousness, echoed the phrases I'd heard earlier today. Daniel begging me to tell my father exactly how I felt. Insisting I couldn't heal until I'd purged this out of me. But how could I purge something so ingrained that it made me who I was?

I sniffled and pulled back, swiping at my soaked face. My nose was snotty and stopped up. My eyes ached, and I had the edge of a headache threatening to burst forth. "Sorry," I said on a low sigh.

Grandma tilted my chin. "Don't you dare apologize." Her eyes were so serious and intense that I was startled. "You *never* apologize for your feelings. Not to me or to anyone else. But please, do think about what we talked about. I know you're afraid you'll lose control. I've seen how hard you work to not let people in—not only to protect yourself, but to protect them out of some misguided fear that you'll turn out like him. But sweetheart, you're not your father, and what happened to him won't happen to you. If you want to be free of this pain, you need to let all of this go. Stop letting *his* mistakes and *his* illness continue to impact you like this. And stop blaming yourself for his actions." She lowered her hand to her lap. "No one can tell you the right way, so search your heart for the truth. Your answers are in there."

My stomach flipped. Her advice was hard to swallow. So easy for people to tell me I should let it go. I stupidly thought I had, in a way. No, I hadn't written my dad a letter and burned it, as the therapist had advised me a long time ago. But I'd stayed in school. Gone to college. Was pursuing my love of music. How was that not moving forward with life?

Why couldn't that be enough?

The kitchen timer went off.

Grandma pulled me off the couch. "I think some of my amazing meatloaf will set you on the right path."

I gave a watery smile, as I knew she was trying to lighten the tension in the room. But my heart was still far too unsettled. I wasn't able to do the things Grandma and Daniel were telling me. The idea of even talking to my father made my stomach turn, made me want to vomit. Grandma had said my dad's issues were out of my control, that it wasn't my fault, but I still couldn't shake the feeling that I could have done something, *anything* to stop it from happening. Could have saved my mom and sister.

And what would happen if I did as they said but I didn't feel any better? If I faced the truth about my emotions and confronted my dad somehow? Then I'd have no one left to be angry at but myself.

I didn't know if I ever would be ready to release this deep-seated fury. A thought that both saddened and scared me.

Chapter 21

The temperature was dropping daily, it seemed. Now that we were well into fall, I had dug out all of my sweaters from storage and was wearing a fuzzy dark green one on my way to Monday morning's philosophy class. As usual for the last couple of weeks, my stomach was a total mess of nerves as I headed down the sidewalk to my class building. I sipped my coffee and forced my shoulders to unclench. The dub-step song playing through my earbuds throbbed beneath my skin and helped me relax a bit.

Students laughed and jostled around me, some making a mad dash across campus to make it to class on time.

A cool breeze whisked through campus, making my hair dance along its currents and sending a smattering of goose bumps across my skin. Fall was my favorite season; usually, I anticipated it with much excitement. But there wasn't a lot to be excited about these days, it seemed.

When I got into the classroom, I took my usual seat and tucked my bag under my feet. I turned off my music and stowed the phone and earbuds away. The desk in front of me was empty, as it had been since I'd gathered my courage post-conversation with Grandma and gone back to class that Monday. One week off from philosophy was probably too much, and I had to suck it up and go or else I'd be in big trouble grade-wise. But I was petrified to face him.

It still gave my heart a painful pinch to remember how Daniel hadn't been sitting there anymore. That first day back, I'd been shocked to come in and find him sitting in a back corner, hunched over his notes, not paying attention to anyone else in the room before our professor started the class. He hadn't looked over at me once.

It also didn't help things that I'd felt like a total wreck, and he was still devastatingly handsome. His hair curled softly, and his green eyes were even more vivid than I remembered. Something in my soul throbbed, as if a piece of it had been ripped out and thrown away. I'd been torn between wishing I could ignore his presence and wishing I still had the liberty to drink him in.

After that Monday class had ended, he'd grabbed his stuff and taken off. And every class period since then had been the same.

We were strangers now. No texts, no calls, nothing. Like we'd never been close or shared secrets. Like I'd never smelled his scent on the lean muscles of his throat, or he'd never kissed me, or we'd never been as intimate in our bedrooms as two humans could possibly get.

Daniel was giving me the space I'd demanded of him. Respecting my wishes and not pushing me anymore.

And my stupid heart was bitterly sad about it. That love I'd felt for him hadn't gone away, despite my simmering anger at his pushiness. It hadn't faded with the distance. In fact, I had a hard time concentrating in any of my classes. I kept replaying our times together, layer upon layer of memories that haunted me. My bed was so empty without him. It was killing me that I couldn't read his face anymore. What had once been an open book to me was permanently closed.

The professor strolled in and began writing on the board. I dared a glance over at Daniel. My heart stuttered when our eyes caught, then he looked away blankly and focused on the front of the room.

I never imagined I could hurt this much over a guy. Especially over one who had betrayed my trust, who had pulled all those dark secrets from me when I wasn't ready to deal with them. I halfheartedly scribbled some notes on my notebook. Tried my best to pay attention to the lecture. But the class was dull.

I was dull.

It was like my inner spark was gone now. All that was left was a shell of a person, getting up and going to classes and eating and sleeping and repeating the whole process again and again. But with no passion. Even my music sucked when I tried to compose something new. The song I was working on felt trite, meaningless, like there was resonance missing that I didn't know how to recapture. Deejaying felt like a regular job, too, and I counted the hours until my shift ended.

I sighed and tucked my hair behind my ear. Good grief, I was tired of feeling so down. It wore on me, rubbed off layer after layer of skin until I was a raw bunch of nerves. I listened to party girl Amanda whispering with another girl, talking about parties they went to the past weekend, funny things that happened to drunk attendees, what they were going to have for lunch.

Class ended. I stayed in my seat as the crowd around me slowly left. When the room was empty, I gathered my things and stepped into the hall, then outside into the cooler autumn air. Leaves had changed with brilliant speed, our campus decorated in hues of reds, oranges and yellows. The sight momentarily lifted my spirits.

Ahead of me, I saw Daniel strolling away, bag slung over his shoulder, head up and shoulders back. I was filled with a strong burst of longing.

I couldn't help it—I followed him. Not closely, but I just felt this crazy urge to see him more, even if he didn't see me. My heart thumped, and my hands shook a little, so I crammed them into my jeans pockets. That bitter sting of anger I'd felt after the cemetery incident had started to fade away with the passage of time. Now I was left with a whole lot of remorse.

Remorse and loneliness. I missed him. Missed the way he'd smile at me, take my hand, make me laugh. How he saw me, knew me.

Had I been wrong to shove him away without talking things through about the cemetery trip? Upon thinking about it all, I knew Grandma was right. I needed to let go of the pain so I could heal. But I wasn't sure if I was too damaged now, if all this resentment and animosity and fear about my father had poisoned me to the point where I couldn't get over it. It had caused me to push away everyone, whether they deserved it or not.

My eyes stayed fixed on Daniel. He stopped to talk with a tall Latino guy, so I slowed my pace and lingered by a tree, pretending to check something in my bag. I'd been so sure Daniel was 100 hundred percent wrong, that I'd been justified in demanding he leave me alone. But time was making me revisit the incident with a different eye. And suddenly it wasn't so crystal clear. Sometimes people did the wrong things for the right reason. Had that been the case here?

When I looked up, he was gone. And that ripping ache in my chest widened just a fraction more.

I curled my legs underneath me on the couch and flipped through the channels. There was nothing on TV on a Tuesday night. I'd gotten bored of just sitting in my room, staring blankly at the walls. Earlier I tried to work on my song, but all it had done was make me depressed because it wasn't fitting together right. None of the samples I layered in clicked. I'd never had music fail me before, and it was crushing to realize I was losing all my safe spaces. There was nowhere to turn to feel better now. On impulse, I'd listened to the one Daniel and I had made and started crying. So I'd disgustedly shut everything off and come into the living room, needing to get out of my own head for a while.

I settled on some random sitcom and tucked a pillow on my lap. Time slipped by in a dull numbness.

After a while, the front door opened. "Oh, good. You're home," Megan said as she walked in, bearing two full grocery bags. She went into the kitchen and unloaded her items.

"How was your day?" I asked politely.

There was silence for a moment, then she plopped down on the couch beside me. In her hands were two pints of ice cream. She thrust one at me, along with a spoon.

I took a good look at her, maybe for the first time in weeks. I'd been so caught up in my own personal misery that I hadn't seen much of my roommate. There was a strain of fatigue around her eyes, and she was wearing a plain black sweater and jeans. No makeup either. None of her usual flair.

I peeled off the top of the container and dug in. Chocolate ice cream with peanut butter cups. The girl knew what I needed. "Are you okay?" I asked her after I took a bite of ice cream.

"Are you?" she retorted, taking her own bite. She moaned with pleasure, then twisted her body to face me. "Casey, have you noticed that in the last few weeks, this apartment has been horrendously depressing?"

A bubble formed in my throat, and I tried to swallow it back. I gave a short nod. My old friend, guilt, flared up again. "I'm sorry."

Megan grabbed the remote and flipped to AMC. Some old black-and-white thriller was coming on, the opening credits scrolling. "Look," she finally said with a heavy sigh, "I know there's something up with you. And I know it probably has to do with Daniel, since he hasn't been around here lately. And I *also* know you probably don't want to talk about it. But it's killing me to see you so sad. How about we overdose on ice cream and movies for a while?"

Tears burned the corners of my eyes. I blinked, set my ice cream on the coffee table. I spent so much of my life keeping people at arm's length, yet people still kept trying with me, even if I didn't deserve it. I felt alone, but I wasn't alone.

I gave her a shaky smile. "You're awesome, do you know that?"

She laughed. "Actually, yes, I do. But I'm glad you're finally realizing it. Took you long enough."

"Are you okay? You seem . . . tired," I said tentatively. I wasn't used to seeing her like this.

She shrugged, her mouth curving into a slight frown. "Bobby and I broke up."

I offered her a sad smile. "I'm sorry to hear that."

"Don't be. I'm better off." She shoveled in another spoonful of ice cream. "I caught him in bed with two girls after he got trashed at a party last weekend. Not having that." She glanced down at the container. "The only threesome *I'm* interested in is with Ben and Jerry."

I couldn't help it; I laughed. I popped my hand over my mouth. "I'm sorry—I shouldn't, but . . ."

She looked up at me and laughed, too, shaking her head. "Why are guys so stupidly messed up? Don't they ever get tired of being assholes?"

Daniel's green eyes came to mind. The lightness faded, replaced by a pressing heaviness on my chest.

In that moment, I needed to get all of this out of me. I had this strange ache for Megan's friendship. I needed to confide in her, to show her she was important, that I appreciated her continued efforts at drawing me out. Her honesty and willingness to share her family and her life with me. Friends did that for each other, and though I didn't deserve it, she was still there for me.

"Can we talk?" I asked her.

She put her ice cream aside, then reached over and squeezed my arm. "Of course. I'm here for you."

I spent the next half hour telling her everything. Although it was hard to do so, I lifted the bottom of my shirt and showed her my stomach scars. Her eyes had grown wide, then filled with sorrow and grief as I relayed what had happened to me.

I told her how my grandparents had been my everything for so long that I didn't know how to let others in. That I was afraid of trusting—not just because my father had committed the ultimate betrayal, but because I didn't know if I would turn out like him in the future. Tears started dribbling down my face, but I let them fall, unchecked. My hands were clenched on the pillow, but still I talked.

About Daniel. The way he'd drawn me in, how we'd kissed and I'd pulled away at the drive-in. His slow wooing of me, how I'd found my barriers crumbling. How we'd made love after he'd taken care to make me feel comfortable and sexy and wanted, and I'd realized I'd fallen for him.

Megan stayed quiet, just listening. Her eyes flared with all her naked emotion, but she kept silent, letting me speak my peace.

When I got to the part about exposing my secret to him, and our trip to the cemetery that had ended our relationship, my body throbbed with all the emotions stuck inside of me. It was hard to keep talking because I still felt so hurt about it, but I made myself put it all out there.

Finally I finished. I drew in a few slow breaths to help ease the pain in my chest. I gave an awkward chuckle and grabbed my ice cream, which was pretty much chocolate slush by now.

"Wow," she said as she shook her head. "It's been a rough semester for you, hasn't it."

"I don't know how to fix anything," I admitted. "And I feel like I can't. Like I'm going to be stuck in a pain cycle because I'm . . ." I bit my lower lip, blinked back fresh tears. "I'm too jacked up to ever be fully happy. The way I'm so desperate to. All I wanted was peace and safety. A normal life."

Megan leaned over, took the ice cream from my hands and wrapped me in a warm hug. I slipped my arms around her and squeezed, let myself cry on her shoulders. Strange how I was starting to grow used to this now—finding comfort from others. Not just bottling it all up.

She pulled back but held my upper arms. "I'm proud of you, you know," she said. "You've gone through a hell most of us will never experience. But here you are. Despite all your challenges, you're going to college. You have a great job you love. You're working on music."

Her words were a balm; tension seeped from my knotted shoulders, and my stomach stopped clenching. In her eyes, I didn't see judgment over how I'd handled things with Daniel, how I'd been trying to cope with my life. There was no awkward pity or deep sadness that would make me want to run.

Instead, I saw empathy and caring. Genuine emotions. The surprise of it shocked me into silence.

"Casey," Megan started in a gentle voice. "Listening to you, you sound like you're just waiting for your life to start. For everything to feel better inside your heart so you can finally be happy and feel whole. But honey, your life already *has* started. You've been living this whole time without actually owning it. Carving out a place for yourself in this world, taking risks. Finding those things that make you happy and chasing them down. No shame in any of that, girl. Life isn't going to be perfect or safe or peaceful, so you have to grab hold of those things that give you pleasure when they're here."

I opened my mouth to retort, to say that I couldn't possibly be the person she described, then snapped it closed. She was right. I huffed out a surprised breath.

All these years, I'd been mentally waiting for some magical moment when suddenly I wouldn't feel "damaged" anymore and the world would make sense again. Telling myself I was simply treading water, playing it cautious, not rocking the boat so I could settle, telling myself I craved the safety net I'd created in my head.

And yet, I'd jumped on the chance to deejay, even though there had been no guarantees it would work out. I'd entered into a relationship with Daniel, had fallen for him. I'd opened myself up to the chance of getting hurt and rejected with my music. With love.

Those were not the actions of a person who craved safety and security.

I *was* living, not just getting by. My life wasn't safe, despite thoughts to the contrary, and it never really had been. I was fooling myself to long for something I'd never even had—a steady and boring life. And frankly, now that I was examining myself this closely, I didn't think I'd want that anyway. What would my life be without the risk I'd taken with music? With finding love?

The pressure in the middle of my chest faded away. I stared in awe at Megan. How was it that I hadn't realized this stuff before now? There was something about her easy acceptance of me, the way she hadn't pushed me, that made me able to open up and listen to her.

Listen to myself.

Fresh tears sprang to my eyes—but not of pain. These were of gratitude, relief. "Thank you," I managed to whisper. "I really needed this. Thank you."

Her own eyes filled with tears. "Thank you for trusting me.

I know that was hard for you. I promise, your secrets are safe with me."

And I knew she meant it. I reached over and hugged her. "You've helped me, but I feel like I haven't helped you. Want me to slash Bobby's tires or something?"

She laughed, swiped at her tears. "Nah, it's okay. I wasn't in love with him or anything. Besides, the double penicillin shot he'll probably need from that night will be payment enough."

A laugh barked out of me. "Good point."

Megan grimaced as she eyed her ice-cream container. "Damn. Half of it has melted." She stood up, took both of our containers. "Good thing I bought plenty of backups. I can pop these in the freezer until they set again."

As she made her way into the kitchen, humming some song under her breath, I sank back into the couch. Something had shifted in my chest. Something had changed. Where there was darkness, I now felt an edge of hope. A breath of life filled my veins, bubbling within me. I wasn't doomed to failure and misery, like I'd feared. I wanted happiness, could take it in my hands.

I craved more of this good feeling. But if I was going to really make this work, if I was going to turn over a new leaf and take my life by both hands, there were a couple of things I needed to do first.

Chapter 22

Saturday morning, I slipped into my car, sat behind the wheel and fired it up but didn't move. I dragged several deep breaths into lungs that had squeezed to the size of grapes and stared blindly ahead of me at the row of brick apartment buildings.

I was scared shitless.

To bolster my nerves, I kept Megan's encouraging face in the forefront of my mind. I'd told her where I was going. She'd ordered me to call her if I needed anything, had even offered to come along, but I knew I needed to do this alone.

After a full ten minutes of waffling—should I do this, or should I wait? Was it a bad idea to go alone, or should I have taken Megan up on her offer?—I finally cursed at myself to just drive and pulled the car out of the parking lot.

I tried to keep my mind off where I was going and focused on my surroundings instead. Dark brown, crunchy leaves blew across the street. The soft morning glow of the sun slanted across trees, houses, grass. The highway was strangely open with little traffic as I buzzed along. It was too cold this morning to even think about having the windows down, so my heater was cranked up to drive away the chill in the air.

The closer I got to the cemetery, the more that sickening ringing in my ears picked up.

I finally reached the entrance, the iron gates flung open to allow visitors in. My heart was stuck in my throat, throbbing a pulse that made my hands jitter. I couldn't remember the last time I'd been this nervous. *Dear God,* I said in my head, *I'm not much of a praying girl, but please let me get through this without crumbling apart.*

The car's tires crunched over the long gravel drive. I studied the path markers and made my way to the appropriate area. There were rows upon rows of graves, straight little lines like jagged stone teeth thrusting from the ground. I parked the car and shut off the engine.

My lips began to tingle. A wave of panic smashed me right in the gut. *No.* I bit down on my lower lip to startle me out of an attack, clenched my hands together, drew in more slow breaths. It was going to be fine. And I had to do this.

After drawing the scarf a little more securely around my throat, I grabbed the small box in the passenger seat and made my way to the row that held the graves of my parents and sister.

I stopped right between my sister and mother and dropped to the ground. Stared for a long minute at the smooth, clean etching of my sister's name, LILA, dug into the stone. Wiped away a few errant leaves that were scattered on top of their short, grassy plots.

The grounds were empty right now; I was alone with them. A few birds chirped in nearby trees, their voices loud in the echoing silence.

"Hey, sis," I said. My words were so awkward, but I made myself keep speaking. "I've missed you so much. Not a day goes by when I don't think about you and wonder what kind of person you would have been if you'd had the chance to live." I ran my fingers over the carving of her name, like it would bring us closer together. A memory of her young, bright smile popped in my head, and my heart squeezed in agony.

I dug into the box and brought out a tiny, porcelain princess doll I'd found while at the mall with Megan yesterday. The figurine reminded me of my sister, with huge brown eyes and a wide grin. Her hair was pulled back in a bun, and she wore a bold blue dress. As soon as I saw it, I knew I had to buy it.

Lila had loved princesses.

With trembling hands I scooped a handful of dirt out near the headstone and popped the princess in the hole, burying it completely. "Got you a gift. I don't want anyone taking this, so I'm hiding it. It's our secret." Then I took out a plastic baggie I'd labeled "Lila" and dropped a small handful of the cold graveyard dirt into it. That would be going home with me later.

"I really miss you," I continued, throat hoarse as I attempted to talk through a closed-off windpipe. Hot tears began to sting my eyes. I let them fall, made myself unlock the pain I'd kept hidden away for all these years. "And . . ." I paused, swallowed. "I'm so sorry I never came back here. It was wrong for me to stay away for so long. But I was afraid to face the truth. Afraid I'd fall apart and never put myself back again. Crazy, huh." My whisper was rough, burned my throat.

I swiped a hand over my damp eyes and glanced over at my mother's grave. Silent as the rest of them. She wasn't in there anymore—I knew that. Her spirit had left her body that night she'd been killed. My sister's too. But I should have been more respectful of them and visited, instead of running so hard from my past.

Which meant running from them, as well.

"I'm sorry, Mom," I said. A sob ripped out of my chest. I clenched the sides of the frozen headstones and bowed my head. "I can't seem to forgive myself for so many things. Surviving when everyone else died. Being a burden on Grandma and Granddad—they've been great to me, by the way. I'm not trying to make it sound like they weren't." I paused, trying to shake off my bone-deep sorrow. This visit wasn't about wallowing in my own guilt. It was about letting all of that go.

"Anyway." I cleared my throat, dropped my hands to my lap. My fingers were freezing, so I rubbed them together. The chilly ground pressed on me from below, an assault of cold everywhere. I shivered a bit. "I'm in college, living in an apartment with a really nice girl. I'm going to graduate this year, actually. I think you guys would be proud of me. My grades aren't perfect, but I've done a solid job so far. And . . . I'm a DJ too. I work in a dance club, and I'm good at it. I know, that's crazy, right?" I sniffled and wiped at my nose, which felt like it was running nonstop now.

My gaze drifted across the graveyard. A brisk breeze whipped through, danced the edges of my scarf. Although I was by myself here, I didn't feel alone, strangely enough. I knew they were here with me. Listening to me.

A bittersweet pang made my stomach tighten in a knot. Talking to them wasn't nearly as painful as I'd been afraid it would be. I should have done this before now.

"I love music, Mom," I admitted. "I've written a few pieces of my own. Never would have guessed that, would you?"

No, that actually wasn't true. How often had Lila and I danced around the house, singing at the top of our lungs to whatever song was on? We'd even tried to write a couple of our own, though she'd been terrible at rhyming.

And if I remembered right, one night Mom had patiently sat as we'd put on a musical performance for her—Lila playing the recorder while I sang and smacked a plastic tambourine against my hip. She'd applauded us at the end like we were a Broadway performance.

My father's tombstone loomed over there to my right, but I didn't want to look at it. Not yet. I wanted to bask in the warm memories of my mother and my sister just a few moments longer. I kept my attention on the rest of the cemetery. Let my gaze wander around the serene landscaping.

"So, I met a guy," I confessed. "His name is Daniel, and he goes to school with me. Mom, you'd love him. He's pushy like you." A sudden, watery laugh burst from me. "He tried to get me to come here before, but I got so pissed at him. I felt like he'd betrayed me, like he'd disrespected my wishes and brought me here.

"But he was right. He forced me to face my guilt and shame. Made me realize how I was keeping everyone at arm's length and shutting myself down because I was scared to let anyone into my heart. I wasn't ready for him and his honesty. For him to bring me here and make me face the thing I've been running from for so long—my darkest, scariest feelings about your deaths."

God, I missed Daniel. A big part of me wished he was here right now, holding my hand. Telling me I was brave, that he was proud of me. I'd do anything to feel his strong arms around me.

"I fell in love with him and I pushed him away and messed everything up." A cry bubbled in my throat. I wrapped my arms around my chest. The cold seeped in through my jeans, but I barely felt it. "I'm *so* tired of hurting, Mom. I'm tired of being sad and lonely all the time. Daniel and I haven't talked in weeks. And it's killing me. I'd give anything if I could ask you what to do to fix it."

Big, ugly sobs ripped out of me, and I let myself weep. I didn't try to fight it anymore or mask it. I embraced all the pain and finally wailed. "I miss you guys so much," I repeated. My voice broke as I talked. "I wish you were here to go through life with me, because *nothing* has been the same without you."

The cemetery was silent for a long moment except for the gut-wrenching sounds of my misery. I drew in a sniffly breath and tried to get myself under control. I cast a tearful glance at

Mom's grave, at Lila's, and then I stood and wiped off my jeans. Letting all of that hurt go was liberating. I wasn't smothering down how I felt, trying to pretend I was normal and whole. I needed to stop pretending I ever would be. At least, not anytime soon.

A tingling sensation of self-awareness trickled over my soul. I needed to accept myself for who I was. Flawed and scared, scarred, yet with the capacity to still love, despite the way my world had been shattered. I'd rebuilt myself one day at a time. I'd opened my heart to my grandparents, to Megan. To Daniel.

I moved over to the front of my father's grave and stared down at it. Tendrils of guilt warred with that familiar deep, searing anger. For so long I'd smothered those feelings too. I'd told myself if I was going to heal, I had to shut him out of my head and my heart.

But my father was still in there, like it or not.

Words struggled to free themselves from my mouth. "I . . . will never understand you," I finally said. I clenched my fists and shivered against another cool breeze that whipped through the area. "And I don't think I want to. Were you evil the whole time and we just didn't know? Were you insane? Was it untreated severe mental illness?"

I paused and gasped in a lungful of cold air. Something in my chest exploded, and I yelled to his grave, "What the hell was wrong with you? If your life was so miserable, if you were so damaged in the head that you could never be right again and you wouldn't bother trying to help yourself, why not leave us? Why not walk out of our house and never look back? Or why not just kill *yourself*? I hate you for this!"

A swell of guilt-ridden release spiraled out of my torso as I spoke. It was horrible, the things I was saying, yet I couldn't take the words back. I wouldn't. I'd bitten them back for eight years. That was long enough.

"Why did you have to hurt me and Lila and Mom?" I continued. I wrapped my arms around my trembling torso. "What did we ever do to you? We just tried to make you happy. Everyone around you tried to help you, but you shut us all out." My knees grew weak, and I dropped down. A bite of pain surged through my legs at the impact with the ground. I didn't care.

"Why couldn't you love us the way we loved you? You messed me up, Dad," I said. My damn voice broke again, and a sob ripped out of my throat. "You messed me up, and I don't know if I can ever forgive you for it. You stole away the people I loved the most, in the most selfish way possible."

I stayed there in front of my father's grave for several minutes, soul aching, heart splintering into pieces as I faced my demons. I shook and I shuddered, but I stared hard at his headstone through puffy, aching eyes. My father couldn't hurt me anymore, I told myself again and again.

Nor could he hurt Mom or Lila.

No, I couldn't forgive him—at least, not right now. But that was okay.

The brisk breezes stopped, and a warm strip of sunlight peeked through a nearby tree and slid across me. My shivers subsided as my emotions started to level out. I turned my face to the sun, closed my eyes. The sunshine seeped into my skin, warming my flesh, warming my heart.

This moment felt like a gift to me from my mom and sister. Their way of telling me they were with me no matter what, that it was all going to work out. My breaths slowed, leveled out.

I stood, knees aching from contact with the cold ground, and opened my eyes. My tears had dried, leaving stiff, salty streaks down my cheeks, but that didn't matter. Those dark recesses in my heart were dissolving right here in the light, and I felt a sense of slow acceptance.

Mom would want me to live and be happy. Lila would want me to have fun and follow my dreams.

I would do so for both of them. And for myself.

No, the shadows weren't all gone inside of me—not yet. Even as I dug out a small chunk of ground at my mom's gravesite to put in a bag I'd labeled "Mom," I could still sense the dregs of anger lingering in my gut. But somehow, that was okay. I was *allowed* to feel angry.

And when I did in the future, I'd find someone and talk through it. No more bottling things up. No more hiding myself.

"Good-bye," I whispered to my family as I headed back to my car, box in hand bearing the two small bags of dirt.

I'd entered the graveyard one person and exited someone different. No, maybe not different. Someone . . . lighter. Like I'd left a hundred pounds of personal agony behind me. My shoulders weren't so slumped in self-protection anymore. My chest wasn't so tight.

No matter what happened from here on out, I could be proud of what I'd done today. I started the car and headed back to my apartment. An old song came on, and I turned it up as I let music wash over me. My limbs were cold, and my jeans were damp from the ground. My back ached, and my eyes were throbbing.

But I felt better. Tired, a little drained, but ready to move forward for real. My father couldn't hurt me anymore. I wouldn't let him have power over my emotions, over my head space. *This* was what it felt like to let go.

To reclaim myself.

I wasn't going to turn into my father—keeping people at a distance, never dropping my walls and telling anyone I needed them. Festering in the darkness alone, despite others begging me to let them in. My fears hadn't protected me from getting hurt; they'd hindered me from connecting with others. But I understood it now, and I was ready to stop living like this.

Now I had to convince the guy who had my heart to give me another chance.

Chapter 23

Monday morning before philosophy class, Amanda turned to me, a strong pleading in her eyes. "*Please* tell me you have Friday's notes," she whispered. "I didn't make it to class because I caught a horrible stomach bug. I'm already behind as it is and starting to panic."

I dug through my notebook and flipped to the appropriate pages. I ripped them out and handed them to her. "Here ya go—you can get them to me before our next class. And if you have questions about anything, just let me know." I went to turn my attention back to my notebook, but a sudden memory from last Friday's class flashed in my head. "Oh, and we have a quiz this Friday, by the way. We're covering the whole chapter on Immanuel Kant."

Instant relief washed over her face. She gave me a genuine smile. "I had no idea. Thank you so much for the head's up—I really appreciate it. Maybe we could get together this week? Like, do a little study session and grab coffee or something?"

I blinked in surprise. "Um, sure. That would be . . . fine." And I was even more surprised to realize I meant it.

"Thanks." She ripped off a corner of her notebook and scrawled her name and number on it. "Here's my cell. Let's make plans to meet up."

I gave her my number, too, and she beamed in pleasure as she typed it into her phone.

Amanda's gratitude and desire to hang out with me, despite my attitude toward her all semester, chipped away at something in my chest. Since yesterday's visit to the cemetery, I'd been feeling . . . different. I'd woken up early this morning and made breakfast for Megan. She'd been floored when she'd emerged from her room and saw the kitchen table all set. It made me realize how few truly unselfish things I'd done for others over the years. No wonder I had no real friends. At least, not yet.

So when I swung by the coffee shop before coming to class, I'd bought my drink and then secretly paid for the harried-looking guy's coffee behind me, leaving a nice tip as well. I didn't stay around to see what happened—after all, it wasn't about fulfilling my ego. It was about trying to put myself out there and not be so closed off to the world.

I shifted in my desk and glanced over at where Daniel sat now. He was staring at me with an unreadable expression on his face. But unlike the other times when our eyes had connected, he didn't tear his gaze away. His jaw was smattered with a sexy five o'clock shadow, like he hadn't bothered to shave this morning. I wanted to brush my fingers along the soft stubble. Breathe him in.

My heart throbbed with a painful intensity, but I didn't blink, didn't move.

The professor came in, breaking the moment. Daniel turned his attention forward, fiddling with the pen in his hand.

I sighed and made myself begin to take notes as Professor Wilkins wrote all over the board. Daniel hadn't looked away immediately this time . . . was that progress? Would he be willing to talk to me?

Last night I'd lain in bed, staring at my ceiling, replaying the day's events in my mind. After the visit with my parents and sister, I finally understood what Daniel had been trying to do for me. He'd wanted me to shed my fears and take a leap of faith, but I'd shoved him away. I'd been so hurtful in my language.

I'd shut him out completely.

Did he hate me now? A knot formed behind my rib cage. So much time had passed since we'd last talked. Maybe if I'd come to him weeks ago instead of waiting this long, wallowing in my own pity, we could have repaired things.

If I attempted to reach out to him and he shut me down, it was going to kill me. Which was probably the biggest reason I was paralyzed in my seat at the moment. And yet I knew that was the coward's way out. I wasn't going to be that person anymore.

My eyes trailed over the classroom and found their way back to his corner. A blond girl with a confused face was leaning close to his desk as he whispered and pointed toward the open book. She nodded a couple of times, and I saw her give him a grateful smile.

A fresh bout of pain grabbed my heart, twisting it right in my chest. I bit my lower lip. Daniel was always quick to step up and help someone who needed it. He was generous with his time, his affection. How could I have thrown all of that away so easily, like he hadn't mattered to me?

No wonder he was shutting me out. I'd made him feel unimportant, unworthy of my affection or secrets. Yes, I loved him. But with the way I'd treated him, how could he ever have known?

Now Daniel was protecting himself. And could I blame him for it?

My hand shook a bit as I clenched the pencil. Daniel was worth the risk. He deserved someone who put forth everything. I didn't know if he'd be willing to talk with me again—to listen to why I'd freaked out and possibly accept my apologies—but I knew I had to try. And I had to give this effort everything I had in me.

If he rejected me after that, then I could hold my head high and know I gave it my best. I would be proud of myself regardless. But God, I hoped it worked. Because all of that love for him that I'd been afraid to look at too closely over the last few weeks was still right there inside of me, simmering beneath the surface. I ached for him. I needed him.

And I wanted to let him know that it was safe for him to need me too. That I could be there for him the way he'd tried to be there for me.

Suddenly I couldn't wait for class to end. Anticipation bubbled in my veins. It was hard to focus on the lecture when my heart and head were locked on thoughts of Daniel. I made myself take notes, though the effort was halfhearted.

When our instructor released us to go, I grabbed my stuff as quickly as possible and stood outside the door. Students filtered out while others for the next class slipped in. Daniel was in the back of the group.

My heart slammed against my rib cage as I reached out and touched his arm. "Hey, can we talk?"

He blinked in surprise, then his face grew expressionless. "I don't have time right now, sorry."

"Tonight, then? Are you free this evening? For coffee, even?"

My stomach sank when he shook his head. His flat eyes glanced on mine, then turned away, Adam's apple bobbing when he swallowed. "Look, I just . . . I can't."

"Five minutes." I could hear the begging in my voice, but I didn't care. "I promise it won't take a lot of your time."

He gave a heavy sigh, then finally peered down at me. I saw a flicker of emotions before he seemed to pull into himself, to hide behind a smooth mask. He scrubbed the back of his neck with the hand not holding his backpack strap. "I can't do this anymore, Casey. I can't keep riding the roller coaster with you. I'm sorry."

Then Daniel walked away from me, down the hall, out of the building without looking back.

Wow. Despite the way things had gone with us in the cemetery, I'd thought he would at least talk to me. But he'd shut me out.

Crushing defeat cramped my belly. I leaned against the wall for several minutes and fought the urge to cry as the beginning of a headache pounded my temples. No, this couldn't be the end of us; I couldn't let him go without a fight. I just needed to get him to listen, to see that I was changing. I knew Daniel was afraid to be vulnerable with me, for good reason. But if I opened myself up and did it first, if I showed him I was willing to put myself out there and risk it all, it might convince him to drop his walls and give me a chance.

The stirrings of an idea began in the back of my head. I drew in several slow breaths to sooth my tattered heart. I could do this. I'd give it everything I had . . . and pray like hell that it would be enough.

My phone buzzed. With shaky fingers I dug it out, hoping it was Daniel. But I didn't recognize the number.

Hey, it's Amanda. Study today? Pleeeeease? I'll buy coffee. ;-)

I bit my lip. My impulse was to run back to my apartment and curl up in bed with my headphones on, to nurse my aching heart for a while. But old patterns weren't going to help me in my quest to change. Besides, it wouldn't hurt to study now so I could focus later on my plan for Daniel.

Free now? I texted back.

Her reply was quick. *OMG YES. Coffee Baby? 10 mins??*

See you there.

I wrapped my scarf tighter around my neck and headed outside. Students dashed by in a mad rush to make it to class. Couples held hands as they crunched along dead leaves on the sidewalk. My breath puffed out around my face. I tried to not think about walking with Daniel on this very path when we first went to the coffee shop.

God, I missed him so much.

When I got inside the warm café, packed with students, I found Amanda already sitting at a nearby table, two cups of coffee waiting and a pile of sugar packets in the middle.

"I got here early," she said in an apologetic tone. "And I didn't know how you'd like your coffee, so I got black, but if this doesn't work, I can get you something else."

My smile was genuine. "I appreciate it. And you didn't need to buy me coffee. That was really nice of you."

"It was the least I could do. I'm petrified of flunking this class."

I took off my coat and settled into the chair across from her. I grabbed two of the packets on the table and dumped them in the cup, stirred, then sipped the coffee. "I'm not an expert in philosophy," I warned her.

"Are you passing the course?"

"So far, yes."

"Then you're probably doing better in it than I am." She laughed. "But I'm gonna try as hard as I can to at least pull a C."

"Then let's get started." I dug my book and notebook out of my bag, and we spent the next half hour comparing notes. Despite Amanda's flakiness around guys and her protests about how badly she was doing in class, she wasn't dumb. Which made me feel bad for judging her so harshly all semester. Her questions showed she was internalizing the material.

I couldn't help but think about studying with Daniel in this very place, discussing Nietzsche. My heart gave a sad lurch.

"What's wrong?" she asked, brow furrowed.

My throat was too tight to talk for a moment, so I silently

waved off her concern and offered a small, brittle smile. "Oh. Just . . . personal problems."

"Sorry. I didn't mean to pry." She turned her attention back to her notes.

Guilt flared up. *Stop pushing people away.* Amanda just wanted to make sure I was all right because that was what people did. "No, I'm sorry. I'm . . ." I swallowed. "I'm really awkward at this. Getting to know people, having casual conversation. You know, being normal. It's not you, it's me."

She gave a small laugh at the clichéd line. "Wouldn't be the first time I've heard that one," she replied in a droll tone.

I laughed, too, and the knot of tension in my chest lightened.

Amanda leaned forward, and her face turned serious again. "I don't want to put my nose in where it doesn't belong. But . . . you've seemed off lately. Even quieter than usual. Is everything okay? Did you and Daniel break up? Is that why he changed seats?"

I blinked. "You knew about us?"

She quirked a brow, and a dimple popped out. "Seriously, I'm a girl, and he's hot. Of course I noticed who he was hanging out with."

I rubbed my neck. "I messed up," I confessed, eyes glued on my notebook as I talked. "And now I'm scared I've lost him for good. I pushed him away for so long that he's afraid to be around me, afraid I'm going to hurt him."

"So what are you going to do about it?" Her voice held a hint of a challenge. "You're not going to just let him walk away without a fight, are you?"

I jerked my head up. "Um, I think I have an idea. But . . . if it doesn't work—"

"No, don't do that." She shook her head, and her eyes filled with passion. "Don't defeat yourself before you've even tried.

Daniel's a great guy. He'll listen to you because he cares about you. Real love doesn't just fade away after a few weeks. Trust me. He'll listen." She sipped her coffee, and in that moment my heart swelled with appreciation for her strength, her confidence.

"I hope you're right," I murmured.

"I am. If there's anything I know, it's men." She winked as she put her cup down to reach over and squeeze my forearm. "Something about you drew him to you in the first place. You have to trust in it. Trust in him too."

My eyes stung. "It's so hard to trust," I admitted. "My past kind of . . . screwed me up, and I'm still struggling with this."

"You're trusting me right now," she pointed out.

That was true. I couldn't believe I was having such a deep, personal conversation with a girl I barely knew. Before I knew it, I found myself telling her a bit about what happened when I was thirteen, how I lived with my grandparents. I skimmed on some of the more painful details, though I found it didn't hurt as much as I thought it would to admit what had happened to me.

Amanda's face showed every emotion she felt. As I talked, she sipped coffee, commiserated with me. Then she shared that her mom was an abusive drunk who went on weeklong benders. She and her older brother had moved out as soon as he'd turned eighteen, and they hadn't seen her since.

My heart lurched in sympathy. It was so easy for me to get swallowed up by my own pain. But others out there hurt, too, yet they got up out of bed every day and lived past the pain. *Despite* the pain. Amanda kept smiling, kept flirting and laughing and having fun.

"How do you do it?" I asked her. "How do you keep going?"

She nibbled on her thumb and thought for a moment. "I keep going because that's what you do. That's life. And I'm not going to let *her* issues hold *me* back. I want more for myself." She paused. "People are stronger than they realize. And you're gonna get through this, Casey. I believe it. You're a good person with a good heart."

Despite the lingering sting from Daniel's dismissal, the day hadn't been bad. In fact, opening myself up to others hadn't been too painful at all. And it was getting a little easier every time I did it.

"I'm really glad we decided to get together. Thank you," I told her, pouring every ounce of sincerity into my voice.

She sipped her coffee, then gave me a wide smile. "Please. It's the least I can do for all the help you're giving me. Now let's get back to studying so we'll both pass this stupid quiz. That'll give the old hag a shock. Though with my luck, she'll probably think I cheated." Amanda winked.

We spent the next hour studying and talking. When it was over, I invited Amanda to come to the club this weekend while I deejayed. Her responding smile and quick acceptance filled me with warmth. I knew my mom would be proud of me—for reaching out, for trying.

For living.

Chapter 24

This was going to take everything out of me. I just hoped it would be enough to work.

It was after three on Friday morning, and I'd been working since after dinner. In a little less than six hours, I'd be handing my song over to Daniel. The piece I'd been working on almost nonstop for the last several days. The one that would show him who I was and how I felt in no uncertain terms. My heart on a platter, his for the taking. No other guy had made me want to bare my soul so fully.

I hunched over my computer and propped my elbows on my desk. My eyes were gritty with fatigue, but I was almost done. Another hour or two of work, and it should be ready.

I chugged the dregs of my coffee. The drink had gone cold hours ago, but I needed the caffeine to help me stay awake so I could finish. My lower back throbbed in agony from sitting like this for such long periods over the last several days. But none of that mattered right now.

I was in that zone, and I was determined.

I pulled a memorable harmony from the song Daniel and I

had composed together. With a click of my mouse, I pasted it into my piece and fiddled with the key so it blended in to my song.

Would he recognize it? Did he remember that day as vividly as I did?

I stood and stretched my back. Snuck out of my room and poured another cup of lukewarm coffee. Memories of Daniel were everywhere—on my couch, peeking through the fridge, sitting at my kitchen table.

Haunting my lonely bed. God, how many weeks had it been since I'd gotten a good night's sleep? Too long.

I took a long draw from the mug, then headed back to my room. I grabbed the mic and flicked it on. Time for the last element of the song.

I drew a long breath and spoke.

The walk to class that morning was equal parts anticipation and trepidation, mixed with a dash of utter exhaustion. All of my free time this week had been spent on classwork and my project. I'd barely eaten or slept.

The hand clutching the iPod began to sweat from clenching it so hard. I made my fingers relax a touch, since they ached from being locked so tightly. Cold autumn breezes floated in and out of building breezeways, scattered crackly, brown leaves along sidewalks and stretches of frost-covered grass.

My pulse pounded in my throat as I walked into the building, made my way to philosophy class. I'd purposely come early to ensure I was there before him. Sure enough, the room was empty and the light off. I flicked it on and headed to his desk.

After putting down the iPod and the earbuds that had been wadded up in my coat pocket, I dug the note I'd written asking him to listen to the song and placed it on the desk, covering the equipment. I didn't want everyone else to walk in and see it or think they could just take it. My hand wouldn't stop shaking, and my breath was coming out in ragged huffs.

Then I darted to my seat, whipped out my pencil and a notebook and tried my best to not faint.

Students began to filter in. I didn't dare look up—if my eyes connected with his, there was no way I'd be able to get through this. It was so unbelievably scary, knowing he would either listen or just toss it all away. If it was the latter, I couldn't bear to witness it.

The seats filled up around me, though there might as well have been no one else in the room at all. When Daniel entered, my skin practically crackled with awareness. Still I kept my gaze on my paper, digging my nail into the wooden surface of the pencil. *Keep it together*, I ordered myself.

"Hey," a soft, feminine voice said from in front of me, making me jerk my head up. "Thanks again for the study session. It was a huge help."

I gave Amanda a tremulous smile. "Sure, no problem."

Her eyes narrowed, and she gave me a concerned look. "Everything okay? You look like you haven't slept in days."

My hands were clenched so tightly, I didn't think I'd ever be able to loosen this pencil from my grasp. It seemed like it was permanently welded to my fingers by now. I forced a smile that I knew didn't look genuine, but I didn't want her worrying about me right before the quiz. "I'm . . . just nervous, that's all."

The worry in her eyes faded away. "Oh, you'll be fine," she said with a wave of her hand. "You totally got this—the quiz *and* the other thing. I'm rooting for you." She squeezed my free hand. "Holler if you want me to pin him down so you can talk. Just speak from the heart—he'll listen because he still cares."

God, I hoped she was right. "Thank you," I said in a quiet whisper. "And I'll let you know if drastic measures are needed."

For the next few minutes, I flipped through my notes to refresh my memory. My brain was exhausted, running on fumes. The words started to blur together.

Professor Wilkins came in, and the class suddenly got quiet. I dared to look up and saw her eyeing all of us, her thickly braided hair slung over her black sweater-clad shoulder. "Quiz time," she announced in her typical emotionless way.

There was a soft groan from behind me, which made me shake my head, a small smile curving on my face. Some things never changed—like guys who thought somehow the teacher would forget. Not this prof.

Quizzes were handed out, and we began. Time both dragged and ran by far too quickly. I was anticipating the end of it, yet also fearing it. My brain wouldn't stop screaming at me as I scrawled my answers on the paper. What would happen when class was over—had Daniel listened to the song yet? Had he decided to wait until later?

Was he just going to dump it somewhere on his way out of the room?

Anxiety ate away at my stomach. I couldn't concentrate. Shit, I was totally going to blow this quiz.

It took everything I had to draw my attention back to the paper on my desk. The questions were all essay, which were mentally exhausting, but at least I was forced to focus on them. I shoved thoughts of Daniel aside and tried my best to answer. Logically, I knew essay questions were good because she'd give partial credit for effort.

As I worked on the last question, Professor Wilkins announced, "Time! Please put your writing utensils down and pass your quizzes to the front."

I groaned. I hadn't gotten to finish, but hopefully it had been enough.

A hand tapped my shoulder. I took the papers from behind

me, adding mine, and handed them to the black-haired girl two seats in front of me. My heart began its irregular thumping again as I moved out of quiz zone and back into my reality.

Professor Wilkins walked across the front of each row. She gave the quizzes a cursory glance. "From the looks on your faces as you took this quiz, I have a feeling it won't be fun grading these." She leaned back against her desk and glanced at her watch. "Okay, your homework is to read the next chapter this weekend. We'll start discussing it on Monday. You are excused."

I barely heard her last words over the deafening roar in my ears. Oh God, class was over and it was time to face everything. I was locked in place, frozen with fear. My head felt a little light and my vision blurred.

Papers rustled as students crammed belongings into their book bags and began filing out of the room.

Amanda stood and turned to me, rolling her eyes. "That was grueling."

All I could do was nod.

She slung her bag over her shoulder and cupped my shoulder. "Be strong. Text me if you need anything, okay? I'm wishing you luck!"

My fingers fumbled as I tried to put my stuff away; I had to lean over a few times to avoid being plowed into by guys running up the aisle for escape. My gaze so desperately longed to look over and see if Daniel was still there, though I was petrified of it.

I couldn't remember the last time I'd been this scared.

Finally the sounds died down. I swallowed, closed my eyes, gathered my strength. I could do this. I was in control of my life, and it was worth the risk. The music had been for him, yes, but it had also been for me.

I looked up and allowed myself to scan the room. Every desk was completely empty.

Daniel had left the room without saying a word to me.

My heart fell into tiny pieces, and a small cry threatened to erupt. I'd tried so hard, but in the end it hadn't mattered.

I'd failed.

I gave myself a full minute to feel the misery welling in my soul. But I wasn't going to cry here. I'd scrape together my pride, walk out the door with my head held high and be proud of myself.

I'd laid it all on the line for someone with no guarantee of response. I'd opened up and let myself be crushed into sand-sized fragments, had taken a risk for love. I sniffled and threw my bag over my shoulder. I was going to be proud of that.

Megan would be too. She and I could curl up on the couch and cry it out. And knowing her, she'd probably try to drag me out of the house to help me feel better. I still didn't want to, but the thought no longer made me almost break out into hives. I knew her efforts came from a place of caring.

I slipped on my coat, walked down the aisle and through the door. And then stopped in shock when I reached the hallway.

Daniel was standing about fifteen feet away from the entrance, back leaning against the opposite wall, an earbud in his left ear. His face flashed numerous emotions I couldn't read.

I cleared my throat, shifted the bag on my shoulder.

"Hi." He shuffled in place a bit, then pushed off the wall as he pulled the earbud out. "Um. How are you?" His tone was polite, oh-so polite.

I opened my mouth to say fine, wanting to hold on to those last vestiges of pride and not let him know how badly I was hurting. But something stopped me from lying to him. I stepped closer, out of the path of traffic, and dropped my bag by our feet. I visually devoured everything about him—the dark green of his eyes, his shaggy black hair, those damn beautiful freckles. I let myself absorb it all in.

"Actually," I said. My voice faltered, so I cleared my throat and repeated, "Actually, I'm doing horribly."

He blinked.

"I . . ."—*say it, Casey*—"I miss you so much. I miss everything about you." I kept my eyes locked firmly on his face as I let every drop of emotion pour from my gaze into his.

He didn't move from his spot, though his back stiffened. His face remained frozen while he stared at me in what looked a bit like shock.

"Do you wanna know what I miss about you?" I continued. I was filled with a strange sort of bravery now, the foolish type those who know they're plunging headfirst into something painful adopt because they have nothing left to lose. "I miss the way you hog the sheets in bed and the way your arm draped over me, protecting me. How your hair smells right when I'm drifting off to sleep."

His eyes shuttered, and the side of his jaw ticked. "Casey," he began in a strangled tone, then stopped.

"I miss how you push me out of my comfort zone." I gave a small, bittersweet laugh. "I'm sure that's as much a surprise to you as it is to me. But it's true. You challenged me, helped me grow. I'm not as afraid anymore of living, and that's because of you." The knot in my chest grew larger, but I pushed myself to keep talking, blinked back the slight burn in my eyes. "I miss the way you make me laugh, how you shock me with your strange questions."

I paused and drew in a shaky breath. I couldn't read his face right now, the strange darkness in his eyes, and that killed me. I dropped my gaze down so I wouldn't chicken out of the last things I had to say to him. My hands shook hard, so I pressed them to the sides of my legs. "You're such a good man, and I didn't appreciate you the way I should have. And I miss . . . God, I miss just talking with you about everything and smelling your skin and the way you made love to me like I was beautiful—"

Then a hand was on my chin, and my mouth was captured in a deep, soul-rending kiss that swallowed the last of my words. I was too stunned to move at first, and it took me a second to realize Daniel had pressed the length of his lean body to me, was wrapping a possessive hand around my waist under my coat, was *kissing* me like he was intoxicated by my mouth.

My body responded instantly, skin tingling with an ache so strong it almost hurt. I clutched his arms, tilted my head, tasted him. Every molecule in me craved his closeness with an intensity that scared me.

A low whistle rang down the hallway, and a guy off in the distance laughed. "Whoo! Happy Friday to you guys too!"

Daniel and I pulled back, panting and flushed. The grin on his face matched the one on mine. I felt lightheaded and dizzy from the intensity of that kiss.

He grabbed my bag with one hand and my hand with the other. "Come with me." Then he tugged me out of the building and led me toward a bench in the grassy commons. Since it was chilly outside, there weren't a lot of students lingering.

"You don't have a coat on," I protested.

"I'm fine." Daniel tugged my hand until I sat with him on the bench. Then he scooted close so that our knees touched. He kept my fingers wrapped in his. "Casey, I . . ." He drew in a slow breath and when he exhaled, I saw a little bit of tension leave his shoulders. "I loved your song."

My heart gave a small stutter of relief. "I'm so glad."

"No one's ever done something like that for me before." His eyes were earnest; he wasn't trying to hide his feelings from me anymore. I could see everything, and the intensity of it all dumbfounded me. "And I really liked that you put our song in there too. It made it even more special."

So he did remember. "Look, Daniel, I . . ." My throat tried

to close up, but I swallowed and forced myself to keep speaking. "What happened at the cemetery . . ."

"I'm so, so sorry about that." His grip tightened. A red flush worked its way over his cheeks, and his gaze scattered away. "It was wrong of me to do something that stupid and impulsive without thinking things through. I was trying to get you to open up to me—to face your feelings and let all that pain go so we could move forward together. But I shouldn't have sprung it on you like that, out of the blue."

"It's okay."

"I hurt you." Simple words, but so raw; I could feel his anguish pouring out of them. "Do you have any idea how many nights I've lain in bed, replaying that scene over and over again? Seeing the absolute misery on your face, that betrayal? I was angry with myself about it—I'm still angry, in fact. I'd pushed you away, which was the last thing I'd wanted to do."

"It wasn't the best way to approach it," I admitted. I released one of his hands and touched his cold cheek. "But it was the right idea. I wasn't ready then, but I ended up going back to the cemetery. On my own."

A line drew up between his brows. "And . . . are you okay? What happened?"

I nodded. "Yeah, I'm okay. Well, I mean I will be. I talked to my father and got all that anger off my chest. It felt good to yell at him, to let him know how much he'd hurt me. And I took a bit of dirt from the gravesites of my mom and sister and used them to help pot two orchids I bought. They're in my room." The bold purple and pink petals made me smile every time I saw them. "I know that's kind of morbid, but I wanted to keep them closer to me."

He shivered just a touch, and I moved to stand. "No, I want to stay right here." With careful scoots he inched beside me until the lengths of our bodies were touching on one side. His arm darted under my coat, and he leaned in and breathed deeply.

The soft breath on my ear made me shiver, but not from cold. "I've missed this."

"Me too." My throat was hoarse with unspoken emotion.

His lips grazed my ear. "I'm so sorry I hurt you—I was trying to help, but it was the wrong way to go about it. I just wanted you to find some happiness, even if it was without me."

Yes, I could survive without Daniel; I'd proven that to myself over the last few weeks. I could live, but I wasn't happy. I reached over and wove my fingers through his. "There is no being happy without you."

"I love you," he whispered in my ear, like it was our intimate secret, and I felt my stomach pinch in a surge of unexpected pleasure. "I love you, Casey, and I'd do anything for you."

I turned to face him, saw that love flaring in his eyes. "Forgive me for pushing you away?"

"Nothing to forgive," he instantly replied with a firm shake of his head. "Your past is a big part of you. I accept it all, even if I can't help but want to ease the pains. And I know things won't be perfect, but I'm here for you. Just . . . please don't shut me out. I'll try to not push you anymore. I don't want to go through this ever again." His honest, ragged words splintered my heart.

"I won't. Daniel, I love you so much," I told him, releasing the words I'd been dying to say directly to him for so long. I pressed my mouth to his, and our cold lips warmed instantly.

There was rustling of my hair, and then an earbud was pressed inside the shell of my ear. I pulled back a touch and saw Daniel had done the same with his side. The soft strains of my song, the one I'd written for him, started up.

It wasn't a dramatic piece. It wasn't fancy or overdone. But its simplicity captured my emotions. At the end, as the last notes faded away, were the words I'd spoken to him: *"Daniel, you changed me. You showed me what it means to truly live, and I'll never be the same. Thank you for sharing so much of yourself with me, even when I didn't deserve it. I love everything about you. I love you."*

"I snuck and listened to it the whole time I took the quiz," he admitted with a crooked grin on his face. "I couldn't stop replaying it. I wanted to stand up, grab you and kiss you senseless right in the middle of class."

"Professor Wilkins would have loved that," I said drolly, but on the inside my heart flipped with glee. I removed my earbud and tucked it in his hand. "That's all yours," I said. After I'd bought the mini iPod, I'd also filled it with a few songs I thought he might like, including the one we'd made together.

He brushed a sweet kiss across my brow. "And I'm all *yours.*"

Yes, he was. And he knew my heart was nestled right in his large hands. Our fragility with each other just made us stronger.

We both stood, donned our bags and headed toward the sidewalk, bodies pressed side by side, steps in unison. I didn't have anywhere else I had to be right now. And there wasn't a place in the world that could hold more appeal for me than being right by Daniel's side.

Our steps crunched in time across brittle fall leaves skittering on the sidewalk. The wind picked up, and I tugged Daniel closer to my side.

Contentment. That was this feeling warming my chest, lighting me from the inside out. That elusive bliss I'd been seeking for so long.

Daniel and I walked in total silence as the wind picked up and warned us of colder days to come. It made me think of all the memories we'd start making together from this day on. We headed no particular direction, just hand in hand, our emotions filling the scant space between us.

I squeezed his hand, and he squeezed mine back.

Acknowledgments

Thank you to my editor, Peter, for taking on this book and giving me savvy guidance on how to make it as strong as it can be. And to all the folks at Kensington, I'm grateful for your support.

Thank you to my writing friends. I'd be huddled in a corner crying myself to sleep if I didn't have you all to lean on, haha. You keep me sane in this insane industry.

Thank you to my wonderful family and friends. You rush out and buy my books, and you nag everyone else to get them too. I appreciate you so much.

Lastly, thank you to YOU, the reader! I hope you enjoy this story.

The *Scratch* Playlist

Here are some songs I thought would make a good sound track for *Scratch,* either lyrically or thematically, and some others I imagine Casey would play at the club or listen to on her own. You can find it online by following the link SCRATCH by Rhonda Helms or by searching for "SCRATCH by Rhonda Helms" on your Spotify interface. (Note: This requires a Spotify account to access.) I hope you enjoy this mix as much as my editor, Peter, and I enjoyed putting it together!

—RH

"Concrete Angel"—Gareth Emery and Christina Novelli
I think this song could be the theme song of *Scratch,* kind of how Daniel might see Casey. An instant EDM classic.

"Rewind"—Emma Hewitt
There are some awesome remixes available on the single, but I like the Mikkas one best. I saw this as a song Casey and Daniel dance to when they check out the DJ at the club.

"Lovers (Pure Mix)"—Solarstone featuring Lemon
"Love me into life, take away my pain . . ."
This song strikes me as something Casey would play when she DJs, and I love the Depeche Mode feel of the vocals.

"Live for the Night"—Krewella
Another song I see Casey playing. There are some good

remixes available, but the album version is dance-pop as it is. Krewella's "Alive" also has some lyrics appropriate to *Scratch*.

"Welcome to the Jungle (Original Mix)"
—Alvaro and Mercer

In my head, I saw Casey playing this at the club, maybe when the dance floor is crowded and a little steamier.

"Red Lights"—Tiesto

I think this is something that Casey would listen to on her own time, away from the DJ booth. I like the Extended Version; it has some great peaks and valleys to dance to.

"Frost Nova"—Aqua & Arctic

This is a pretty great EDM instrumental track. It sounds like a piece I imagined Casey might compose.

"Under Control (Extended Remix)"
—Calvin Harris featuring Alesso and Hurts

I could also see Casey listening to this walking across campus between classes. I like the build-up especially.

"Need You Now (How Many Times)"—Plumb

Her voice on the chorus of this song is so emotional and pleading, and setting it against the electronic dance background gives it a great anthem feel. I like the J-C Club Mix. It sounds like something Casey might compose for Daniel, infusing so much emotion into the music.

"Back to You (Wach Remix)"
—Fabio XB & Christina Novelli

Christina Novelli's voice on "Concrete Angel" led me to this song, another that seemed to fit the book's themes so well. "No matter what I do, this current pulls me back to you . . ." Beautiful and haunting.

"Moves (Vinny Vero & Steve Migliore Radio Edit)" —Bright Light Bright Light

The lyrics again thematically fit the story: "Moving on is the hardest thing to do . . ." It has a great groove, and I think it's a fantastic remix of a brilliant song. Look for the Blueprints Version for a more tender acoustic tone that underscores the words.

"In the Dark"—Tiesto and Christian Burns

An older Tiesto track, but the lyrics seem fitting for Casey and Daniel:

"Cause I will be there / And you will be there / We'll find each other in the dark"

"Swagga"—Excision and Datsik

Like "Welcome to the Jungle," this might be something Casey would put on after midnight when the vibe of the crowd became a bit . . . grindier.

"Like Satellites"—Manufactured Superstars

I could easily envision Casey playing this in the club, too.

"All of Me (Tiesto's Birthday Remix)"—John Legend

This is a beautiful, heartfelt song, and the remix really hits its stride halfway in. It would definitely be on Casey's personal playlist, and again fits the themes of *Scratch*.

"Steal You Away (Club Mix)" —Dash Berlin, Alexander Popov, Jonathon Mendelsohn

I like the buildup in this song as well, and I could see this as something Casey might write and even play.

"Parachute (tyDi Mix)"—Ingrid Michaelson
"I don't need a parachute, baby, if I've got you / You're gonna catch me . . ." On the flip side, I feel like this is something Daniel might put on a playlist for Casey. And her voice is beautiful, as always.

"Say Something"—A Great Big World
This is another song I think would be a theme song for *Scratch,* especially toward the end. There are some good remixes out there, but the rawness of the lyrics seems best served by the simple production. It gives me the sniffles whenever I hear it.